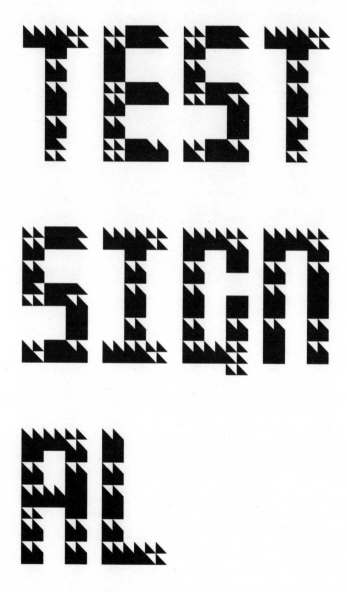

TEST SIGNAL

**Northern
Anthology
of New
Writing**

Edited by
Nathan Connolly

dead ink

BLOOMSBURY PUBLISHING
LONDON · OXFORD · NEW YORK · NEW DELHI · SYDNEY

Test Signal is a co-publication from Dead Ink
and Bloomsbury Publishing

DEAD INK
Cinder House Publishing Limited
Northern Lights
5 Mann Street,
Liverpool,
L8 5AF

BLOOMSBURY PUBLISHING
Bloomsbury Publishing Plc
50 Bedford Square, London,
WC1B 3DP, UK
29 Earlsfort Terrace,
Dublin 2, Ireland

BLOOMSBURY, BLOOMSBURY PUBLISHING and the Diana logo
are trademarks of Bloomsbury Publishing Plc

First published in Great Britain 2021

A catalogue record for this book is available from the British Library

ISBN: HB: 978-1-5266-3091-9; eBook: 978-1-5266-3088-9

Typeset by Laura Jones   Cover design by Luke Bird

Printed and bound in Great Britain by CPI Group (UK) Ltd,
Croydon CR0 4YY

2 4 6 8 10 9 7 5 3 1

To find out more about Bloomsbury's authors and books, visit
www.bloomsbury.com and sign up for our newsletters.

To learn more about Dead Ink, visit
www.deadinkbooks.com where you can find out about our latest releases.

CONTENTS

CONTENTS

INTRODUCTION

Open submissions to *Test Signal* closed on 6 February 2020. On 16 March, the Prime Minister, Boris Johnson, began encouraging social distancing. A week later, he announced the first nationwide lockdown.

From the start, *Test Signal* was envisioned as a wide-ranging and collaborative project that bridged the gap between the North of England and the publishing industry largely based in London. The idea was to create opportunities and build lasting connections through collaboration. Aside from the book you hold in your hands, *Test Signal* was about events, networks and participation.

Obviously, we were forced to swiftly reconsider our plans and adapt to an ever-changing environment. *Test Signal* ended up being put together in isolation – judged over Zoom, edited from home, produced in an environment where many of us naturally wanted to bury our heads under duvets and scream into the void. But good news is something that we always need and, however small, the production of this book is good news.

It took 281 Kickstarter backers, C&W Literary Agency, New Writing North, Bloomsbury Publishing and my own press, Dead Ink Books, to bring *Test Signal* to fruition, but here we are: twenty-two writers in the North compiled into one book showcasing the talent, variety and originality of literature in the North of England.

There were open submissions that invited anybody residing in the North of England to enter their work, we approached literature organisations in the region for recommendations, and we begged some of our own favourite writers to take part. The result is a book that highlights writers from a number of different disciplines, at different stages of their career and from every corner of this beautiful and inspiring region. Unlike anthologies you have read before, this one will not hold together as a whole united by a single theme or cause. Instead, our goal here is variety. The only condition for consideration was that an author be based in the North when they submit. This book is a snapshot of Northern writing at a moment in time, and that is how it is intended. If in future years we are to repeat this endeavour to the extent that we have a series, I hope that series provides a stop-motion montage of changing tastes, preoccupations and trends. If the North is anything, it is alive and it is always evolving, adopting, reinventing.

It may be that not every entry in this book is to your liking, but we hope our efforts towards variety are appreciated and every reader can find more than a few writers contained within these pages that they can become passionate about and champion.

I say champion, because if *Test Signal* demonstrates anything, it is that the literary landscape is malleable, and you can participate in it. I do hope that this project demonstrates that to you and you feel empowered by taking part in it – and by reading this book you *are* taking part. To those not involved in the industry, literature and publishing can seem like far-off things that exist within gated compounds and are fiercely guarded by people who are not like *us*. How many times do we hear the metaphor of 'knocking on doors'? This book, if used for anything, should be used as a wedge to keep that door open.

Literature is participatory. On the most basic level, all you need to take part is a pen and paper. That might be somewhat of an over-simplification that ignores the connections, networks and cultural capital that actually make things move within the industry, but it does hold true to an extent, and everything else is just a matter of organising. Books exist to serve readers, and it is ultimately the reader that holds all of the power in the sometimes antiquated processes that come together to make books into an industry. But power must be recognised to be useful, so we're thankful that 281 people recognised their power and supported this project when it was nothing more than an idea.

The events of 2020, and now 2021, may have forced us to reconsider our original plans for *Test Signal*, but in one respect we already know that it is a success – you hold it in your hands! I hope that this book inspires you to support the writers you believe in, the literature in the area where you live, and yourself and your ability to enact change. Power within publishing ultimately lies with the reader, and through organisation it is possible to use that power for positive change.

In the great scheme of things, perhaps that doesn't mean all that much, but change comes from a lot of small victories, and today I feel like a small victory is valuable enough to cling to. Perhaps it can even inspire more small victories?

Test Signal has been a joy to work on, even if that work has been done beneath a tremendous pressure from outside. Despite all of the chaos and the uncertainty that has come our way since we began this project, working on it at my desk from my home *office* has always been a refuge – a small place in the world in which I can place my efforts into something positive and forward-thinking. It took a great deal of collaborative effort to bring this book to this point, and although I'm not at all sure what the future holds for anything at this point, I am sure that the connections, relationships and collaborations that formed during this project will continue to grow, and positive change will emerge from them.

Nathan Connolly
Editor

CLAVICLE WOOD

ANDREW MICHAEL HURLEY

eaning

On the Ordnance Survey map, it has no name, but we've come to call it Clavicle Wood, my family and I, on account of my eldest son breaking his collarbone there twice when he was younger. The first time falling from a rope swing, the second time after coming off his bike on a BMX track built by the collective labour of local kids.

It's nothing to look at, Clavicle Wood. A half-mile, L-shaped strip of trees that first parallels a railway cutting and then dog-legs along a stretch of Sharoe Brook, a cloudy urban stream which twists its way through the north side of Preston. But when the COVID pandemic struck and we were forced to find natural spaces closer to home, it became something of a sanctuary, a place where the long weeks of lockdown could be charted not by the graphs of cases and casualties but by the progression of floral changes: snowdrops to celandine to bluebells to the swirl of downy cottonwood seeds let loose on a warm afternoon in May, making it seem as if it had snowed.

Its fate, however, might already have been spelled out. During the building of the new housing estate further along the railway line, all the poplars that once bordered the embankment were ripped out (a vicious process, I remember, in which cranes yanked at the trees as if they were stubborn teeth) and a high wooden fence put there instead to deflect the noise of the passing Pendolino trains.

In the same way, the land next to Clavicle Wood – part of an old golf course turned to wild meadow – has long been earmarked for development (that vague but ominous word), and so at some point the maple, beech, hawthorn and sycamore here might well be deemed just as unimportant and inconvenient too.

It brings to mind Blake's line, 'The tree which moves some to tears of joy is in the eyes of others only a green thing that stands in the way.'

For those of us who love and need these natural spaces between the bricks and concrete, the thought processes that might lead a person to be so unconcerned about the destruction of a wood are unfathomable. It's baffling that the same place can, to someone else, have no *meaning* at all. But then if there's a profit to be made, meaning can be expunged from pretty much anything.

On the plans for Beech Crescent or Cottonwood Close, or whatever name they give to the roads that might eventually replace and recall the trees that are uprooted, the wood will no doubt be nothing more than a set of measurements. So many acres to be cleared away. There will be no note of the name we've given it, nor of the memories that it holds for us, or for anyone who has spent time here. It will be 'valueless' in that sense.

Although it will be upsetting to be reminded of this year, it's important that the wood remains. Because once life experiences, good or bad, are tangled up in a particular place, that place becomes precious, or at least significant.

It's the site where some of our roots are planted, somewhere which shows us that we have lived and what we've lived through.

In his book *Common Ground*, Rob Cowen talks about this 'emotional intertwining' of people and locality, and explains how 'time spent in one place deepens this interaction, creating a melding and meshing that can feel a bit like love'.

I'd always thought this sort of idea more than a little quixotic, the preserve of the minority who'd spent their entire lives in timeless rural places, but by retracing my footsteps through the wood during lockdown, in various states of numbness and apprehension, I began to see how that reiterated path-making might begin to bind emotion to physical space. When so much thinking and feeling has occurred in one place, it's hard not to be reminded of those contemplations on future visits.

But memory is a diminishing return, of course, and recollections come to us rosy with nostalgia, or perhaps wholly inaccurate. Yet we expect that. It's the ability to feel that our emotional lives are associated with and expressed by place that matters.

It's a feeling that John Clare voices in his poem 'Remembrances', one of several penned in opposition to the Enclosure Acts:

Summer pleasures they are gone like to visions every one,
And the cloudy days of autumn and of winter cometh on:
I tried to call them back but unbidden they are gone
Far away from heart and eye and for ever far away...

The memories he speaks of here have not only been made to seem distant by the passage of time but, we discover, by the wide-scale devastation of the landscape in which they were formed. Clare talks of seeing places special to him torn up by the 'never weary plough' and describes how a beloved tree 'To the axe of the spoiler and self interest fell a prey'.

The feeling of 'belonging' that we're talking about here requires that the physical appearance of a place doesn't change all that much; that the past – collective and personal – feels alive; that it remains embodied in the landscape and decipherable by those who live there. Yet, this is almost impossible in suburbia, the edges of which are always being added to, and where the past, especially the recent past, is usually removed in its entirety. Once work on a new housing estate gets going, it's hard to picture what the land used to look like before, and the speed of it all doesn't give us enough time to process what's being lost. This is why during lockdown, when there was a hiatus in building work, it was possible to see more clearly the importance of preserving somewhere like Clavicle Wood, in words if nothing else.

Interior
It's a damp afternoon in early September, and now that things have returned to a semblance of normality, the main road by the wood is back to a constant flow of cars and lorries.

But step into a wood and everything changes, every sense is altered.

The immediate and unexpected feeling for a place as small as Clavicle Wood is enclosure. It's all trees. Suddenly. A few paces in and they've sprung up behind me in a tousled screen: sycamore, elder, hawthorn, sapling oak and sapling ash and the huge cottonwood trees above them all. The effect is so complete that even though the wood is only twenty or thirty feet wide here, I can't see the road or the houses of my estate anymore. There is only the BMX track that did for my son's collarbone winding between the trunks, the trees that came down in Storm Ciara in February incorporated ingeniously into the course.

The birch that I'd watched from my house being decked by the wind still lies where it fell, however, too heavy to move, its splintered trunk rotting and soft and covered in bracket fungus. Other trees have toppled more recently, making it necessary to clamber over them or under them. But the blockade invites touch: smooth skin, hard, rutted bark, knotholes, splits, forks. I'm close enough to sniff the different trees. None of them are as fragrant or pungent as pine, but there's something almost homeopathic about the smell: a faint hint of vegetation at the back of a water-pure cleanness. It's potent enough, whatever it is, to subdue the exhaust fumes from the road outside.

A few yards on and the clamour of the traffic is starting to be replaced by the sound of the treetops moving in the wind, of the rainwater pattering down through the leaves and branches as if from broken taps. A robin sings above me and is answered by another further off. I walk on, stop, walk a little further, trying to pinpoint the moment where the sound of the road disappears completely.

During lockdown, it wasn't only how far we could go
that changed but how we *moved* too. In taking our allot-
ted daily dose of fresh air, we were urged not to linger
but to simply exercise and return home. The wood was
then a place to pass through; now, there is a certain
freedom to be still and loiter. Which I do. When all
man-made noise ceases, I stand and close my eyes and
try to listen only to what's here, what *this* space and no
other contains. If the wood offers us meditative seclu-
sion, then it seems proper to accept. As Thoreau says,
'What business have I in the woods, if I am thinking of
something out of the woods?'

There's a tone of veneration in his words that alludes to
the ancient analogy of the wood as sacred, the wood as
temple. And certainly in April and May, when it seemed
that every day here, there was something new and vibrant
growing, it was easy to understand how the arrival of the
summer might have once been considered a visitation
from the divine.

It's that the interior of a wood, like that of a man-made
place of worship, is differentiated from the outside by a
feeling of closeness with some (more powerful) *other*.
Immersed in a wood, we can describe its contents taxo-
nomically, we can explain biological processes, but the
experience of *being* for the living things here is utterly
incomprehensible to us. Trying to imagine what it is like
to be that robin in the branches, how it experiences the
wood, other creatures, its own song, the air, is like trying
to imagine a different dimension. We simply cannot grasp
how the things of the natural world conceive themselves.

Even the idea of self-conception is misleading. An ego is a human burden. The 'harmony' that we seem to notice in nature is achieved through an intelligence or a knowing that's beyond us.

Which is why in so many folk tales we resort to anthropomorphism to make sense of it all, and why the plot of many a fairy story is concerned with defeating something threatening. The Big Bad Wolf represents a literal and physical hazard inherent in the forest, but he also personifies (and so makes more governable) the otherness that stems from our feeling of separation.

It's this disconnectedness that makes us feel exposed in a wood, perhaps; as conspicuous as Little Red Riding Hood. Along with the abundance of hiding places and the silence, it's what accounts for the feeling of being watched.

Aware of the noise I'm making as I come into a clearing deep in fallen branches, I wonder if this self-consciousness partly explains our instinct to build dens.

Bringing my children here (or to any wood) when they were younger, it was the first thing they wanted to do, not only for the pleasure of constructing something to their own specifications, but to hide themselves away. All the painstaking lifting and carrying, jamming and balancing was never as exciting as the moment of crawling inside. Suddenly you've blended into the trees, you're part of the wood. The Big Bad Wolf might pass by and never know you were there.

Strangely, if my children returned here to find their den knocked over, they always preferred to construct a new one rather than commandeer one that had already been assembled by other kids. Perhaps a den is only truly safe if it's been built by your own hands.

Here, some have been skittled by the wind, but one remains, well anchored to the trunk of a maple tree, the body of the shelter a solid warp and weft of deadwood. It's dry inside, and if it weren't so small I might be tempted to curl up in there and wait out the rain.

Trespass

But I move on, using boughs as brakes as the woodland starts to slope down towards the brook. The path runs with sludge and is overgrown with bright pink, hyper-invasive Himalayan balsam. People have tried to pare it back by pulling up some of the plants in a session of 'balsam bashing', and the track is strewn with uprooted stems that snap underfoot like celery. As with the hand-built BMX track, it's another way in which this place is shaped by those who use it. There is a democratic curation here.

Yet any sense that, because of collective care and affection, it *belongs* to us in any way is an illusion. Just as I have, I'm sure many other people have wandered through the woods and further afield across the old golf links thinking of it all as our local common, but that name is entirely wrong. We have no right to be here whatsoever, no lordly concession to use these fields. It is, on paper, private land, and a more legally accurate term for what we engage in every time we set foot here is trespass – an intrusion which is becoming less tolerated, it seems.

Making my way down to the stream, I see that two new signs have been nailed up, each reading:

Polite Notice. This wood is private land. Please respect that!!! Do not put anything in the brook to aide [sic] *crossing.*

The 'private land' referred to is a beautiful, bowl-like grove scooped out of the bank, full of sturdy sycamores and beeches, the floor of it scattered with last year's jennies and mast. It's a place where, all summer, children have played hide and seek or made pendula of themselves on the rope swings, just as my son did years ago; it's where families have come to paddle in the water. Now, this glade is to be looked at in passing but not touched.

Little by little, the acres of open, natural space around Clavicle Wood are being closed off to the public. Only last week, I found a new fence erected in one of the former fairways. Eight feet high, it sliced up the meadow diagonally, preventing all but the most determined, like me, from passing through into the next field. This too was ringed by barriers that appeared to be guarding nothing other than more fencing piled up and waiting to be distributed.

It's the same elsewhere on the course. Dozens of acres have been barriered off, some for several years now, the empty space sitting behind bars and watched over by twenty-four-hour CCTV.

There's no particular reason for it, other than a statement of possession. And when the only function of a fence is to carve off some piece of seemingly disused natural space that might otherwise be enjoyed, we resist.

*

The effect of natural light, colour, air and shapes on our well-being is as known to us as the effect of water on thirst. So when a faceless 'someone' – a fellow being, of all things – keeps them out of reach simply to prevent you from appreciating them, the affront is sharply felt. Someone might as well have cordoned off a percentage of your lungs to keep for themselves.

Perhaps I stopped short earlier. These fences aren't only statements of possession, but of control. For 'authority', in whatever guise that appears – landowners, local councils – there is often great anxiety over empty, natural space. Away from roads and houses, there's scope for sedition. There have been reports in the local news lately about kids riding motorbikes across the grassland, and periodically the broken record is played about the threat of travellers commandeering any field that doesn't have a gate.

It's travellers, in fact, that the present Conservative government is using as collateral in their argument about the need to crack down on trespass. Some choice lines from their 2019 manifesto read:

> We will tackle unauthorised traveller camps. We will give the police new powers to arrest and seize the property and vehicles of trespassers who set up unauthorised encampments, in order to protect our communities.

The prejudice here isn't even coded in dog-whistle politics. It's a straightforward association of an already well-marginalised minority group with inherent criminality. But whipping up antagonism towards the travelling community is a means to a far more disturbing end, and many other 'undesirables' will be moved on when the ultimate goal is reached and trespass becomes a criminal rather than civil offence. It will mean that rough sleepers who set up homeless camps or those who protest by occupation can be more heavily punished.

It's in the debate about land usage and land ownership that the same ancient battle lines are drawn time and again between those who see the natural world as a common treasury, to use Gerrard Winstanley's words, and those who see it as a thing to be divided up and owned. That there is such a thing *at all* as private property, that it is possible for someone to own earth, water, grass, trees and (up to a certain height) airspace is so entrenched in our society that it is often assumed that the legal right to acquire land comes with the privilege to demand obedience. The tone of superiority in 'This wood is private land. Please respect that!!!' is centuries old. The outrage expressed in the three exclamation marks is concerned with a perceived lack of deference to the principle of private ownership itself, rather than any anxiety about what people might actually *do* should they ford the stream and venture into the trees. There's nothing there to steal, nothing to vandalise or a livelihood to disrupt.

It's with a sense of satisfaction that I see that one of the Polite Notices has been impolitely defaced.

Escape
At the root of all this is a suspicion about what people might use such open space *for*. We're not to be fully trusted. Away from scrutiny, we act differently (perhaps

not always legally), we move differently, we think differently. Shortcuts and desire lines are often severed so that we can't transit from one place to another unseen. It's what's happened near Clavicle Wood. The previously unbroken greenway between the various estates around the edge of the old golf course is being gradually sectioned off into single acres here and there, so that to walk into one of these fields is to be kettled by mesh.

The establishment of so many cul-de-sacs diminishes what's therapeutic about walking, which is the ability to do it continuously and at length. Rather than going in circles, it's necessary to feel as if we're escaping something, leaving routine behind and abstaining from the roles we're obliged to play most of the time.

I think of my great-grandparents and their generation, and how the West Yorkshire moors provided respite from the mills of a Sunday. But whereas escape for them meant that they didn't have to labour, escape for me means that I don't have to consume. They turned their backs on the factory's rhythms; I turn off my phone and walk away from algorithms.

In his book *A Philosophy of Walking*, Frédéric Gros says, 'the walker considers it a liberation to be disentangled from the web of exchanges, no longer reduced to a junction in the network redistributing information, images and goods.'

It stands as proof to the declaration by the Director for Hatcheries and Conditioning in *Brave New World*, who says that 'a love of nature keeps no factories busy'.

Walking with pathlessness, aimlessness, for extended periods of time, is the antithesis of capitalism's intentions for us. If we wander, we can't be governed.

*

Right now, there's a pressing need for green space. Social distancing is routinely cited as the way in which we will slow the pandemic. Therefore, it stands to reason that it's in heavily built-up towns and cities that we most need places like Clavicle Wood or common land. It's especially vital in the towns and cities of the North, in which living conditions are the poorest and coronavirus infections the highest. Put a map of England's most deprived areas next to a map of COVID hotspots and they are almost identical. Manchester, Burnley, Blackburn, Oldham, Salford and Rochdale, for example, feature on both.[1]

Many of these places have parks and open green spaces, but there have been stories recently of local councils being forced to sell them to pay for frontline services, the budgets for which have been systematically cut by central government over the years of austerity that followed the crash of 2008. It's one of the cyclical ironies we have to deal with that the spaces which might well provide some palliative for physical and mental ill health are being flogged off to fund services over-stretched by physical and mental ill health.

---

1   This was an observation made at the time of writing, and of course plenty of other places in the country have been as badly affected since. However, a report in *The Observer* on 7 February 2021 pointed to the fact that regions in the North are seeing the slowest decrease in infection rates. Cases in my home town of Preston declined by only 9% between the first and last week of January 2021. In Bradford West it was 14% and in Rotherham 18%. Whereas, in more affluent constituencies, such as Surrey Heath and Abingdon and Oxford West, the decline was 70% and 72% respectively. This suggests that, for a variety of detrimental socio-economic reasons, the poorest places in the country, as well as being the first to be overwhelmed by COVID, seem likely to be the last that are released from its grip.

*

Despite everything that occurred during lockdown, there was a degree of optimism that the shock and upheaval of the pandemic might prompt us as a country to take stock; that this crisis might lead us to tackle other longstanding issues and engender a new era in which we thought differently of one another and of the places where we lived.

Many of us *have* felt this desire, but to translate this calling to live more compassionately and thoughtfully into widespread and lasting societal change is almost certainly doomed to failure. More democracy, more collective ownership, more spaces in which people can just 'be' remain anathema to those who control the system.

The 'self interest' that John Clare decried is still with us, and the folk song of those who, like him, objected to the Enclosure Acts is, sadly, as relevant now as it was then:

The law locks up the man or woman,
Who steals the goose from the common,
But leaves the greater villain loose,
Who steals the common from the goose.

Pessimistic as it may sound, in the post-COVID world the relentless pursuit of power and money by the self-serving plutocracy at the top will continue unimpeded, blind and deaf to any concerns about the environment or our well-being. If what's happening to the fields around Clavicle Wood is anything to go by, then if and when the next pandemic comes, there will be fewer places to escape to than there are now.

Change

I come to the meadow on the other side of the wood and find it, for now at least, unencumbered by fences. It's still knee deep in grass and thistles, there are bees and damselflies, but things are starting to die off in the quiet unstitching of summer's work. There's little birdsong, apart from the robins, the ragwort is wilting, and the flowers of the cow parsley have desiccated to little brown rattles. I pass a sycamore, one half apple-green, the other half yellowing to the colour of Bartlett pears.

I don't think I've ever been as attentive to the smaller increments of change as I have this year.

It's this intimacy with place which allows memories to be pinned to it more intensely. In Cecil Day Lewis's poem 'Walking Away', the memory of his son starting school is associated with – and perhaps prompted by – the 'leaves just turning'. And so for me, when I see this sycamore at this point in its transformation next year, or the year after, or for as long as I'm here to return to it, I'll recall the feelings that I have now about my son leaving for university a couple of days ago. Pride, parental anxiousness and a longing – for something I can't quite identify.

But it's being *here*, specifically, that gives those emotions weight.

In Clavicle Wood he is a little boy making dens, an older boy with a broken collarbone, and he is also, astonishingly, a man.

It's no coincidence that Day Lewis's poem is rich with natural imagery. The son is first a 'half-fledged thing' and then a 'winged seed'; the new place in which he finds himself is a 'wilderness' where he must tread his own path. We've long seen ourselves, our brief lives, mirrored in the natural world. It is the oldest metaphor for the necessity and normalcy of change. 'Nature's give-and-take,' as Day Lewis puts it. 'The small, the scorching / Ordeals which fire one's irresolute clay'.

Natural metaphors appeal to us because the change they allude to is cyclical rather than permanent. In fact, because nature always appears to be in the act of returning to where it was, we perhaps feel it has a kind of perpetuity. Its patterns endure whatever.

Even if that's untrue, it's a seductive idea and one that's given me a great deal of solace throughout my life. Whatever was happening, I could rely on nature to be there and allow me, for a time, to align myself with its behaviours and so become something else, or nothing at all.

In *The Living Mountain*, a memoir of her life spent among the Cairngorms, Nan Shepherd expresses a similar feeling: 'The mountain gives itself most completely when I have no destination, when I reach nowhere in particular but have gone out merely to be with the mountain as one visits a friend with no intention but to be with him.'

The natural world often feels like the best of companions – reliable and available, welcoming even after long periods of separation, never wanting anything from us.

Which is why the first few days of lockdown felt like a sudden bereavement. Everything had changed without me having had time to prepare for it. The plans that I'd made to spend some time in the Lake District to diffuse a gnawing sense of restlessness had to be abandoned. And just as I might have recalled time spent with a loved one, I began to relive certain walks: Helvellyn the previous May, Bowfell on a glowering October afternoon, the long trudge I'd made from Grasmere into Far Easedale only a few weeks before everything came to a standstill.

As much as it was comforting to escape into those memories, it was distressing to think that I had no idea of when I'd be able to return to the fells. From the railway bridge near Clavicle Wood, I'd look north on clear days and pick out the ridges of the Langdale Pikes. They seemed ineffably distant.

At the very moment when I needed the constancy of those places amidst the upheaval, they were out of bounds. And this is the anxiety we feel when any natural space which has been so vital to us in that way is made inaccessible. To imagine a life which consists *only* of the very things which make us seek out the moors, mountains and woods in the first place is unsettling. It would be unbearable to have no distance from which to look at how we live and see that the thousand things we dress up as imperatives are actually insignificant. A life lived among nothing but what is man-made, and therefore shaped in order to shape us in return, feels limited and futile, whereas if we experience life happening in wild, unmanaged places, it can feel expansive, even transcendental, no matter how small the physical space. It's not by accident that in Buddhist stories, *satori* – that glimpse of true 'seeing' – often occurs in a natural setting.

There's a Zen koan from the writer Dōgen that goes: 'Before one studies Zen, mountains are mountains and waters are waters; after a first glimpse into the truth of Zen, mountains are no longer mountains and waters are no longer waters; after enlightenment, mountains are once again mountains and waters once again waters.'

Koans are not unlocked by logical thinking but by awakening a truth already dimly known. In this example, the first observation and the last seem to be identical, but although the act of looking is the same, the perception of what is seen has changed. The journey begins with indifference – the mountains and rivers are merely background scenery – but this isn't where we end up. Enlightenment does not return us to apathy but shows that things simply are as they are, free of the religious or metaphysical concepts we lay upon them, alive in the same way that we are alive.

I hesitate to use the word 'oneness' only because of the connotations attributed to it as being specious or pseudo-spiritual. But I can't think of another word for those moments alone in a wood, or on the ridge of a mountain where I've felt that little 'I' inside the skull evaporate. To say that we are part of the nature we (falsely) perceive to be 'out there' isn't poetic or philosophical, but a statement of fact.

It's a few days later and I'm back in Clavicle Wood on what will probably be the last warm day of the year. The sun comes in at all angles like crossed swords of light. Where it's sieved by the leaves, it ripples on the trunk of a dead oak tree, itself liquid-looking from the gnarled repairs to its bark. The twists and eddies of colour make it seem as if it were poured into shape.

In the shade here it's noticeably cool, the air a little damp in the encroaching autumn. Even in the space of a few days, more leaves are looking singed and mottled. The sycamore at the edge of the meadow has changed again, more yellow than green. The feelings I had about my son leaving home are bound up in a moment that has now passed. But they will be returned to me, if the wood remains.

Buddhism teaches that suffering arises from attachment and, following that logic, I perhaps shouldn't rely so much on Clavicle Wood. And yet it feels important that it stays as it is. Not only because part of my life is here, not only that it has the potential, like all natural spaces, to check our sense of self-importance, but because we flourish by spending time with what is strange to us. It does me good to know that on the other side of the railway line, there are miracles.

September 2020

Postscript

It's now February 2021, we're in the midst of another lockdown and Clavicle Wood is all but gone. Tree-felling began on my eldest son's birthday in December and has continued on and off ever since. Not to clear the way for more housing, as I anticipated, but to remove trees along the cutting before they cause problems on the railway line. Everything within about forty feet of the track has been chopped down, reducing the wood to little more than stumps and sawdust. Because it has been such an excessive, insensitive cull, it's hard to think of this as anything other than a preventative surgery of the crudest kind: like cutting off a person's hand on the pretext that they might assault someone, sometime in the future.

Perhaps the hope is that those of us who loved the wood will be assuaged by the fact that this area of the defunct golf course is now being regenerated. A billboard heralds the arrival of 'New Village Parklands' with twenty-seven wildlife ponds and five miles of footpaths.

Part of me is glad they aren't just going to build over everything, but it's clear that this 'improvement' of the landscape is geared towards selling the new houses that are springing up in the vicinity. The old fairways have always had a monetary value, but now that they are being remod-elled there's a more tangible sense of their profitmaking potential. They are slowly being reshaped with revenue in mind; pruned and groomed to attract prospective house buyers. Neat 'parklands' are far easier to sell than a scruffy woodland or miles of sprawling, open fields.

So much is lost in this gentrification, most notably the freedom to wander and be spontaneous. Now that Clavicle Wood has been decimated and many of the grass-lands around it fenced off, our routes through the green space that is left will be much more prescribed. We'll be funnelled between the boundaries of private properties, directed around driveways.

But this is our lot. Seeing how quickly the space around me has been physically altered, I think now that we suburbanites will have to arrive at a feeling of belonging not through what is fixed, but through a constant recalibration of our relationship with topographical change. Perhaps there is a response to be made in the form of the *dérive*. By finding new ways to navigate whatever parcel of land we're eventually gifted by the planning committees, by disrupting and disorientating in some way the lines that we're supposed to follow, we can continue to know the difference between a path that's made for us and one that we discover for ourselves.

MAKING MONSTERS

AMY STEWART

I 'm floating in the water like a dead thing. My belly is breaching the surface, a thin layer of webby water over the top like ripped tights, and there's nothing above me but wide skies I could fall up into. My leg has been throbbing for the last ten minutes, and I let the sensation tingle and spread. I haven't felt anything in so long that the pain is delicious. I cradle it in my body, begging it not to leave.

When I finally swim back to shore, my sisters prop themselves up on their towels. Leigh's eyes widen at the red welt on my thigh.

'You've been stung by a fucking jellyfish.'

Have I? That makes sense. My sisters look worried, but I read about jellyfish stings before we came to the island, and I know I just need to clean it. I make a show of dabbing it. It'll be fine.

Everything'll be fine, now we're here.

How long have we been on this island? It could be a week, or a month. We lie out on the beach most days, baking ourselves in sun and salt among the grizzled locals, who eye us with interest, wondering why we don't leave. I think about how we look on the outside. Milky and innocent as lambs, perhaps: Orla is the smallest of us, a child from the back though she's in her late teens, while

Leigh is athletic, boyish. I'm somewhere in between in all things; an amalgamation. A compromise.

Today's hours pass slowly. We measure our time in moons and tides. When I tell my sisters that I'm going for ice cream and some vinegar to clean the sting, they nod lazily. A drip of sweat rolls over Leigh's lip. Orla throws an arm over her face, afflicted.

The path from the beach to Chora is beaten and dusty. I think again how far we are from home – but we're not running away, as we've been told. We've just come somewhere else, to feel a bit better. We chose Serifos because we'd never heard of it but could get there easily from Athens, and really, we could have done worse – the island's abandoned blue-and-white churches and tiny tavernas expect nothing. I like the way the coast looks all jagged and broken up, like teeth gnashing in the water. There's something lonely about the place, but it's lovely all the same – it's a moon on a night I'd thought barren.

Stou Stratou is my favourite place for ice cream in Chora. It's a tiny white building sitting right at the top of the hill, and by the time I arrive my back is wet with sweat, blisters burning. My stung leg feels a bit strange. I like it, and think I'll leave the vinegar for a while. There's a couple sitting out on the terrace who I've spoken to a few times before – Maria and Nicholas. They wave as I take a seat.

'Ah, Julia,' Maria says good-naturedly. I love how she says it: a 'y' instead of a 'j'. 'Exploring alone again?'

I nod, rubbing at my scaly arms. 'I've been at the beach.'

There's a map of the island unfolded on the table between them. They're on holiday from Athens, escaping the summer tourist hordes. I can't tell how old they are, but they're beautiful, with twinkling eyes and weather-exposed skin. When they see me around the island, they tell me things about Serifos – how it was once the home of the Cyclopes, that it's where Perseus returned after his famous quest, how it was once occupied by the Turkish. Nicholas is tall and thin and has a strange way of speaking English – a little formal, archaic. Elegiac, even. He told me once that Athenians are graceless and tasteless people, and grinned when I replied that that's my favourite kind.

My sisters don't know about Maria and Nicholas. It wasn't a conscious decision not to tell them, not at first, but now I like that they're my secret. They don't remind me of home, or the things that happened there.

Maria is taking great sweeping licks of her ice cream. She's the kind of person who eats passionately, as if she can never quite get enough. 'I'd recommend the pistachio,' she grins.

Nicholas is the more measured, the more perceptive. He sees my vacant look and asks, 'Are you okay?' The sun is in his eyes and he peers at me from beneath a peaked hand. I think perhaps they worry about me. As much as strangers can, anyway.

'Better today,' I lie.

They share a glance that I can't translate. Maria digs into the pocket of her cargo shorts. 'I bought you a present from one of the little boutiques in Chora,' she says. She unfurls her palm and there's a precious stone of some sort there. The colour – it's how I imagine the inside of a volcano would look, all swirling magma and dead ash.

'It's agate,' she explains, taking hold of my wrist and placing the stone in my upturned palm. 'Famous Greek stone. Good for healing. Will make your pain softer.'

Tears are pricking at my eyelids. I don't know what they think has happened to me – I don't think they'd even be able to begin to guess, but their simple kindness makes something inside me swell.

'Thank you,' I say quietly.

Nicholas smiles at Maria and sips his dark espresso. The bitter smell carries on the breeze.

I head inside, counting out the coins into my palm. It's cooler inside the shop, and it smells like freshly baked bougasta. I order a double scoop of the lemon sorbet in a cone, and by the time I've paid, it's already started to melt. I suck drops off my fingers, feeling clumsy, and when I look back outside, Maria and Nicholas are still watching me. Perhaps we'll all go for dinner together. Somewhere with cheap wine and pictures on the menu. I'll just tell my sisters I got carried away wandering around the island; it's happened before. Anything's better than sitting in that hotel room, counting down the minutes until sunrise. The dark hours are the worst for us. They're when memories wake up.

*

The next morning, I look at myself in the mirror and am taken aback by my ugliness. I'm not sure if my sisters see it, but my skin's cracking in the Greek heat; my body wasting, ribs sticking out of skin like gnarled fingers. My hair is clumping, serpentine, coarse as hay. My skin has a green tinge – not Starbucks green, the colour of money, but the grimy hue of river water. I know it's because I'm wearing them all on my face – the things that happened at home. I open my mouth in the mirror, bare teeth, frighten and repulse myself. There's a power in it. I only stop when my sisters come up behind me.

'You love looking at yourself,' Orla jibes. Her skin is clotted cream compared to mine. 'It's because you're the prettiest.'

The sting on my leg hurts, but I'll wait to tell them. We're going out on a boat today to have a look at the little scattering of islets around the coast. We need to leave now to be on time, and I don't want to ruin the mood.

But there's no one else at the harbour when we get there, just shabby motorboats bobbing at the end of a jetty. We dangle our legs over the side, toes skimming the water. We're still getting used to the island's concept of time – it's half an hour until a Greek man comes up behind us with a clipboard. We've met him before; as well as leasing the boats, he cleans the hotel we're staying at.

'Sisters,' he says warmly, accepting our money. 'Don't go too far out, no?' He helps us each down into the boat and I'm touched by the chivalry. His hands are surprisingly soft for a man's. Leigh takes control of the wheel, always best at this kind of thing, and the motor splutters into life.

As we pull away from the harbour, I find myself thinking about Maria and Nicholas. I cradle the agate in my palm, marvelling at the way it retains warmth. Last night I had too much wine and I think I cried a little as they walked me home. They both linked an arm through mine, and I was a child between them.

The coast stretches away from us, and soon we're surrounded by nothing but water that's clear as a mirror. Leigh lets the engine idle, resting one hand on the wheel, watching the horizon like a captain. Orla lies down in the belly of the boat, shiny legs propped up on the seat. David Bowie is playing tinnily from my phone. I stare down into the water, my reflection contorting with the waves and light. I marvel at my greying skin, the coarse ropes in my hair. I'm beginning to scare myself. My sting twinges – I never did clean it.

Something arcs into my vision: a fat-bellied fish, whiskered and twisting. Without thinking, I reach a hand into the water and grab it. I keep it submerged and its staring eyes fix on mine. It wriggles. I'm about to let it go when I get a strange feeling in my fingertips. The fish solidifies in my hand, scales giving way to stone. It's rough, cold, eyeless. Nothing but a rock. I pull it out of the water and lay it on the bottom of the boat.

'Where did you get that?' Leigh asks, sounding bored.

I don't answer. My body is too full of feeling – confusion, fear. But not just that. I feel strong, for the first time in such a long time. Maybe Maria and Nicholas were right: the island is healing me. But I look at the stone, its uncompromising lifelessness, and I know it's doing something else to me, too.

*

I dream of him. Joe. Hands in my hair, pulling it back. Breath on my neck, hot as a slap. *Fuck*, he'd said, *I'd follow you anywhere.* I thought it was the most romantic thing I'd ever heard in my life. Now I know better.

Something feels wrong when I wake up. My sisters aren't in the room, for a start, but there's a note: they've gone for lunch and will be back in a couple of hours.

I look down at my leg. The sting is scarlet, whip-like, fringed with a red rash. There's barely any pain, though. I could easily drift back off into a nap, sleep the day away. There's a spaciness in my head, lazy and hypnotic, that's not unpleasant. My phone buzzes on the bedside table.

We're passing your hotel. Lunch? M&N x

I get butterflies when I read the message. I stand to look in the mirror. I'm a little unsteady, like I'm drunk. Then I see my reflection, and bile creeps up my throat.

My hair has turned the same dirty green as my skin, which is now threaded with fine red lines – like veins, like jellyfish tentacles, like earthquake-scarred earth. My teeth are pointed, yellow. When I move there's a hissing sound, like something trying to escape through a gap. My heart starts to hammer.

I'm horrific. I'm monstrous.

I turn away from myself and go to the bathroom to pour a glass of water. But I can't escape myself – when I blink I still see hair writhing, skin sinking inward. I need my sisters. I need to get out of this room. My phone beeps again.

Last chance! Beach picnic. M&N x

*

I suggest Livadakia Beach – it's close and as bustling as Serifos gets, and I'm craving as much company as I can get today – but they'd prefer to go to Ganema.

'There's never anyone there,' Maria tells me with a wink. 'Not a tourist trap like Livadakia.'

I wonder absently if they notice how my body is disintegrating. I can't quite bring myself to ask. I put a hand to my hair, self-conscious, and pull away when I feel something thick and ropey. It seems to move under my fingers, as if invoked. My heart slows as we walk along the dusty road to Ganema, though. There's a strong wind today and my hair whips around my head while Nicholas playfully pushes Maria off the path, catching her every time. I feel a stab of something bitter, watching their arms entwine.

They've brought so much food with them and they lay it out with precision: scarlet strawberries speckled with seeds, fat olives stuffed with pimento, multiple types of sweating cheese, two bottles of warm white wine.

As we eat, I show them my jellyfish sting.

'Ah, yes,' Nicholas says, squinting at my leg. He touches a tentative finger to my skin, lifting the hem of my dress ever so slightly to reveal the full wound. Maria watches, finishing her second glass of wine. 'That looks bad. Hospital?'

I can't tell them why that can never be an option. That the last time I was in hospital I had a broken jaw and blood dripping down my legs. I promise them I'll go, but after that I can't eat much. My appetite has dried up like skin in the sun. Maria frowns. 'But you're so thin,' she says disapprovingly. 'And we bought all this food, just for you.' Nicholas nods in agreement.

I swallow, feeling awkward. It's the first time they've been anything but gentle with me. Now they watch closely as I bite off the tip of a strawberry. The beach suddenly feels very empty.

'There's a party happening tonight,' Nicholas says. 'Lots of locals – a big feast. Party. Drink. On a beach near here. Some of our other friends told us about it.'

I don't know why those words hurt so much: *other friends.* Maria and Nicholas are outgoing, social – why should I think I'm the only one they've befriended?

'You should come,' Nicholas continues. 'You and your sisters.'

That word from his mouth makes me start. My sisters are my own. 'How do you know I have sisters?' I ask, voice small.

Nicholas laughs, shrugging off the question as though it's a mosquito. 'You told us,' he smiles. His eyes land on mine and he takes a swig of beer. 'Silly girl.'

*

I walk back to the hotel alone, paranoia pulling at my nerves like a fish hook. But that's all it is: paranoia. I remind myself that people are good and kind. That not everyone wants to hurt me. That not everyone swarms around pain like it's bait.

On my way back over the coastal road, I see a lithe man on the rocks, poised to dive into the waves. My stung leg aches but I pause to watch him. The sea swallows his body greedily and then he resurfaces, pushing his hair back over his head, clambering out to dry off. The sun dazzles my eyes, relentless, and I squint. The man is gone – there's only the rocks he was lying on, the same rich sepia as his skin.

When I get back to the hotel, Leigh and Orla have returned. They're sprawled out on the bed like cats, tanned bellies to the ceiling. They've brought me some fresh marathokeftedes, my favourites, crispy fennel fritters prickling with salt. They sit sweating in their carton on the side. The ceiling fan whirs loudly, but it just seems to move the heat around the room.

'You've been gone ages,' Leigh says, propping herself up on her elbow, one eyebrow raised. There's a slick of sweat on her upper lip.

'I needed a walk,' I say.

'You've just missed Mum and Dad – they called.'

Those words shouldn't make my stomach sink, but they do. They'll be asking when we're coming back, and I wonder what Leigh and Orla told them. Mum and Dad feel like they should have access to that kind of information again, because we moved home for a little while after everything happened. I felt their goodwill like a drug – they wanted to care for us, to parent us again. And I was so ready to let them. I wanted to collapse back into them, to let them know everything that had happened so they could wrap it up and sell it back to me as something much less frightening. But they expected me to understand it, to be able to put it into words, and I couldn't. So I became all sharp edges, cutting them at every turn, until we had to get away. Until we had to come here. It was an inevitability – I don't know why they were so surprised.

'I told them we'll probably be home next week,' Leigh says carefully. 'They think that's a good idea. We need to start getting on with things.'

My sting prickles and I stagger a little, woozy. I feel as though someone is trying to rip my skin away from my body, and I have to concentrate to hold on to it all. 'Next week?' I manage to say. 'You want to leave Serifos?'

Orla dangles her legs over the edge of the bed. 'Did you think we'd stay forever?'

I'm not sure – not exactly. But I do know I'm not ready to leave yet. I think of Maria and Nicholas, left alone with their new friends, and it makes my stomach roil. I think of the fish in the water, how it became stone in my hand. How I immortalised it with my touch. Or did I kill it? I was a broken, desperate thing in England. Here, I'm something else.

'We're not so sure that the island is good for you,' Leigh continues. 'You've been … weird.'

So they have noticed: the tinge to my skin. The writhing of my hair. The way my gaze is flat and staring. But I need to make sure. I feel like some kind of spell would be broken if I were to utter the truth out loud.

'What do you mean?'

'You're keeping secrets. You don't sleep, you barely eat. It's like what happened last time. You didn't tell us what was happening until it was too late.'

'This is nothing like last time,' I say under my breath.

'How would we know? You don't tell us anything. You're always sneaking off to meet someone – don't think we don't notice. We came out here to help you heal after … after everything with Joe.'

His name cuts through me, quick and sharp as a cleaver. 'Please don't talk about him.'

'And we're running out of money,' Leigh continues, as if I haven't spoken. 'We need to get back into the world again. Get jobs. Pay tax. Start our lives, properly.'

Somewhere underneath layers of fear and frustration, I know that she's right. The island is timeless – nothing changes, nothing evolves, there barely seem to even be seasons. But somewhere else in the world – *everywhere* else in the world – time is passing. I'm getting older. I'll be thirty next year. It's a thought I can't face. I'd prefer to stay here forever with the dusty roads and the skies of endless cornflower blue. But still, the only words that bubble up to my lips and feel true enough to say are, 'I won't leave.'

Orla's delicate brow furrows but Leigh rolls her eyes. 'Do what you want,' she says, words barbed. 'We're booking a flight for Monday.'

The fan continues to whir. It's so hot in the room that I feel the tops of my thighs sticking to each other. My sting is oozing. I don't say anything but turn and leave, feeling their eyes on my back as I go.

*

I'm going to the party on the beach. Maria and Nicholas didn't even tell me where it's happening, and for a while I wander around Chora. The main square is lonely and echoing at this time, the shopfronts shuttered. The tiny cobbled lanes seem to have gotten tangled up with each other in the dusk, like lovers under sheets. From my vantage point on top of the hill, I can see frothy lights down by the bay. I follow them and the sound of building music down to the beach.

There are so many people here, milling around in the dying light. It casts a golden glow across their faces, their exposed shoulders, backs, waists. There's a DJ at some decks, as well as long trestle tables topped with platters. Everything is festooned with bulb lights, and over it all is the gentle hum of the ocean lapping at the shore. I scan the crowd for Maria and Nicholas, finding them quickly. They're standing alone beside a large group, heads in close, faces serious. I go to wave but then decide I want to watch them for a minute – how they are when they don't know they're sharing a space with me. They seem older somehow, more serious. Nicholas looks up, his eyes sweeping the crowd, and sees me. It's a funny thing to see his face transform; the watched becoming the watcher. They beckon me over and I obey, picking up a flute of Prosecco from a nearby table first.

'You came, Julia,' Maria says, her hands on top of my hands. They're slightly cool. 'But where are your lovely sisters? Did we not say that they were invited, too?'

I don't want to talk about my sisters. I don't want to think about them sitting in that hotel room, booking flights to get away from here, away from a peaceful life that feels so hard-won. 'No, I'm alone.'

They give me that look I'm so familiar with now. A strange land between pity and understanding. Maria takes my hand and pulls me towards where a crowd of people are dancing. Grinning, she spins me underneath her arm. I'm not a natural dancer, I can't move my body effortlessly to the beat like she can; my hips are stubborn and I can't stop thinking about how I must look. Maria doesn't seem to care. She pulls me in close, so close I can smell sweat and jasmine on her skin. She whispers in my ear, 'Let go, Julia.'

Nicholas is watching. He raises a glass, drains it, then approaches. Together they frame me, their bodies surrounding me, until I'm no longer sure whose arm is whose. For a minute, two minutes, it's perfect. My head sparkles with alcohol and I feel as if an anchor has come loose – that I'm drifting freely, pleasantly, into an ocean that never ends.

Then I feel Nicholas's palm on the small of my back. Maria's hand is on my cheek, quickly replaced by her lips, wet and hot. My ribcage contracts. My breath quickens. I want to be fine, but I'm not because here are the memories again, furiously clear and unapologetic. Joe's strong arms pushing me, forcing me into a dark room with no way out.

I sway, feeling faint. Maria is there to catch me before I've even doubled over. Gently, they lead me out of the crowd, across the beach and around the bay, to a quieter stretch behind the rock. There's a carcass of something here. It's been picked clean.

'Julia ...' Nicholas stretches out a hand, but all I see is Joe's – I smell his whisky and cigarette breath, the soft tan of his skin in the half-light. I think I hit Nicholas's hand away, but I can't be sure.

He reels back, surprised. His eyes snag on my hair, and I have the sudden sense that he *sees* me now: the ugliness inside, the wasting skin and the viperous hair and the irises of granite. I need to tell him to stop looking at me, because I can feel something happening. Something dangerous and damaging and out of control. But I keep a hand on his, and I don't look away.

'Nicholas?' Why does Maria's voice sound so fraught? 'My love, what's happening?'

I feel a tug of guilt, but I can't stop now. Nicholas's hand is already cold underneath mine, and it's spreading all the way up through the veins in his arms. Each one is submitting to me. Surrendering.

When I've finished, he's a single, sad monolith. Another rock on the beach, toppled. Maria takes one look at me, makes an ugly guttural sound, and then begins to move backwards, hands grasping at the sand. I don't want to hurt her, but what else am I supposed to do? Who would she tell about what she's seen? How would I even begin to explain?

Gently, I place a hand on hers. I repeat what Joe said. His last words to me.

'Don't struggle, and it won't hurt.'

*

The coach doesn't have air conditioning, so the ride to the airport is stifling and intense. Orla falls asleep on my shoulder while my head lolls back and forth. Leigh keeps her eyes strained to the front of the coach. She doesn't want us missing the stop. She is sensible and steady as a stone, my sister.

The last week has passed quickly. When I got back to the hotel after the party, dazed and stumbling, Leigh and Orla took one look at me and called a taxi straight to the hospital. My sting was infected, and I had a fever that needed antibiotics. After a couple of days in bed, heaving through dreams of poison and whisky and music and festoon lights, I started to feel better. I told my sisters I wanted to go home.

The airport is air-conditioned and so we drape ourselves across the plastic seats, drinking freshly squeezed orange juice and feasting on the last bougasta we'll ever eat. I let the sugar coat my tongue, my teeth, trying to make myself sick of it so it won't be so difficult to leave.

I will the flight to be delayed, but we take off on time. The plane pulls our skulls back into the headrests as it arcs upwards and away from the island. My sisters let me have the window and I crane my neck to look back. There it is, Serifos, nothing more than a craggy lump of rock in the ocean. A heart of green surrounded by endless blue. We're still close enough to make out figures on the beaches. And down there, facing us, a bay like the one of the beach party. Could it be that same nameless beach? I scan for rocks, toppled in the sand, see nothing. I pull the agate Maria gave me out of my pocket, cradle it in my hand. It's still warm, but cooling now.

I look past and through the island to see myself reflected thinly in the window. I'm not sure what I expect to see, but it isn't the person who stares back: clear-skinned, blue-eyed, young-looking. It feels as though none of it was real – that I haven't been alive for the last month, simply dreaming. I desperately want to have something of Serifos, to know that somehow it healed me. That I'm different to when I came.

I close my fingers around the agate, and when I open it again, there's nothing but an ocean-smoothed pebble. Grey and cold. My body hums with energy, blood hisses in my veins, and I think, perhaps, the island left its mark after all.

BIRDIE IN THE BIG SMOKE

MELISSA WAN

The Operation

Birdie is on the 10.55 to London. Her train has departed and she sits alone with a notebook on her lap. The carriage is not crowded and her suitcase is on the floor in front of the seat beside her. She is going to London to see a friend who lives in Brussels now but who is in England to attend a wedding. As the train whizzes past fields neatened by speed and distance – a blur of colour and repeated patterns – Birdie thinks about the friend, whom she has not seen in a long time. They remained close after graduating and for a while they wrote to one another. They sent long handwritten letters of love and missing across the Channel but Birdie can no longer remember who last did the writing. Outside the window the cows lie low on the grass, their legs folded neatly beneath them. Until today Birdie had no idea that Crewe was so far away from Manchester: past Stockport, Wilmslow, even Alderley Edge.

Reckoning

Instead of making a start on the new story that has been
on her mind for almost a month, Birdie uses the blank
pages of her notebook to make calculations. Birdie
cannot afford to be in London for six days but the friend
said she could stay with her in the room she has booked
in the youth hostel. Until payday, just over a week away,
Birdie has £62.61. On Google Maps she checks how long it
will take to walk from the station to the youth hostel and
she receives a message from her telephone provider: 'You
have used 80% of your data.'

Kindling

While Birdie is on the train she receives an email from
the Norwegian she worked with not long ago. He says he
will no longer be coming to England as initially planned.
He will be staying in Norway. Birdie is disappointed. The
prospect of seeing the Norwegian again had rekindled an
attraction she once felt quite strongly. It is an attraction
that resurfaces with proximity or the prospect of it. He is
tall, blond and blue-eyed – not her type – but after spending so much time with him, Birdie began to understand
why people married their colleagues.

A Lapse in Decorum

Across the aisle, a man in a green checked shirt sits at
a table by the window. He has just been asked to move
because he is in someone's reserved seat. He is sure one

of these was available, he says, and the seat owner says perhaps, but that she would prefer to please sit by the window, in the seat she had especially reserved. The man in green moves into the seat beside hers. The train is empty with available seats and Birdie cannot understand why he makes the choice to stay cramped beside the stranger. Now he no longer has the view from the window, the man in green takes out his phone and tries to lose himself in its screen.

A Wake-up Call

Birdie is staying in the friend's private room in a youth hostel on Noel Street, even though the room has been booked only for one. The friend is paying £400 for five nights. For that money you get to be in Soho, crowded and expensive. The room has a double bed and security is lax. Nobody looks at Birdie, let alone asks what she thinks she is doing there, but the friend is paranoid they will be caught. This paranoia overshadows any joy at seeing one another again and almost instantly their reunion feels like an anticlimax. That evening the friend wants to go to a cocktail bar and eight of Birdie's pounds go on a Long Island Iced Tea.

Closer

Halfway through her drink Birdie begins to look intensely at her coaster which is swollen with liquid. She has the desire to tell the friend about the Norwegian, about her confused feelings and disappointment, but feels it won't be of any relevance. Also, the Norwegian is married and Birdie anticipates the friend's moralising. Over the loud music the friend shouts that she and her husband were recently in a car crash. Though they are okay, they both came very close to not being. Birdie knows they have been thinking about breaking up for almost as long as they've been together, but the friend says the crash has brought them closer.

Beauty Sleep

The friend does not want to attend the wedding tomorrow. After their cocktail she lies flat on their bed in the hostel and complains. She does not like the couple and says they are always talking about money. Does Birdie even know how much this wedding cost? Birdie does not. When the friend tells her, Birdie keeps her eyes closed and mutters something conciliatory. That night Birdie will learn the meaning of the phrase 'paper-thin walls'. She can hear the couple next door having sex but the friend is wearing her earplugs. Her eye mask says, 'I need my beauty sleep.'

Thief

The next morning Birdie waits in the room while the friend goes down for breakfast. Birdie can hear a man on the phone in the corridor outside. He says, 'Hello, James here,' and Birdie thinks he has a voice you could fall in love with. When the friend comes back having eaten, she says nobody took her breakfast token. Birdie smiles in the presumption that the friend will offer the token to her. Instead the friend judges Birdie for wanting to steal breakfast too. Birdie is always stealing something she shouldn't be. She is stealing the youth hostel's electricity and hot water. She is stealing a pillow and one side of the mattress and duvet. The friend tells Birdie she can stay for one more night, but then she should probably leave. The room is booked only for one and, anyway, doesn't Birdie have plenty of friends she could stay with in London?

The Stomach Versus the Wallet

On her third morning in London, Birdie packs her suitcase and leaves the hostel at 8.30 a.m. She trawls the streets to find an affordable breakfast that might also fill her up until dinnertime, when she is meeting a friend who will put her up on his sofa. A steady stream of Londoners pass her by, fractious and defeated from their commute. Birdie sits in a cafe called Fiori. Because it is in Covent Garden it is expensive despite being low quality. Birdie spends £7.20 on a toastie and a pot of tea and stays there for three hours. She chews slowly and asks for a refill of hot water. Birdie tries to write but is distracted. She cannot stop thinking about the fact that she is now alone in London, with little money, having to rely on the generosity of others until her return train on Sunday. Fuming, Birdie writes three angry pages in her notebook.

The Walk

Birdie walks from Covent Garden to Deptford. Deptford is six miles away and it takes her two hours and forty-five minutes, in part because every thirty seconds she has to stop to realign the wheels on her suitcase, which catch. For much of the way she walks along a main road. Birdie learns that this part of the city is not made for pedestrians. Google Maps can no longer calculate a walking route. Birdie is completely surrounded by cars and machines and by the time she reaches New Cross, she has been driven almost to the point of tears.

The Hungarian Cafe

Birdie checks prices through the windows of cafes before she decides whether or not to go in. A cup of tea at the Hungarian Cafe is only £1.80. When she enters, there are two women sitting in the window, but they soon leave and Birdie becomes the establishment's sole customer. The waiter is an old man in a waistcoat, his hair and moustache religiously white. He stands behind the counter and spritzes the leaves on a money plant. After an hour Birdie feels so guilty about only ordering a cup of tea that she buys a muffin for £2. It is tasty but small and dry, and she resents having to pay twice what she had intended. She phones her mother but her mother cannot talk. Birdie can feel her eyes prickling but is determined not to be so pathetic as to cry. Instead she looks out of the window at the road and makes a list of 'At Leasts':

At least I'm not a bus driver always stuck in traffic.

At least I'm not an HGV driver always stuck in traffic.

At least I'm not a taxi driver always stuck in traffic.

At least I'm not a woman who has to shop for her whole family and carry this shopping in heavy bags hanging from the crooks of her elbows.

At least my knees still work.

At least my brain still works.

At least I have never been in a car crash.

At least I have the choice to take contraception if I want to.

At least I can buy flowers if I want to.

At least I sometimes find a pound on the street and even €100 that summer in Naples.

At least I'm not homeless.

At least I could have caught a bus if I really wanted to.

At least I could have caught the tube if I really wanted to.

At least I could even have taken a taxi if I really wanted to.

At least

Laura

A day later, staying with her friend Laura, life looks up significantly. In Laura's presence the world becomes a better place. Once, Birdie was in love with Laura. When they first met, Laura had long hair down to her waist. She has now cut it to her shoulders but of course this does nothing to mar her beauty, her intelligence or her kindness. She makes Birdie cups of tea and shares a tin of sardine paste with her. Laura reads Birdie a message in which her girlfriend, who lives in Austria, says hi hi hi and sorry she missed her. Birdie likes Laura's girlfriend. This feeling of warmth towards the girlfriend despite her previous feelings for Laura has been one of the best things to happen to Birdie and she hopes it says something about her character.

Yellow Pears

In the late afternoon Birdie and Laura go for a walk around Laura's new neighbourhood of Swiss Cottage. They walk and walk without knowing where they are going, stumbling down cobbled streets, often into each other. They feel drunk without having had anything to drink. They walk past the Freud Museum and Laura shows Birdie the house where Rabindranath Tagore once stayed. They buy a bag of chips to share, which they coat in salt and vinegar, and walk down a small alley where pears have fallen from their trees and onto the stairs. The pears are yellow and the leaves too are yellow and orange and red. Everything is beautiful. When they find a pub, Laura even buys Birdie a pint.

Raclette

Birdie and Laura buy cheap wine, potatoes and salad from the supermarket to accompany the cheese Laura brought back from Austria when she went to see her girlfriend. The groceries come to a total of £9.51, which Birdie happily pays for on her card. The cheese is for the raclette machine. They debate over whether raclette is a French or Dutch invention. Later Birdie will discover it is Swiss.

They listen to music and Birdie introduces Laura to Bill Callahan. In her bedroom they listen and laugh to 'Eid Ma Clack Shaw'. They talk and listen to music until late in the night. Birdie thinks it is funny to joke that Laura's bed is a piece of crap, but for her remaining two nights in London she sleeps the best she has slept in days.

The Final Supper

Birdie sees the friend she travelled to London especially to see once more in the capital, at breakfast on the morning of their return journeys. The friend tells Birdie she seems 'off'. They are at an expensive cafe so Birdie only orders a coffee and watches the friend complain about the size of her egg. Birdie finds it hard to remember why they were ever friends. Things have changed so much that their friendship, now, is based entirely on the past and what they once shared. Birdie wonders for how long history and obligation will be enough.

Balance Carried Forward

In total, while in London for five days, Birdie took two buses and one tube ride. That is a total of £5.40. Had she not worried she could have spent at least three or four times this amount, which would still not have been enough to worry about but which would have depressed her on her return to Manchester. In the end her expenses come to £41.24 and Birdie is thrilled to arrive back home with £21.37 still in her account when she had expected to be deep into her overdraft.

Aftermath

The friend changes her profile picture to one Birdie took of her on their first night in London: the friend is smiling, red double-deckers blurring behind her. Birdie neither likes nor comments on the photograph. She thinks about the fact that she and Laura took no photographs together. Two years later, Birdie receives a message from the friend out of the blue: 'David has decided to put an end to our relationship.' Birdie turns off her phone.

ANGEL OF THE NORTH

KIT FAN

'Do you have any questions for us?' the Chair asked.

Tenshi was fixated on the idea that everyone was staring at his sweat patches. To wear an undershirt or not wear an undershirt was the question he had asked the misted mirror in the morning.

The fact he had over-prepared for the interview didn't help him recall the questions he'd rehearsed the night before. He wrote a whole page of them and thought each one was a key to open doors he'd never dreamed of touching. Now the job interview was ending with the awkward silence that comes when the interviewee is invited to ask questions. No one would believe the last thirty-five minutes had been a jolly conversation between friends, rather than an official inquiry into his competence, character and dedication to taking up a new role he felt completely incompetent for. It was too responsible for someone like him.

His mind went blank, then somewhere else.

Somewhere above the left shoulder of the Panel Chair, through the sash window, under a copper beech tree, there was a pigeon sitting on the wing of an angel whose chipped nose had been weathered by Islington rain and lichen.

Quite a sizeable angel even at a distance. Why did people put angels on their tombs?

The pigeon fastidiously groomed her wings. Since childhood, Tenshi had been frightened of pigeons. Everything about the bird – the mad swarm, the constant pecking, the coo-cooing noise, the grey-green poo, the way they nosed around stealing food, their shameless-ness among humans, their matter-of-factness in cities. The most maddening thing about them was their yellow-black eyes – lidless like scandals, naked like nipples. He had always been fascinated by the unique character of nipples – other people's and his own – but while nipples stiffened, those bottomless pigeon irises widened and deepened, drowning Tenshi's confidence.

She was eyeing him now and he had nowhere to hide.

His stomach rumbled. One of the interviewers in the assertive blouse with Sicilian lemon-prints smiled.

The growling got louder the second time. He took a deep breath to stop the noise of emptiness. He didn't know if he should smile back to the lemons which were acidifying in his mouth.

'I'm terribly sorry. I didn't manage to have lunch ...'

'It is absolutely fine if you don't have a question for us.'

A sportier pigeon crash-landed on the angel's wing, pushing the weaker one away.

'Actually, I do have a question. What do the children think about the cemetery?'

The headteacher arched her already peaky eyebrows and put down her ball-pen.

'Sorry, I mean ... isn't it a bit unusual for a school to be right next to a cemetery? Are the students curious about who's buried here?'

He remembered the heavy silences in classrooms when a teacher asked a question and the whole world stopped until a pupil was stupid enough to raise their hand.

The interviewers all looked puzzled. He needed an exit strategy: a joke, the fire alarm, an earthquake. It would have helped if he could make his stomach gurgle on cue.

'*Non est ad astra mollis e terris via*,' the lemony teacher on the panel said and smiled warmly at Tenshi.

'Sorry, I don't have Latin.'

'We're not interviewing you for a Latin post,' the lemon assured him. 'It's Seneca. It means there is no easy way from the earth to the stars.'

The words sent shivers up Tenshi's spine. He wanted to grow a pair of wings to flee from the high-ceilinged, ornately corniced interview room that smelt of beeswax and antiques.

*

By the time the interview was over, he had completely lost his appetite.

The sun re-emerged after a long spell of low clouds. He had time on his hands before his train to Darlington and took a detour to walk along the canal towards Angel. The last time he had followed this beautiful path was nearly two years ago when he'd first moved to London. He watched the wind stealing a few leaves from the trees, the algae blanketed around some houseboats, the cyclists zooming past. He brushed a fly from his forehead. The surface of the rippling water caught him off-guard and he saw himself looking at himself.

'Coward,' the reflection stared back.

The sun was fierce, and water was a super-absorbent of thoughts.

He popped by his favourite Japanese cake shop on Islington High Street, picked up an order for a special cake he had made the week before and asked for an extra ice pack for the journey north.

King's Cross on Friday afternoon was far from heaven. All the destinations on the departure screen were place names north of London, mapping out a major eastern artery linking two nations. But where was the heart pumping the blood?

'Twenty-four-hour CCTV recording is in operation at this station for the purposes of security and safety management.'

'Please do not leave your luggage unattended on the station. Luggage left unattended may be removed without warning, or destroyed or damaged by the security services.'

'The next train to depart from Platform Two will be the 16.00 LNER service to Edinburgh. Calling at Peterborough, York, Darlington, Newcastle and Edinburgh ...'

The dense crowds on the concourse moved like a murmuration of starlings – forming, dispersing, and then re-forming abstract patterns. It reminded Tenshi of the famous Shibuya crossing in Tokyo. He wished he had access to the CCTV footage of the concourse, could immerse himself in the dance and observe the hidden beauty of hundreds of people making fluid, split-second decisions to keep their distance – not having any eye contact, not bumping into each other, not stepping on someone's toes. There was freedom in the art of prohibition. He would put a monochrome filter on the film, juxtapose it with early nature documentaries about bird flight and punctuate the narrative flow with abrupt blackouts. He would call the short film *The Starlings of King's Cross*.

A loud gang of middle-aged women, seasonably blonde, with fake tans and plastic tiaras, were blocking his way to the platform. One with turquoise acrylic nails put her hand over Tenshi's shoulders and wrapped her baby-pink and gold TEAM BRIDE sash around his neck. He was attacked by a heady dose of perfume and lager.

He sneezed.

'Oi, our Charlene like salmon sushi,' one of the many bridesmaids shouted in a fake Japanese accent.

The woman with acrylic claws now had her tongue out, pretending to lick him.

'Com' on, lassie, I'm clamming. Leave the gent alone.' The bride disentangled the sash from Tenshi and smiled with a hint of self-knowledge.

The train was hellishly packed. The customer service manager with his charming Geordie voice apologised for the disabled toilets being out of order and the catering carriage unable to serve hot food. Just when some of the passengers were rolling their eyes, a further announcement was made: 'We're so sorry that gremlins have hacked into the systems and stolen the seat reservations in coach C and D – C for Christian and D for Dior. But not to worry, we've laid on a brand new coach P – P for Prada – with loads of unreserved seats. Oh, I forgot, there is a hidden Prada bag in that coach too. Welcome and enjoy!'

The humour seemed to soften the blow for many, except for a tall, delicately tanned man in a summer linen suit who stiffened his lips and kept mumbling 'ridiculous' in an accent people would recognise in Harrods. Many passengers gave way to him, and Tenshi too made room.

The Dior coach was a real mess. An argument had broken out between two men about overhead luggage, while a group of teenagers refused to turn their music down. A Chinese couple struggled to understand the ticket restrictions of the different train operators. Somewhere a baby was screaming his heart out. The air filled with the sweet pungency of soiled nappies.

Tenshi couldn't find his reserved seat. At the last minute, he jumped off the train and ran along the platform to find the Prada coach. He grabbed the last table seat and tried to secure the cake on the overhead luggage rack.

'Is it a birthday cake?' the young mother opposite asked. 'You can put it on the table. Plenty of room here. We like a birthday cake, don't we, Daisy?' Her daughter stopped colouring in a butterfly, gave Tenshi a quick glance and nodded.

He put the cake down and the condensation from the ice pack made a small pool on the table. The train engine started and the water spilled over his trousers. Tenshi thanked the man sitting next to him for handing him a tissue, and through the black hat, bushy beard and curly side-locks, he found a handsome young man with no facial expression, moving his eyes back to the iPad and mouthing verses from the Hebrew Bible.

None of his fellow passengers at the table spoke a word. Tenshi felt the train trembling and dragging the air in and out of the many tunnels north of London. At British Rail speed, England gradually blurred into a hedgeless, wheat-yellow horizon dotted with cattle and sheep. Here a golf course, there a town defined by its out-of-town shopping centres. Semi-detached redbrick houses, tennis-ball-coloured rectangular lawns sanitised from weeds. A Ford Mondeo and a Mercedes A-Class waiting at a level crossing. A woman walking her dog on a country lane. The Union Jacks and the occasional Saint George flags punctuating the flat skyline. This was the country he knew, and truth be told, the England he thought he'd known since birth. Until everything changed that night. He felt severed, though not sure from what.

'Mum, the train's stopping.' Daisy pointed at the outside world with her purple pen.

'No, sweetie. It isn't.' Her mother kept her eye and finger on her Candy Crush Saga.

'Yes, it is!'

An uneasy calm descended on the Prada coach when the brakes were pressed increasingly hard until the train came to a full stop.

Tenshi was undisturbed by the loudness and stillness. His face was glued to the screen, swiping his photos at that familiar speed you see zoned-out people doing on their phones in a mindless bubble.

The young Jewish man glanced at Tenshi's mobile, and when Daisy's mother noticed, he turned back immediately to the sacred text.

'Is that your daughter? She's beautiful.' The mother put her game on hold. 'Sorry, I shouldn't have intruded on you like that.' She smiled at the Jewish man before looking at Tenshi, who found her eagerness slightly disingenuous.

'Yes, that's my angel.' Tenshi was reluctant to establish proper eye contact, but he did eventually out of politeness. The mother sensed this, though she pretended she hadn't.

'Can I have a look? Oh, she's gorgeous. I like her red bikini.'

'Mum, let me see.' Daisy had already latched on to her mother, blocking her view. 'I want one of those. Mum, can you buy it for me? Please, I really like it.'

'You're too young.'

'Charlotte got a bikini from Zara. Please, Mummy, I really *need* it.' Daisy was all over her mother, touching her cheeks, stroking her hair, hiding in her cleavage.

'The sea looks beautiful. Is it Costa del Sol?' She ignored her daughter.

'No, it's actually the coast near Staithes.' Tenshi realised she hadn't heard of Staithes.

'Sorry, I've no sense of geography. I've lived in London all my life. Just visiting my nan in Glasgow.'

'I hate you, Mum!' Daisy pouted and dropped her head on her half-coloured butterfly.

'How old is your daughter?' She was stroking Daisy's head to cheer her up.

'She's nine in the photo.'

'Mum, I need to go to the toilet.'

Daisy gave Tenshi a naughty smile when her mother picked her up and carried her across the table to a safe landing as if she were on a roller coaster.

Not far from Peterborough now, Tenshi thought, and returned to the beach near Staithes. It had been an unseasonably hot May bank holiday but the North Sea was perishing cold. The tide must have been low and there was a boy on his own, building a sandcastle with a red bucket, the same colour as his daughter's swimsuit. She insisted on a swim and ran straight into the blue-grey sea. She screamed like a baby and in less than a minute jumped out of the water. Her skin was flamingo-pink.

'I am sorry I looked at your photos. I shouldn't have done that.' The young man sitting next to him put his iPad down.

'Oh, it's okay. I didn't even notice.' Tenshi waited for a reply and couldn't stand the awkwardness. 'Where're you travelling?'

'Back to Gateshead.'

'What are you reading? I mean ... which chapter is it? Sorry, I don't have Hebrew and I reckon you must be reading the Bible.'

'Yes. I have been rereading this passage all week. Moses sees the burning bush and asks what Yahweh is to his people. Yahweh replies, *"Ehyeh asher ehyeh,"* which is often translated as, *"I am who I am."* But the English translation is problematic.'

'In what way?'

'There is no present tense of the verb "to be" in Hebrew, so strictly speaking it should mean, *"I will be what I will be."'*

'That sounds strange but also straightforward.' Tenshi glanced at the iPad densely packed with Hebrew words, which looked worlds apart from English and Japanese ones. 'Why does this phrase bother you so much?'

'God is speaking but it's a conundrum, isn't it? The state of being is full of familiarities, and yet we know almost nothing about it.'

'Hello!' Daisy put her hand on the cake box, licking her lips and rubbing her tummy.

Her mother looked flustered and embarrassed. The young man tilted his iPad back up.

'Dear passengers, I am so sorry for the delay,' the charming Geordie man announced. 'We have been informed there's been a fatality near St Neots and British Transport Police are involved. Our thoughts are with their family. We managed to change track and will soon be on our way to Peterborough.'

'Mummy, what's a fatality?' Daisy put the purple crayon in her mouth.

'Don't worry, sweetheart. Everything is all right. It's just a short delay.'

'But he said police are e-volved.'

Tenshi and the young man smiled. The mother picked up a black crayon and started colouring in the butterfly's body for Daisy, who took the darkness out of her mother's hand and cheekily replaced it with orange.

The train started moving and no one spoke again until Tenshi said goodbye to everyone at the table, just before he got off at Darlington.

*

Tenshi pressed the doorbell once. No answer. He could smell fried garlic and possibly roast chicken. The two climbing roses he had insisted on planting at the front of the house – *Tess of the d'Urbervilles* and *Madame Alfred Carrière* – looked healthy. He tried the bell again and finally knocked on the door.

Footsteps drew nearer. Then paused. He heard a voice whispering inside. After what seemed a lifetime, the door was half-opened.

'Hi, Tenshi. What're you doing here?'

'Hi, James. How are you?'

'We're having dinner.' James had a new haircut. The familiar parting had been replaced by a closer shave around the sideburns. He looked as stylish as a hedge-fund manager in the City.

'Why are you whispering? I didn't know you were eating. I'm sorry.'

'It is dinnertime, though.' James thought he might have been unjustly harsh. 'Do you want to come in and join us?'

'Thanks for inviting me. I don't want to disturb you and Michael.'

'Don't be silly.' James turned around and shouted through an immaculately painted vestibule in subtle greys and off-whites, decorated with a mahogany hall table on which some blue hydrangeas were floating in a large crystal bowl. 'Mike, it's Tenshi!'

'Hi, Tenshi!' It took at least ten seconds for Mike's sturdy voice to reach the front door. James bit his lower lip, a nervous twitch Tenshi still found adorable.

'We were just finishing dinner, so he must be busy or something. Come on in. I've made roast chicken.'

A faint buzz of electricity warmed the glass above. Suddenly the sodium street light was switched on.

'These are antiques, you know.' Tenshi's face was painted ochre. 'They've changed all the street lights to LED in London. It's better for the planet but I prefer the softer yellow.'

Fifteen years ago, when they were walking hand-in-hand on the quayside in Newcastle, all the street lamps came on unexpectedly, and Tenshi had said it was a good omen and kissed James for the first time.

'Sodium street lights are one of the perks of living in Darlington.' James smiled and saw his shadow overlapping Tenshi's. Just when he didn't quite know what he felt, he noticed Tenshi was carrying a box. 'No, no, no. I can't fucking believe you've done this again. I told you not to last year.'

'I'm sorry, James. I didn't know what I was doing. I ...'

James sniggered. 'Don't play dumb. You knew exactly what you were doing. You went into the shop, ordered the cake, travelled over two hundred miles and delivered this fucking birthday cake that nobody fucking wants. You know what? You're a master of self-deception.'

James was grinding at a patch of gravel with his house slippers. Tenshi buried his head in the shadow of the house he'd once lived in.

'What's wrong with you, Tenshi? What's in your head? Tell me. You do know she's gone. She's never coming back.'

James reached out, and when Tenshi recoiled, he dropped the cake on the path.

A neighbour's dog barked and a bird dived out of a sycamore.

'Is it because you're lonely?' James regretted asking but his anger outran his tongue.

With his head down, Tenshi stood under the lamp from the past. His shadow looked like a comma.

James picked up the cake and put it back in Tenshi's hands. The ice packs left a watermark on the concrete.

'I'm sorry, Tenshi. I was rude.'

'You were cruel.'

'Yes, I was nasty because I'm cross. You're cruel too, showing up with the cake just like last year.'

'The world is cruel.'

James bit his lip again and touched Tenshi's shoulder.

'You nasty piece of shit. You think you can get away with murder.' Tenshi kicked the gravel at James like two boys playing tricks on each other.

'Ha! I'm pleased I managed to bring a smile to your grumpy face.'

Tenshi couldn't stop beaming.

'Don't move. Let's have a walk.' James headed back to the house. 'I'm just going to get a jacket and change my shoes.'

*

They walked and walked, without any plan or direction, without exchanging a single word or eye contact. They passed rows of dull suburban family homes and endless parked cars, until they reached the concrete banks of the river reflecting a champagne-coloured sky, one of those rare midsummer moments in the fickle northern weather. It was savoured by the few Darlingtonians who'd found time for a stroll in South Park after dinner.

'Have they got rid of the fountain?' Tenshi frowned. 'This is scandalous. This park is Grade-II listed.'

'It's there.' James pointed at the kidney-shaped pond. 'The council switch it off after eight.'

'I've always wanted to live by the water.' Tenshi took a deep breath.

'You have a lovely lake in Crystal Palace Park.'

'You mean those cheesy dinosaur statues in the murky pond?'

'I loved seeing the Tyrannosaurus rex next to the roses. We had such a hilarious afternoon paddling in our little boat among the London dinosaurs. Was that last summer?'

'No, the summer before last.'

'Oh, yes, when you first moved to London.'

In the distance, a boy ran like a bullet round the outside of the merry-go-round, while a girl held on to the handlebar, laughing, shrieking and screaming as if her head had spun off her neck.

'How's life in London?'

Tenshi found a broken branch and threw it into the pond with the beautiful arm movements of a professional softball player.

'London is London.' Tenshi crouched down to the ripples. 'The world looks more homely when we see it from less than three feet above the ground. Do you remember watching Ozu's *Tokyo Story* together at uni? I really miss sitting on a *tatami*.'

James squatted down to share Tenshi's point of view.

'How's life with Michael?'

'Good. He wants to find another house with a bigger garden in Darlington. He is restlessness personified.'

An early evening breeze tiptoed over the water's surface and disappeared through the small gap between them.

'*Tess* and *Madame Carrière* look happy in front of the house.'

James smiled. 'I had nothing to do with their well-being. Michael is the one with green fingers.'

'Well, Michael is Michael.'

'He sure is.' James sat on the ground, trying to get rid of the pins and needles in his left leg.

'I'm sorry to show up at your front door. I really didn't mean to be cruel. I was on autopilot.'

James started humming and singing the familiar melody of 'Que sera, sera'. He gave a big sunny smile to Tenshi, who wanted to grasp the moment with some-thing stronger than words, but held back.

'I met a young Jewish man on the train up. He was reading the Bible in Hebrew and told me something strange, something God said to Moses when he saw the burning bush.'

'What did the Almighty say?'

'*Que sera, sera.*'

'No way!'

'Yes way! He said, "*I will be what I will be.*"'

'When did you fall for Christ?'

'My fellow passenger was quite hot.'

'Hot like muscle-hot?' James puffed up his chest and showed off his big biceps.

Tenshi laughed ironically, 'Actually, more like brainy-hot, not something you'd understand.'

The pond was calming the agitation in their minds without them noticing. There was a muscular loosening in the atmosphere as the residual heat of the sun rose from the ground, mixing with the cooling evening air, as if they were on a Mediterranean holiday, having a stroll after a candlelit dinner by the sea. Tenshi looked sleepy but his mobile phone rang with a terrible siren-like noise.

'Jesus! That gave me a real fright.' James was stroking his pecs. 'Why can't you have a normal ringtone?'

'Sorry, I have to take this.' Tenshi answered the call and walked swiftly uphill.

Looking at Tenshi in the distance, pacing his way round a majestic horse chestnut tree and totally absorbed in the conversation, James realised the last time he'd seen him was exactly a year ago when he appeared at the front door with a birthday cake. It had been raining that night, the first anniversary of their daughter's death. He let Tenshi into the house and gave him supper. After a few glasses of wine, James lost control of his breath, cried, coughed and choked in Tenshi's arms. When he woke up at four in the morning with a terrible hangover and dragged himself to the kitchen sink for water, he found Tenshi curled up like a kitten on the sofa. A cloud passed and the moon lit up the room and the furniture they had accumulated together through thick and thin – the two IKEA Poäng armchairs they'd bought at university, the sixties teak kitchen table extendable for dinner parties, the poster of Mark Rothko's *Black on Maroon* picked up on their first visit to the Tate, the lava lamp their daughter had insisted on getting for her birthday ...

Then, one day, out of the blue, Michael had appeared. He sat opposite James across the table at a work do, smiled at him as if they had known each other since the beginning of time.

When James had asked what furniture Tenshi would like to take to London, the answer was 'none'.

Now, seeing Tenshi leaning against the tree, completely engrossed in a conversation he was not party to, James couldn't distinguish jealousy from relief. He untied the ribbon on the box and found a matcha chiffon cake in a perfect O, the hollow centre filled with summer raspberries, strawberries, red and blackcurrants. On the emerald brim, there was a piece of dark chocolate half the size of a credit card, with *To J & M* written on top in white chocolate, and next to the initials, a cartoon portrayal of a house with a slanted roof, a window and a door.

'Sorry, Tenshi, I didn't know ...' James's voice was breaking.

'Oh, that's fine.' Tenshi stood there, frozen. The mobile phone was trembling in his hand. 'I got the job.'

'What?' James propped himself up on the ground. 'What job?'

'I can't believe it.' Tenshi's mouth was as wide as the O-shaped cake. 'The lemon lady just rang from the private school. She said it was the unanimous decision of the panel. They said I was impressive and imaginative, and they liked my question about the cemetery. What the hell! I'm going to be a teacher.'

'Congratulations!' James jumped up and embraced Tenshi. He could hear Tenshi's heart going pitter-patter, and his own, too. 'Of course, you *are* impressive and imaginative!' James wiped his eyes before releasing Tenshi back to the cooling air.

'Let's cut the cake to celebrate.' James managed to use the flimsy plastic knife and handed Tenshi a nice piece with plenty of berries on it.

They sat down by the pond again. Tenshi realised how hungry he had been, now that the sweet sponge, light as clouds, reached his stomach.

'Who's this lemon lady?'

'Miss Armstrong, the Latin teacher in the school. She was wearing a bright blouse with Sicilian lemon-prints.'

'I see. What are you going to teach?'

'Digital media and visual culture.'

'What the hell is that?'

'Anything digitally visual, like films, videos, photography.'

'But you haven't got a teaching qualification.'

'You don't need that to teach in a private school.'

'Wow, what a world we live in.'

Tenshi finished his piece and helped himself to another.

'So are you quitting advertising?' James asked, picking some blackcurrants out from his slice of cake and putting them on Tenshi's. He knew how much Tenshi liked them.

'I'll do freelance work one day a week. I think the school likes the connection with industry.'

'I can't believe you're going to be a teacher in a posh school. It's exciting. A watershed moment.' He put his arms around Tenshi. 'I'm so proud of you.'

'Sit tight. I might not pass the probation.'

A pigeon bobbed down from a higher branch to a lower one, mounting himself on a female and trying his luck. The cooing and fluttering lasted three seconds.

Tenshi knew James knew he was wary of them, even though the action was six feet above in the foliage, somewhere beyond reach.

'Do you want to sleep over tonight?'

'Thanks, I'm taking the ten o'clock train back to London.'

'You sure?'

'One hundred per cent.'

'Okay, I'll walk you to the station.'

Tenshi picked up the ribbon and carefully tied a butterfly bow around the cake box. A quarter past nine. Although the sun had set, a faint trace of its orange blaze was still visible on the horizon.

Out of the trees, in the fading evening light, a small murmuration of starlings soared up over the middle of the pond and flew in geometric formations like waves, plumes of smoke, yacht sails or the undulating curve of our heartbeat on an electrocardiogram. It wasn't clear why and how their wings moved in perfect synchrony, as in an evening chorus line. Tenshi started filming the movement on his phone.

'It's beautiful,' James said, holding his breath as if he was walking on a tightrope.

'It's like an augury.'

'Can you tell the message? Is it auspicious?'

Tenshi zoomed in and out, following the unpredictable directions with his fingers, while the time-marker on the screen increased second by second. Against the summer sky, hundreds of black arrows converged into a full stop and dispersed in a fluid, elongated shape that looked like a question mark.

WABBIT

MATT WESOLOWSKI

I 'm fuckin mortal. Head's still ringing with music; the dirty bass of the clubs and the good old songs – sloshing round me belly with the lager. *Oh Delilah*. Staggering through the doors of Cosy Joe's out into the street, reeling. I can still feel the lads' arms round us; stink of sweat and aftershave.

Spit and songs in me ears, all out of tune out of key but who gives a fuck cos it's fucking beautiful. Me throat is wrecked. All the old tunes. Oldies but goodies.

Just like us.

Easter fuckin Sunday morning.

There's a couple of lasses laughing in the cold; tab smoke spiralling up into the sky. Lovely. I bum one and stick it behind me ear; it'll probs get all wet with me sweat. Doesn't matter now, like. Not even got a lighter.

I'm off down through the Bigg Market, get a kebab from the van; chips and garlic sauce; loadsa chilli, mate. Loadsa chilli sauce, my mate, he says. Laughing, little beard; some Arabic tattoo on his neck. Pickled cabbage and everything, me mouth's watering. Just need to sit somewhere; eat me kebab; bottle of lager in me inside jacket pocket to wash it down.

Throat's red raw from all the singing and me mouth hurts from laughing.

Taxi and home.

I walk downhill, past the queue of young'uns outside Perdu; every one of em spice-boys and slappers. Pure Geordie shore types. Dead budgies and nee socks; curly tops and short back and sides. I would have been kicked to fuck looking like that when I was their age. They've all got muscles and tatts now, these lads; all the lasses with their fake tits and Botox. I see one lad passing his mate a baggie of coke – he has a snort off his finger. Things are still the same, really, in the bones of it all.

Up all night on the speed and the cider, we were. Right bunch of charvas.

Long time ago now, all that. I take a swig of me bottle to wash the memory away.

Lights all up ahead, the crossing where there's a million fuckin taxis and people all over the road. A load of students are sat on the steps of Cathedral Square, dressed up in flares and fake afros; metal peace signs round their necks. Used to gan student-bashing back in the day round Byker. Remember when they put those poor fuckers in the high-rises in Cruddas Park? Tarquin and Fiona getting taxed off twelve-year-old radgies. Jesus man, what were they thinking? I almost felt sorry for them.

Almost.

Old Queen Vic sat in her folds of stone, watches us pass by, glaring over at the green lights of Subway. Stink of fake bread coming out of there like a fuckin gas attack. They've got to have doormen outside there now; Greggs too. Mental.

It's noisy as fuck down here man; traffic roaring, lasses shrieking and there's some fuckin southern rugby song coming from the students. Fuck that. I'm away over the road; waiting for the green man like a good lad, me kebab still warm. Some cunt's blowing vape in me face, strawberry fuckin billabong flavour or whatever. Fuckin gleaky twat.

But I'm over and past Tup-Tup on the other side; another queue of spice-boys. But now there's the castle and the cathedral. The clock on there, red and gold. Been there for yonks, still looks new. Just gone one a.m. I'm fuckin knackered. I remember when me and the lads were up till all hours at Haddy's. Cans and tabs and a couple hours' kip before we got up with the dogs to go hunting. Class days, them. Just mates and dogs. Couldn't do it now, like. Them days is long ago.

Look forward, not back. Look to the things you can control.

Gonna feel like shit tomorrow. Cannit control that.

Best get this kebab ate.

The road goes on towards the bridges. Hate that walking bridge; the grey cage covered in seagull shit and the iron stink of piss. Feels like you're gonna get stabbed any second. Can't be arsed to walk all the way round to the Tyne either; huge and green with its lamps like summit out of the olden days. The path ahead leads downward; steep; past Empress where all the Toon players used to drink back when we were class; down to the Quayside. Quayside used to be rough as fuck. Just full of wankers and tourists now wanting selfies of themselves on the Millennium Bridge. Sometimes some doylem jumps into the Tyne and nearly dies. Daft cunt.

Me belly's gonna burst I'm that hungry, so instead I go round the side of the cathedral where all the prozzies used to knock about. There's a path made of old gravestones and scabby grass. Dark and quiet down here too. Got to watch it in case there's any smackheads or spice-zombies. Tell ya what, I'd probably even turn down a prozzie right now. Just wanna get me kebab eaten in peace.

It's well better here, away from the road. Everything's a bit faint now. Bit more peaceful. Old here. You could be back in time right now with all the solicitors and law buildings rising up around you. Georgian roofs. Nowt got touched up here during the war so it's all still here. Even the fuckin Nazis were scared of the Geordies, man. People say the north's grim but have you seen the state of London?

I'm down the path and round the back into the square, in the shadow of the cathedral. Empty. Quiet. Stained-glass windows all black, like the TV's been turned off. I sit myself down on a bench; old and knackered, looks like it would collapse under me weight but it doesn't. Me head's not spinning and I can't wait, can't wait for the taste in me mouth, the meat and the chips; the chillies bursting at the back of me tongue, fuckin lush. Me mouth's full of potato and garlic. Can hear it mashing between me teeth. I feel grease running down me chin but who gives a fuck. A swig of me beer.

I'm done. I get up; me knees already stiff and there's a noise up ahead, a *clink* sound, like something's fallen on the pavement. I look round cos if it's me keys I'm fucked. One of the clouds shifts and the moon shines out. Cheers for that but it's nowt. It's warm but I get a little shiver down me spine. It's proper silent, round the back of the church; a couple of scabby trees and some spiky railings. A couple of council bins; great black metal things like sleeping monsters.

I walk across the square, face the back ends of offices. There's a piddly little pavement and locked doors. Square buildings all round, great big windows with ledges like droopy black eyes; roofs and ridges and balconies nee fucker's ever going to use.

What the fuck is that?

It's lying on one of those old, flat graves, glinting in the moonlight.

No. No fuckin way. It can't be.

My belly's tight as fuck, fit to burst, I can feel the lager sloshing in with the chewed-up meat and chips. I don't even feel that pissed anymore, but I've got a pure cotton-mouth on me. This is fuckin mad. It's dream or something. Has to be. Maybe I fell asleep on that bench like a fuckin smackhead?

Look forward. Make sure what you can see is really real. Not an echo of the past.

There it is. It can't be. Sat on the gravestone. I pick it up. It slots into me hand like a memory. That's what it is, an old memory. I slip the blade out with me thumb, an old movement, feel the *click* as the blade locks, feel it all the way through me bones. It's been years. Muscle memory.

Click.

Where the fuck did I lose it? How did I lose it?

Easter Sunday.

All them years ago.

I look up and I swear I'm nearly sick. Right up ahead of us is one of the doorways; beautiful it is; all curved stone on top of stairs and pillars. One of them round windows at the top. Mad cos no one comes here, even in the day. No one's here to see them curling stone flowers. But there's something else, isn't there? There's something that hangs over that doorway; something that clings to the arch with long, red claws. Something that glares down with blazing pale eyes. Two ears rise like fuckin devil's horns over its head.

Bunny ears.

Black it's been painted; with red claws and white eyes and it's glaring down and fuck me, I can see fuckin madness in them eyes. It's only stone, only stone, but in the night it looks like it's quivering, like it's up there ready with its fans and its claws and those psycho's eyes. There's nee fuckin way anyone's making a statue of a fuckin psycho rabbit up there; the size of it as well. If it jumped, it if jumped from its perch up there on the doorway that no one sees, it would take me fuckin head off. Me old knife would snap against the stone and them teeth, them claws would rip me fuckin limb from limb.

I need to turn back, I can feel me kebab fizzing in me gut and I need to get the fuck out of here cos this is just a hallucination, innit? This is just an echo. A memory. Right?

A fuckin dream, alright? Me brother's voice. A fist in me guts.

I've got me old knife in me hand though now, haven't I? Presented to us on the steps of the fuckin church, before the madness gaze of this stone monster.

Why?

I'm clicking the blade in and out, me hand sweaty as fuck, and I remember. I can remember the bitter stink of me hands that day. Fuck. That day that nee amount of lager and kebab's going to let me forget. The day that I've been trying to drink away all these years. I look up the rabbit. Mr Rabbit. Wabbit. What's the fuck's up, Doc? This fucker's more *Watership Down* than *Bugs Bunny*. Looking into those eyes is making me spin out. But I can't stop looking.

Looking back.

Wabbit.

Fuckin wabbits.

That's what me brother used to call them back in the day.

'It's Easter, lads! Let's go get some *wabbits!*' he says in his best Yo-Samity-Sam. Harry his name was but we all called him Haddy. A ginner he was, tall and scrawny; freckles all over his face; Regal king-size hanging out the corner of his mouth. His eyes used to scare us since he come back from the army. Blank; they looked through you.

We all laughed like gutters. It was five a.m. and nee fucker had been to sleep yet; we were still up from the night before.

We could have just gone up to Spar and got some sausages, like. Haddy liked his meat raw since he come back from Kosovo.

He liked it scared and screaming.

It was a 'frisk'.

There was cans all over the floor in me brother's room. Cans and a stink. I was only a bairn, nineteen. Knew nowt. Me mam said I was going to the army when I got kicked out of school but fuck that. Me brother came back from Kosovo with that blank look in his eyes and a black streak of cruelty in his heart.

Some nights I could hear him screaming through me ceiling. I used to dream of the photos he showed us of what they done out there. Couldn't get em out me head. Never forget that shit. He was the one what gave me the knife. I used to sleep with it under me pillow just in case. If I heard him on the stairs, I'd pull out the blade.

Click.

'Get the fuckin *duurg* then,' Haddy says to us.

I fuckin hated that dog. Horrible thing it was. Haddy called it 'Goblin', kept it in a coal shed round the back of our house place, and you could hear it go fuckin radge when you went out there; all the coal clattering about as it threw itself against the door. Goblin was a mack-off lurcher; all skin and bones with nasty yellow teeth. Its fur had gone black from the coal and was all matted and mangey. Haddy was the only one who could control it. He'd hid Goblin in the shed after the thing had bitten the face off some bairn and we'd had the polis round.

'I'm awnly fuckin kiddin man, you daft cunt,' Haddy says. His mates gurgle.

Haddy liked to watch the half-starved thing tearing apart a *wabbit*. Better still, a hare. Haddy said that at least a hare put up a fight.

The lads all thought it was a frisk but I knew why.

We drive north for miles with the sun coming up slow. It's actually fuckin lush out there, where there's nee cunt; just the roads and the fields and the woods. Single lane, Roman road, straight line all the way, well aye. The lads have their army boots on but nee way am I getting me trainers taxed. Haddy's Fiesta fuckin stinks so we have to have the windows down. Goblin's in the boot, knows he's gonna get a kill. Never shuts up the whole way.

Haddy knaas where he's going and we've all got cans and tabs but there's nee daft chat. We bump down some path and park at the edge of a farmer's field. Then we walk for fuckin ages in the woods. Bump of speed each. Mad in there, middle of nee-cunt-knows-where. All the trees look like claws sprouting out the ground. It's wet and there's nee path and we just keep going on and on and on. Even Goblin stops acting the prick. I've got me knife in me back pocket; schitzy as fuck but it's just the speed. Keep thinking I can see shit in the trees; faces. Spiky, furious faces; silent, thorny screams. I jump when something grabs at me leg but it's nettles; leaves a trail of white welts through me trackies. Bastard.

'*Tuurld* ya to wear ya boots man,' Haddy says.

I've got that lock knife in me hand, sweating to fuck. I can smell mud and iron. Smells like blood down here. Blood and shit. Did he fuck, but I say nowt.

'Private property this, lads,' Haddy says and we're gurgling again. Set of drains. '*Lurds* of *wabbits* and that though so howay.'

Down a fuckin hill next; mud and more thorns; ripping me coat. Fuckin treacherous and I can feel hands snaking through the branches, feel wooden teeth snapping at me fingers. I swear to fuckin god I can see shapes now, like little figures; bairns made out of bracken and bark, skipping away from us in the trees. Once we're down the bottom though, it's like it's fuckin night again. Dark as fuck. The ground's not even wet, it's so thick down here; all bumpy and great thick tree roots like Gary Dodd's python he keeps at his mam's house. Tried to feed her cat to it when she grassed him for twoccing her purse.

'Fuck! Look'it!' Haddy says and he hockles on the ground.

There's a bank rising up on the left, humps in the ground and better than that, holes. Too big for wabbits. A badger sett? Goblin's sniffing about, nose to the ground, sides going in and out. Poor fucker'll be starving. Haddy only feeds him what they catch. I wish I had the crossbow, it's giving me the fear down here, in the quiet. In the dark. I hold me brother's knife. My knife.

'How you know about this place?' I ask.

'Din't knaa,' Haddy says and he's hunched over, tab in his mouth, inspecting the mound. We all go quiet, waiting for him to speak. 'Seen it in me fuckin' dreams.'

Nee one dares to ask if he's joking.

I remember that Easter Sunday when we were little bairns when Mam hadn't come back from the pub and the doorbell rang. Haddy told us it was all a dream. He says never to say nowt about it ever again or he would batter us.

I've never said nowt since.

Those eggs with their bows and their shiny paper.

I've never liked hunting wabbits but it's a frisk, Haddy says. It's just a frisk man, divvint be a girl. What else ya gonna do? Collect fuckin stamps? The woods are quiet, the faces in the trees still, watching. I feel like we're being swallowed and I can feel the fear coming; a rushing in me belly. I want to whitey; but if I do, these'll not let me live it down.

Haddy whistles through his teeth, one of them's cracked at the front where he got lamped by a polis and

I see hockle bubble in there for a second. Goblin comes over, whining, belly to the ground.

'Geet'in there,' Haddy says, raising his fist.

Goblin skitters over to one of the holes. It's too big even for a badger. What the fuck lives down there man, a fuckin wolf? He sniffs it then gets down on his front paws, whining again.

'Fuckin *move*.' Haddy goes to kick him and Goblin begins pulling himself into that hole. It's fuckin brutal to watch. It's like no part of his body wants to go anywhere near but his doggy brain knows that he'll get a kicking if he doesn't. Lurchers don't even *go* down holes and we don't know what the fuck Haddy's thinking. But there he goes. The last thing we see is his droopy little tail, all matted like a dreadlock.

Seen it in me fuckin dreams.

The doorbell went on Easter Sunday. Haddy was twelve. I was eight. He was twice the size of us then and I hid behind him when he opened it.

It was a fuckin dream, right?

We wait beside that mound in the earth. We smoke. A few of the lads piss against the trees. Warm, iron stink. Haddy just stands there, beside the hole; his freckled face getting redder and twisting up till I can't look no more. I put me head down, start curling into meself. I need a drink, I need to go home. I need our mam.

That's when it comes. A rumbling out the earth like the fuckin woods's belly's rumbling. I can feel it like bass through me bones and I'm up on me feet. That's when that fuckin bulge in the earth *bursts* like a zit and we're sprayed with soil; grit between me teeth, crap all in me eyes. Goblin comes first, shooting out of there like a fuckin black bullet, his eyes are round and white as golf balls and his tongue's hanging from his gob like a piece of bacon. He goes flying past me so quick, I can only smell him; earth and shit and something else, something raw and meaty.

'What's gannin on?' Haddy screams, turned round, looking at us, like it's my fault.

Those blank eyes.

Before him there's just this black hole in the ground, this fuckin pit like a grave. That rumbling comes again and I see light, two lights behind Haddy, bright below the ground, he's gangly shadow puppet with his mouth open as two black points come quivering and twitching upward out of that hole; followed by two paws like some fuckin mack-off big cat. A panther or some shit. But it's not a panther cos panther's don't have long, twitchy ears and eyes like lamps and they don't come sniffing and snorting out of the earth, great talons pulling at the soil. I can hear meself screaming and I can hear meself begging and I don't want to look cos those lights from them eyes are blinding but I see that terrible blackness reach out of that hole. Whiskers and a shiny nose, sniffing away at the air, at our fear. Breathing it in.

Easter Sunday when we were little and the door opened and it was stood there on the doorstep. Black fur and those pointy ears; little black tufts at the top of each one. Pointing through a bonnet. I remember that wet nose. I knew that it couldn't be a mask, it couldn't be a suit. I remember its eyes as it looked from Haddy to me. Solemn, silent.

Right now, as the sun rises over a cracked sky in fuck-knows-where, the nightmare opens its mouth, that black monster bunny, and I feel me piss against me leg. Fangs like knives closes around Haddy and his black silhouette becomes the back of the thing's fur and those eyes are blazing and the lads are screaming and they're trying to run but it's too quick. It moves like a spider, silent; pouncing and I've got the knife in me hand and all I can think to do is throw it; throw it at that terrible blackness rising out of the ground and run. I'm crying and I'm running and I can hear the lads screaming and I can smell blood and fur and something ancient like old books. I can feel the ground trembling as that great black shadow with its ears and its fangs comes belching out of the earth. I'm up the hill and through the forest and all the faces in the trees are screaming with laughter. Me clothes are soaked in piss and me kegs are slick with me own shit but I'm running and I can't stop and I daren't look round cos if I look into those eyes I'll lose my mind.

Me hands are trembling like fuck and the car door's open. I dunno how I done it but I drove out of there in me minging clothes and I drove all the way back to Haddy's place with the sun rising up behind me down that long Roman road with its wall from fuck knows when.

I make it back there and I curl up on the floor and I wake up with Goblin licking me face.

Me brother's knife from Kosovo. It's gone. Into that blackness.

So has me brother and his mates.

There's a fuckin Easter egg on me pillow beside us. Gold paper and a bow.

Nee good looking back, is it? Nee good. What can ya dee?

That rabbit never spoke one word back then, it just looked at us. It was carrying a basket of eggs; pink and purple and gold foil on them, tied with ribbons, like summit from a kid's book.

It was a fuckin' dream.

That's what they told me in St Nick's Hospital, when I got out of prison. Don't look back, just forward. It's been forty year since I had me face in the papers for all that. They said I done all of them in cos I was a nutter just like me brother. Now here I am. Looking back.

Daft cunt.

Kernt, as Haddy would have called us.

'It wasn't me though, was it?' I say and I point me old knife at the *wabbit* hanging off the doorway with its red painted fangs and its pale eyes. 'Yee knaa. Fuckin Easter bunny.'

But the *wabbit* says nowt. It just sits there, above the doorway. Mad little piece of history. Just like me.

I knaa what I've got to do and it's been a long old time but I knew it'd catch up with us one day.

'Never thought it'd be yee, like,' I say to the *wabbit*.

I look again at it. Fuckin mad eyes, teeth and claws. Who the fuck paints it, I wonder.

Who the fuck comes here and paints that fucker. A mad old gargoyle on the back of a building that nee one can see?

Think about the things you can *control* is what they used to tell us in the hospital after I got out of prison. Walking round on meds all day like a fuckin dafty. *You can't control the past but you can control your future.*

I reached out for one of them eggs that day and Haddy slammed the door on it. Turned round and punched us in the guts.

'Daft fuckin *kernt*,' he called us.

It hurts like that at first when I dee it. Stick that knife into me guts. When I pull it down like me brother showed us, I look right into the eyes of the *wabbit*. I look into the eyes of the *wabbit* and I say sorry.

Nee one'll miss me.

Just another fuckin mad-head hanging round the back of the cathedral in the middle of the night. Anyone who came walking round might just think I was some old alchy or a smackhead. Passed out on Easter Sunday.

But I knew that when I got out those woods, when the polis caught us and threw us in HMP Durham with the rest of the fuckin mad-heads. I knew then that I was someone. I even got me name in the papers.

I hold me brother's knife. The one he used in Kosovo to win a war with and I pull.

Let me insides pour out of us like darkness.

Let all the darkness out.

A stone gargoyle of a monstrous, fanged rabbit has perched above the ornate doorway of the buildings at the rear of the Cathedral of Saint Nicholas, Newcastle-upon-Tyne, for over a hundred years.

No one is quite sure why.

CLEAN WORK

NAOMI BOOTH

I t's the end of summer. I eat my lunch out in the back-yard, trying to hoard the last days of sunshine. The sunflowers that I planted with Rosa in pots out here are just beginning to turn, the petals browning at the edges. The big, radial flower-heads are the same temperature as the air: they feel warm-blooded under my fingertips. The fur at their centres is sticky and glistening with sap. I should go back to my desk already – I'm behind again and I'll have to work tonight, once Rosa's asleep. But I stay a moment longer. The air carries the scent of late-bloom-ing roses and petrol. There are two wasps moving low to the ground. When one of them lands, exhausted, on a paving stone, the other homes in on it, putting its upper jaws straight to work.

I go back inside to make a coffee. It's when the kettle's just starting to boil that I hear it again. That noise. A weird, scrabbling sound, a scratchy, garbled movement somewhere in the dark, internal workings of the kitchen.

*

When I first got the keys to this house, I discovered that the previous owners had left a bottle of champagne

– the real stuff – and small traps set in all of the kitchen cupboards. The house was in a strange condition: a small Victorian redbrick terrace, with a smart new bathroom on the first floor, but the rest of the house left damp and mouldering. The previous owners had bought it as a doer-upper, the agent told me: *But now, sadly, are … divorcing. Doesn't it have great potential?* The wallpaper was starting to peel away in the hallway, and the walls themselves were cold and chalky to the touch. The kitchen was the worst: when I stepped down into it, this low, narrow return at the back of the house, the smell hit straight away: something green and fungal. I was pregnant with Rosa, and the smell made me gag. There were holes in the brickwork that had been badly filled with expanding foam. The floor tiles were laid straight onto the earth. No central heating in here and at every surface edge – the skirting boards, the join with the oven – a thin line of black sludge. When I moved in, I discovered other things. The cupboards filled with a fine powdered mould that coated our plates and bowls no matter how often I cleaned. And there were slugs – great, ponderous slugs with frilled orange bodies – which left trails over the clean washing, across the baby-grows that I had bought in a job lot second-hand, that I had boil-washed and smoothed out on the clothes horse, ready for Rosa.

I had stayed cheerful, at first: the house's quirks were to my advantage. It needed some work, but that's why I could afford it. I was going to save up and scrub up and make the house right. We were going to live brightly, Rosa and I, in a modernised terrace with clean surfaces and tightly sealed apertures. Look, hadn't I arranged everything? Hadn't I gotten a mortgage, by myself, against all the odds? Hadn't I saved and scraped and grafted on overtime? For when the baby arrived. For me and my Rosa.

*

I ring my mum to tell her about the scrabbling sound in the kitchen. I can tell that she's distracted.

Mmm hmmm, she says. Old houses do make strange noises, you know, love.

I tell her that I've a feeling it might be a rat.

How do you know that? she says. Maybe it's a pigeon got into the roof space again and then back out? Can you smell anything?

I stand in the kitchen while I speak to her. I sniff and then I listen for a long time, but there is nothing.

*

The next day, Rosa's at nursery and I'm at my laptop working in the dining room when I hear it again. Scrabbling. A definite scrabbling inside the kitchen. I move into the doorway. Stand stock-still. Listen. The sound is coming from the carcass of a cupboard. I step closer. The sound is definitely inside the cupboard next to the washing machine. Scratch scratch scratch. I'm too afraid to open the door, so I give the cupboard a hard kick and then I hear the creature scramble desperately, claws slipping. Out of the kitchen window, I catch a glimpse of it as it runs across the yard, its thick brown tail disappearing under the back gate.

I call the first pest-control company that comes up online. I am told about the three-stage process for the elimination of rats:

1. The laying of poison.
2. The removal of dead rodents.
3. A full report on how to secure the property against future *infestation*.

I've only seen one, I say. I wouldn't call it an *infestation*.

Well, says the woman, rats never eat alone. If you've seen one, there'll be more.

How much is it? I ask.

For the full three-step programme? That will be £400 in total including VAT. No hidden costs.

That's ... more than I was expecting. I'll have to think about it.

Her: Don't think about it for too long. Rats need to gnaw. They gnaw through electrics and cause twenty-five per cent of house fires. They carry hepatitis. They multiply. You don't want to think about it for too long.

*

My mum comes round with a large rat-trap and wire wool that she's bought at Barnitt's. We listen to the animal moving in the wall cavity in the kitchen and I stamp on the ground until it bolts again.

This isn't going to work, I say. What will we even do if we trap it? Where would we release it? They carry hepatitis, Mum.

I try to make Rosa her tea: the rusks are in the kitchen cupboard at ground level and the porridge oats too. My mum plays with Rosa, bouncing her on her lap. She's telling her the story of the Pied Piper.

Let's go out for tea, I say.

We eat chips sitting on a bench in town and then Mum says, Why don't you ring around in the morning? There must be a cheaper way of doing it. I can always ask for an extra shift over the weekend. You might ask your dad for some help?

I won't ask my dad for some help.

All night long, I'm googling rats on my phone. Infrared videos of them crawling round people's houses in the dark, climbing up chairs and table legs and into toilets to drink. I wake up longing for the rat's total obliteration. Nothing left behind – the house destroyed: scorched earth.

I dress Rosa and take her to nursery. I pray that she doesn't repeat the word *rat*, which she said over and over before we went out, delightedly, pointing to the kitchen.

When I get back home, I put on winter gloves and I clear the cupboards of food. Then I look through an old copy of *Local Link*: adverts for roof repairs and cleaners and clairvoyants and there, yes, there it is: pest control.

While I wait for the rat man to arrive, I code documents into XML. It's my job to make the text clean. I proofread and place tags around parts of articles, around lozenges within sentences, to make sure that they appear correctly when they're published online.

>title< >author< >date< >main text< / Scratch, scratch, scratch.

When I get thirsty, I go to the Londis on the corner and buy energy drinks rather than go back into the kitchen.

*

Just after Rosa was born, I bought a patch of astroturf to lay out in the backyard. The yard is made of rough, uneven slabs, and each crack is filled with shards of broken slate and small stones. I wanted to give her one patch of something safe and green: I thought of her crawling on it, when she was big enough, or lying out in sunlight. At the first touch of springtime warmth, flea eggs began to hatch in the astroturf. It took me a long time to work this out – I thought the fleas were hatching in the carpet inside. I was suspicious of everyone who visited. I even made my mum strip off at the door, in case she was bringing them back from the care home where she works.

One evening, I looked into Rosa's cot and discovered a flea fat with blood on her leg. I became demented: I hovered over her all night with a bar of soap, which my mother said the fleas would stick to. I desired Rosa's cleanness more than anything. I became a scrupulous angel of death. I shook flea powder everywhere. But flea powder is highly toxic: what would I do when Rosa started to crawl? I hoovered the flea powder back up. I mopped and I mopped. Then I bought non-toxic traps instead: a tea light in the middle of a small metal circle covered with sticky paper that caught the fleas fast. But they were still alive then, just stuck. So I crushed their bodies individually between my nails, bursting those little seeds of blood, and scouring my hands after each one.

*

The rat man is small and polite. He pulls gloves on when we enter the kitchen. I walk behind him. He thumps the kickboards until they give way and then he shines a small torch under each of the cupboards. The smell is bad when he does this: warm and close and animal. He finds fur and sweet wrappers that the rat has pulled inside, and, under another cupboard, faeces. That's its toilet, he says. They're clean like that. They keep things separate.

We walk around the back of the house. He looks at the kitchen wall, at all of the gaps that have been poorly filled.

Any of these, he says, could do it. A rat only needs fifteen millimetres to get inside. They can eat through that expanding foam. I call it rat ice cream.

Then he looks around the backyard, finds a round hole in the earth next to the back gate. That's it, he says, that's an active rat hole. You see how smooth it is? How the earth is clear all around it? Their fur is oily and when they're in and out, the oil makes the hole smooth and clean like that.

He lays poison. He puts some of it in the hole. Then he lays trays of bright blue poison under each of the cupboards. He rakes the poison with his gloved fingers. Rats, he says, are neophobes. They don't like new things. We need to leave this ten days or so, to make sure that they've gotten used to it and taken the poison.

And can I block the holes in the back wall now, I say, with wire wool? To stop them coming back in?

Best not to, he says. You don't know where they're nesting. Could be inside. Could be in your wall cavities.

And if you block their escape route, then once they've eaten the poison they'll die inside and the smell is very, very bad and there's no way to get rid of it.

*

My uncle, whom I haven't spoken to since Christmas, phones me: I hear you have a rat, he says. It doesn't matter if you kill it. There are always more. There's excitement in his voice. What you've got to do is work out where they're coming from and seal off the house.

Then my dad, who hasn't visited in months, arrives unannounced all the way from Beverley to walk the outside perimeter of the kitchen. He holds his hands behind his back. I told you this house was substandard, he says. You're living in a Victorian slum. You're bound to have problems.

We have little to talk about these days, almost nothing we can find a consensus on. He sees any problem I have as the inevitable result of my perverse decisions.

I'll come and do some cementing for you, he says, once they've taken the poison.

I tell the neighbours. Ruth from next door says to me, Don't feel bad. Don't feel bad about poisoning it. I'm vegan, and I'd kill a rat if it came in my kitchen.

The old-timer from across the road calls out to me one morning, How are your little visitors?

*

I wait for the smell of death. My sister messages to tell me about the rats her boyfriend had in his old flat. How he laid the poison and then went away for the weekend. When he came back, the flat seemed darker. He turned on the lights and discovered the windows black with flies. The smell, she says, was impossible to get rid of.

She tells me about another friend who used glue traps. For a few days there was nothing. But one morning, there was a single bloodied claw stuck to the bottom of a trap. The rat had gnawed its way to freedom.

I tell her to stop messaging me about rats.

I buy scented candles and incense and spread them all over the house until the air tastes like soap.

*

Before I bought this house, I lived in a top-floor flat in a converted fruit warehouse on the other side of the city with Lucy, my ex. A few months after we moved in, we were burgled by someone who had a key. They had burgled us with a kind of frenzy, rifling through every drawer and cupboard, but also ripping open everything they could find: shirts were thrown onto the floor with the buttons ripped off, sealed packets of spaghetti and washing-up tablets had been torn open and spilled out, as though we might have had our valuables laminated inside them. The woman in the flat next door looked pleased when I said we'd had a break-in. She told us that at least ten people had been sleeping in the flat before we moved in. *Chinese*, she whispered in a significant tone. You'd best call the landlord and get a locksmith in, she said.

You get some jobs you have a bad feeling about, the locksmith said on his knees in the shared hallway, disarticulating the bottom lock. Like, how do I know you're not the burglars? I mean, obviously *you're* not.

He looked me and Lucy over, and we both felt inadequate.

But with other ... clients, you arrive, and they've no proof the place is theirs. Divorces, other shady stuff. You wonder if you're being paid to lock someone out of their own home sometimes. So I'm thinking of retraining. To do something ... decent. Something clean. You know.

Yes, I thought, when he said that. Yes, I know what you mean. My great-grandfather was a night-soil man, collecting shit from outside water-closets as the dawn broke over Bradford each morning. My mother looks after the elderly, sponging and toileting the bodies of frail strangers. My father was a public health inspector, dealing in abattoirs, drains, infestations, pestilent kitchens. All I've ever wanted was clean work.

He carried on working and I brought him coffee and then he said to me: What do you do for work?

I was working a few different jobs back then, part-time, so I picked one. I work in a library, I said. I shelve books at the university library in town.

Have they got valuable books? he asked.

Some, I said, in special collections.

How do you protect them?

We have reading rooms, I said. And you have to apply for access. Some of the rarer things, you can only see if you're supervised by an archivist.

Nah, he said, I mean from vermin. I'm thinking of

getting into pest control. Been doing my research. Rodents, they're a problem in libraries. And moths, too. It's a tricky business, though. You've got to be careful. Even then you can get into trouble. You can't even look at a badger funny. If you catch a bird in a net, you're looking at thirteen months in jail.

*

When the rat man comes back, he asks me if I have any holidays planned. I haven't.

I'm off to Portugal next week, he says. He's cheerful as he checks the poison under the cupboards.

Doesn't it bother you, I say, going under there?

These don't bother me, he says, it's the small ones that bother me. Cockroaches and bedbugs. Wasps. Coming into wasp season now, he says. It'll be fumigations all afternoon.

The rat has taken the poison. The rat has eaten all of the poison in one of the trays, so now it will be dead or dying, he says. And as there's no smell, he's confident it's gone back outside. He'll come back in a few days' time. I've to ring him if I hear or smell anything different.

*

Autumn's here: webs collecting in all the corners of the house, great fragile harvestmen descending from the light fittings. I've stopped trying to get rid of them.

When the rat man comes for the final time, he removes the trays of poison and tells me to seal up all the holes in the yard and the walls with wire wool and cement.

I listen for noises while I'm working, and sometimes I hear a ticking sound near the sink. When I go into the kitchen, I stamp my feet and bang about. I've filled up the gaps as best I can; every hole is stuffed with wire wool, which coated my fingertips and adhered to my cheeks and lips and made them bleed.

I buy peppermint plants and strong-smelling oils to keep in the kitchen: a warding off. I search and search for tiny traces of blue poison, trailing my fingertips along the floorboards for any tiny toxic thing that Rosa might find and eat.

At night-time, sometimes, I still look for rats. In the dark, as Rosa whimpers, I search on my phone and click all the way to a *Rat King*. A rat king is a ball of rats caught-up together, tails matted fast with filth. A rat king is a wheel of animals, trapped together in their nest. Fastened to one another, terminally: the young to the old, the living to their dead.

*

Every day, I clean up the articles that are sent to me, and Rosa grows bigger. The mould in the kitchen is spreading again, and a bright yellow fungus has begun to grow where the paint is peeling off the window frames. The wood there is sodden and comes away when I press it with my thumbnail. I can't afford to do anything about it until next summer. The floorboards are damp now too, swelling and spongy underfoot. I catch Rosa working away at one of them, peeling away a fat splinter with her keen fingernails and pushing it into her mouth before I can stop her.

At nursery pickup time, I watch other people with their children: they're bright-faced in the cold in new woollen clothes. I love winter! one woman says to me. And being all cosy at home with them! Don't you?

The late afternoon is cold blue hush: that deathly hour just before winter nightfall. I walk slowly with the push-chair. The evening rolls out ahead of me: teatime and bath-time, scooping the spaghetti hoops from the floor, wiping Rosa's face, taking off her soiled clothes, folding her fat, damp nappy into the bin. The tender, tedious rituals of making her clean again: the lick of thick cream on her bottom, the fresh nappy, the almond lotion on her belly and legs. I'll nurse her to sleep – that pain when she first latches still like a lance, but it softens as she drifts, until I can barely feel she's there. I'll press my nose to the skin of her scalp then. Baby soap and something else: something new, something sweet and fungal that I breathe in deep.

*

It's the new year when I hear it again. The scrambling sound, the weird, scratchy, garbled movement somewhere in the dark, internal workings of the kitchen. I stand in the doorway. The sound is coming from the carcass of a cupboard. I step closer. The sound is definitely inside the cupboard next to the washing machine. The same place as before. This time, I want to see it. To face it. I reach out. Hand on cupboard door. Slowly, slowly open it. Frozen. Both of us frozen for one long moment. Then: tiny tics of attention. Sleek brown fur rippling with movement.

Sharp eyes. A large, well-fed, supple body. The creature collides with the cheese grater and then drops away down the back of the cupboard.

I'm breathless afterwards. A slight tremor in my hand. I think about calling the rat man. But I don't; not now. Not yet. She looked so clean and fat and bright, our rat.

Fifteen pellets is all it takes.

Lying in bed that night, I try not to listen. I try to pretend there's nothing to hear. Just the little murmurs that Rosa makes in her sleep; the echo of a pigeon in the chimney breast; the house ticking as it contracts inside the cold surround of the night. But there, there it is: a scuttle in the wall. The garbled scrabble of claws somewhere inside the house.

I lie awake until it moves away and then I fall into a dream. Inside of the dream, Rosa is nursing all night long, her mouth smooshed to my breast. Inside of the dream, my milk runs blue in my veins. My milk runs in blue rivulets through my body. My milk runs through the veins of my breasts towards her: luminous, blue and deadly poisonous.

TRANSPLANT

JENNA ISHERWOOD

I smuggle a seed through airport security, passport control and customs. I stand in fluorescent-lit lines, bend myself to bureaucracies. I walk past the signs about fish, cheese, meat, agricultural products and honey. I don't look dangerous, I suppose. My passport is well-stamped; I look at home in airports (activewear, bottled water), transplant that I am. The seed is from my grand-mother's balcony garden, which clings to the side of my parents' flat. The plant is spiky and resilient. It will be able to make a home here, I am sure. Anyway, it's in.

I let the faces on campus wash past me. None are famil-iar, many are indistinguishable. People look at me like I'm a replica of someone else, or an idea they no longer find interesting. I meet with my supervisor and I'm uncertain when I should talk.

'Sorry, it's been a crazy week.' My supervisor has pens in her hair. The buttons on her cardigan don't line up. 'I'm buying a house. Most stressful life experience after death of a parent, apparently.'

I am not sure if this is supposed to be funny. She tells me to make sure I go to the induction talks about safety and well-being.

I show my visa to a Landlord and move into a house with a Physicist and a Historian. When he shows me the place, the Landlord says he likes students like me. 'Very clean,' he says. 'Are you well-behaved? You look nice and quiet.' I feel inspected. 'The perfect woman!' He laughs while looking over at the Physicist, who also laughs but without smiling.

After the Landlord has left, the Historian says I shouldn't let myself be on my own with him. I nod and hope she can see that I have understood her. She fluffs her wavy hair. The Physicist polishes his glasses.

I plant the seed in a yoghurt pot on the kitchen window-sill. My grandmother said the plant likes south-facing light, so here it must stay in the communal kitchen.

The Physicist, the Historian and I overlap sometimes, but not that often. It seems odd to me. Three people occupying a home, living separate lives. There is more space here than we had at our flat. I think about my mother and father returning in the evening, dark circles under their eyes, and my grandmother bringing us steaming bowls that we'd slurp together, squeezed around a table in the hour that was left before we all slept.

I take up running. Physical activity is good for the mind, they said in the talks. So I run and run, as though perhaps if I cover enough of these streets, I will eventually know this place, and it will know me.

I run past a church that has been turned into a night-club. I run past a graveyard that is overgrown with weeds. Who are these people, who would let the weeds grow over their dead? When someone is very special it seems their family dedicates a bench. A man and his dog have stopped by a bench that says *Grandma*. He looks down the path while his animal crouches and shits on the pavement. My grandmother would kick a dog for shitting by her bench. Now this man puts his hand in a bag, like a glove, and scoops up the shit. It must feel warm through the thin plastic. Then he ties up the bag and just abandons it there. Sometimes I notice these bags are left dangling on trees. What is this telling you about these people? They will touch, or nearly touch, their own dog's shit. But still leave it in the street. Why is this better? What do the dogs think? Perhaps that they have left a small gift that has been wrapped and preserved.

After my run I return for a drink in the kitchen and finger out my seed to see if it has germinated. When I discover that it has, I bury it again quickly, in case I jinx it. The Historian comes in as I am wiping my muddy finger on a dishcloth. She checks the fridge and then leaves without taking anything out. Perhaps she is really checking to see that I am still who she thinks I am: quiet and clean.

I submit my first assignment. My supervisor says my angle of appreciation is interesting but could use some definition. I have no idea what this means.

I continue running. In this neighbourhood, front doors open into the street and there are bins everywhere, with colours meaning different things. Rules. Dates. What does and doesn't go where. How do you know? My bin. Your bin. My shelf in the fridge. Your box of cereal. These people want to pretend they aren't living among others. Eyes and ears everywhere, though. As if they want to know what you are doing but would really prefer to live behind one-way glass, like they have at the airport.

By the time the clocks change, the Physicist and the Historian have started cooking together. They often dirty all the pans in the kitchen. The Historian says, 'I always make too much rice. I can never predict how it's going to expand.' The Physicist seems rapt by her insight and analysis. They don't offer me any of their extra rice. They watch box sets, taking up the whole sofa. I come in when I have cooked my own rice, and sit on a floor cushion.

'It won't make sense if you haven't seen season one.'

The nights are suddenly longer – daylight is getting squeezed out. I'm convinced that my bedroom is shrinking. In the safety talk they told us not to go out alone in the dark. How are you supposed to go anywhere in this city after 6 p.m. from November to March? Perhaps you are not. Perhaps you are supposed to stay at home and watch box sets with maximum one other person. If you are lucky then you and the other person will soon be able to stop watching the box sets and entertain each other in alternative ways. This is clearly what the Historian wants to happen. And probably the Physicist too. Although when I sit on the floor cushion near his feet, I catch him looking at me, as though perhaps he'd like me to come and sit on his lap.

When I can't stay in my bedroom any longer, I follow pavements at random as the light abandons the sky. I find an empty children's park made of hard tarmac and metal. Traffic streams on all sides on its way elsewhere. As I wait at a crossing, a group of boys joins and waits with me. They are a head shorter than me, but looming a little too close. From one I recognise the smell of damp laundry. Another is all sweat and cigarettes. I don't know the words they are saying but I hear the notes, the under-tones. The hairs on my legs stand on end. I am angry with them for making me feel scared, and angry with myself for being unsure whether I need to be. The lights change, the traffic stops, and I run, with all the power my muscles will give me. People in cars watch me go. They are all safe inside their own metal boxes. They could save me or they could smash me to bits.

I keep sprinting onto a canal towpath. It is framed by leaves and graffiti, stone and water. A cluster of dried-out flowers wrapped in plastic has been taped to a lamp-post by a bridge. I am breathing hard now. Breathing in the piss and canal smell. Breathing out carbon dioxide. My legs are starting to burn. I can't see anyone in front or behind me. The light is beige brown, like a city fading away in time. Hedge trimmings and sodden pieces of clothing lie abandoned, like dead bodies. I've lived with this premonition for a long time: that at some point I'll discover a cadaver in some undergrowth. My school-friends used to report nightmares of kidnapping or abduction. We'd compare lurid scenarios and plot escape plans while inflating sweet pink-skinned gum bubbles. Secretly, though, I always had different fears. A flap of material would catch my eye, perhaps in the scrubland around the train tracks behind my parents' apartment building. I'd move on past, but a story would thread itself into my mind. I'd imagine looking closer, finding a strand of hair mingling with decaying leaves. Then, nudging those leaves with my toe, I'd start to uncover fingers in the mulch. Now there are corpses on the news washing up on beaches and I sense shapes moving in the trees. The light of a mobile phone. Laughter. I realise this is a place I shouldn't be alone.

Should I turn back or keep going? Behind me could be the gang of boys from the crossing. Or maybe I am imagining them. The towpath curves and I keep away from the bushes, close to the water's edge, until I find an exit route onto a new street. I notice a sign half buried in a hedge that says *Unadopted Road*. I look down the street for clues about what this could mean. A street with no parents? The houses are different from the terraces where I am staying. Detached, they are called. Cars in driveways. The street seems cared for. Square hedges. Different colours and shapes of paving stones and gravel. Alarm boxes. Bins tucked into little spots next to a garage, just so.

I bend over for breath, and check Google Maps for the way home. But as I look up I'm surprised by the sight of an exploding hedge overhanging the pavement about fifty metres down the street. Curious, I jog towards it and then stop. The house behind the hedge is the same size as the others, but everything else about it is different. Most obviously, there is a small tree growing out of the roof. Underneath it a gutter bends down, loose and smiling, and below that white soak-lines mark the bricks, like tear stains dried onto a cheek. I cover the house with my eyes. It's so unusual, this dilapidation, almost enticing. Wooden window frames are softening with moss. They hold grimy glass and shaggy brown net curtains. I sense the other houses on the street looking sideways at this soft, mossy house, bonding in quiet disapproval. But I am drawn to it. I step up to the gate for a better look, assuming the house must be empty, but then I notice a dim light come on in a downstairs window. Inside my chest, the urge to run and the urge to stay push so hard against each other that I let out a gasp. I feel dizzy; the view in front of me seems to bend, but my feet are stuck. Through the net curtains I think I sense movement. A figure in a chair, seeing me looking. I blink. And then I run. My feet suddenly feel light again. I almost fly.

That night I dream about you – the figure in the house. You are a woman, I am sure. You say, *Oh have you come to help me?* You say, *My only child is on the other side of the world.* In my dream I say, *Yes, I have come to help you. You are my friend.* When I wake I can feel that you were there, my friend, but I cannot make out your face. I worry that I have abandoned you. That I have missed my chance and you will not remember me when I return.

The Physicist and the Historian have started doing their laundry together. Black jeans, mutually greying underwear, floral smocks. They festoon them around the radiators in communal areas, like occupying flags. The house gives off a mushroom smell. When the Physicist and the Historian go home for Christmas, the clothes stay out, like they have shed their skin into the space. They will be gone for two weeks.

Two days before Christmas, the Landlord says he wants to come and check the house. Twenty-four-hours' notice. I WhatsApp the Physicist and the Historian.

An immediate reply: 'Don't let him touch our stuff.'

The Landlord sits down on the sofa. Bounces up and down a bit. 'This has seen some action I'll bet! Life in the old dog yet, though.' Is he saying he is an old dog? I look at his face. He is not that old.

I follow him upstairs. In the Historian's room there are black knickers on the radiator. He purses his lips.

'You shouldn't dry things this way. It causes condensation. You know, things get wet inside?' He looks as though he expects something from me. I do nothing. He picks the knickers up off the radiator. 'She's a big lass, isn't she?' He stretches the knickers and I look away. From the corner of my eye, I see him bury his shiny nose in them.

'How are you settling in anyway?' He sits down on the Historian's bed, his legs spread wide like men do. 'Are people making you feel at home?' I nod, and take a step back towards the door.

He smooths his shirt over his gut. His shirt buttons are pulling open to show a gap of skin, a few curls of hair. He sees me looking down and it seems to encourage him in some way.

'Everyone else has gone for Christmas? Call me if you get lonely, okay?' He's not an ugly man, but there is something disgusting about him. Something disgusting that, nevertheless, appeals. Touching him might feel like squeezing a blackhead.

'I have to study.' I imagine pulling on the hairs curling through the gaps in his shirt, stretching his skin into tiny peaks.

When he's gone I go back to straighten the blankets where his arse shape still shows on the Historian's bed. I notice the knickers are still missing from the radiator.

I wonder if he put them back in her drawers. I slide one open. There are socks and bras inside. I hold one up to my chest, trying to imagine such weight on my front. Trying to imagine how her breasts feel in the Physicist's hands.

The house is quiet without the Physicist and the Historian. I watch their leftovers growing mould in the fridge. The colours spread, soft and furry. I miss them. Their discussions about dinner. Their sex noises. And when they come back, I will miss their absence too. Like I miss my grandmother. And when I go back, I will miss this sad, angry freedom. I might even miss being scared in a place where I am not understood. I will miss these people who don't make sense. I will forget what I had to unlearn. I will explore my regrets. I will remember the times I was bold.

On Christmas Day the streets are empty and grey. I run my usual route. Thoughts disentangle from where they've been growing in clumps. Cars cluster around certain driveways where windows are steamed with light and heat. Other houses stand silent and sad.

Your house is dark, my friend. I wonder if you have been swallowed up by a family somewhere. I feel I ought to check. Your front gate creaks when I open it. In the garden the weeds are spiky, sticks poking up through the gravel path. I approach your window. There's a small crack between the net curtains, and halfway up there's a torn piece that I can look through. There are webs between the curtains and the window frames, dead flies on the windowsill, like the ones I would feed to the lizards in my grandfather's terrarium. When my grandfather died I begged my parents to let us keep the lizards, but they said we'd have no room, now that my grandmother was moving in. My father released the lizards in the park. I cried thinking of them alone and fending for themselves in a dangerous new place.

Here at your window, I make out objects: piles of boxes and papers, an old rocking chair, a door at the back of the room. While I am peering in, your shape comes into focus and you look straight at me, my friend. You are in there after all, sitting very still in your chair in your dark house. This time I don't run. I back away slowly while holding your gaze, in case you are trying to tell me something. My heel touches something hard behind me. A small black pot with an iridescent petrol glaze. It tugs at my heart. I want it for my spiky plant. I pick up the pot and return to your window with it. You don't get up from your chair or shake your head. You keep staring straight at me. This time it is a warm feeling. You are telling me I should take it, I am sure. A Christmas gift from you, my friend.

I run home with your pot clutched to my chest, and when I get there I rehome my plant and put it back where it lives on the kitchen windowsill. There is only one fly on my windowsill. I remember all the flies on yours. I wonder if my grandmother still remembers the lizards. Her memories have been shrinking recently, like she no longer has room for them.

For the rest of the holiday I use as much of the space as possible. I write an essay on the sofa in the living room. I eat dinner at the Physicist's desk. I switch round the DVDs in his box sets, then the next day I worry and switch them back again. I take pictures of myself in the Historian's bed and imagine sending them to our Landlord.

Then the Physicist and the Historian are back. I can tell because there's now a note on the fridge: *Can we ALL try to get rid of out-of-date stuff …* They have forgotten the pretty leftovers belonged to them.

I arrive for a new year meeting with my supervisor. Her office is empty. There are greasy smudges on the walls where her postcards used to be. The Head of Department comes in. 'I'm sorry ...' He pauses, and I realise this is an invitation for me to say my own name. He says, 'Your level of supervision has not been, how shall I put this, *what we would have hoped*. I've reviewed your recent work. Well, let's just say you've got a lot left to do.' I can sense meaning in the spaces between what he is saying. Perhaps meanings like this have been there all along.

I work and I work and every day I run past your house. I tell you, my friend, that I am taking care of your pot. It is taking care of my plant. I tell you I am working hard. I put words on pages and the Head of Department says things like, 'Yes, but more.' The Historian keeps long hours and has disabled her Facebook. The Physicist splits activities into 25-minute bursts. The leaves are returning to the trees. I keep running and writing, writing and running, until foliage foams out of paths and crevices, and the streets smell sweet like shampoo. I feel the place changing around me, warming up.

Then one evening, a shock of pink in the kitchen. The explosion catches my eye when I have been at the library all day. My spiky plant is flowering. The Historian sees me staring past the sink, where she stands with a steaming colander.

'Would you like some pasta? I've made loads by accident.' The Physicist's eyes have wandered. He is staying somewhere else this week.

I continue to stare at the pink flowers, so lovely against the sharp leaves and the deep darkness of my friend's pot.

'Yes?' the Historian says, as though she can't be certain if we have ever really understood each other.

I nod. We eat the strings of flabby pasta. I see her trying to swirl the spaghetti around her fork, over and over, and almost every time it slips away. I catch her eye and suck mine up in one long slurp. She sees me, smiles and slurps too. We sit, slurping, not speaking but sometimes letting small smiles break out around our pursed lips.

My friend, many things are different now, but I still think about the last time I visited your house. It had been raining but then the clouds broke. I wanted to bring you back your pot, with my plant in it for you to keep. I didn't run. I walked down the pavements past the nightclub church and the park, along the canal, under the arch and back up to your unadopted road.

Perhaps you know, my friend, that when you are looking at things for the last time, light falls on them in a special way. You see the thing you will remember, which is never really what has been. Perhaps you have never really seen the thing itself, but only how the thing made you feel. The sharp neon sign of the nightclub church. The memorial benches and the silver puddles in the park. The canal water reflecting trees and sky, and the shadows under the arch. I carried my plant in your pot past all these things, holding it out in front of me as a gift.

I can tell you now, my friend, that there are things we can unlearn, but there are things we can't unknow, things we can't unsee. I opened your gate, noticed the new green weeds smothering your garden. I noticed so many more flies on your windowsill as I knocked, ready to tell you my name and that I would be leaving soon. Now, as I remember, I want to tell you that when I peered through the curtains and saw you still in that chair, with a shaft of sunlight across your face, so terribly in bloom, there was a part of me that had always known. But like you, I had no one to tell. Like you, I had started to change beyond all recognition. Like you, I would soon be returning to another place.

GOOD MORNING, VIETNAM

LAURA BUI

The last time I was with my Uncle Bill, I learned that my grandpa was still rummaging around in his house. He had been dead five years, but it seemed that he made appearances at old haunts. Uncle Bill spoke about this during lunch without a flicker of irony or embarrassment, transitioning from my cousin's wedding and his children's educational whereabouts. It was his usual bundle of news, centred on family, and whether I met the relation of interest was irrelevant. In emails, he asked after my well-being, then told me about my grandmother's health and who was going to visit her and when. In phone calls made in between drives from his home to his office to house viewings for clients and to school pickups, he relayed who was poorly when and who would be graduating from what. For my graduations, he had asked if he should book a flight to attend, worried that too few would be there to celebrate. Whenever I was in Seattle, he never failed to make long stretches of time to see me, always offering to pick me up from the airport. And when I called him, on the other end of the line I was met with, 'Good morning, Vietnam.'

The greeting itself is recognisable, as the title of the 1987 film starring Robin Williams as a radio DJ stationed in Saigon for the Armed Forces Radio Service. Probably the most acclaimed comedy on the Vietnam War – although centred on the typical subject, American soldiers – Uncle Bill claimed it as a signature salutation. He first arrived in the US six months past his twentieth birthday, in the early seventies, to join my eldest uncle, an agricultural engineer. But over his lifetime, he often visited Vietnam to tend to the family who stayed. This lifestyle produced a cultural mishmash that normalised local monastery visits and wearing of traditional garbs alongside a prideful display of a Ronald Reagan calendar and partaking in snowball fights.

I listened politely as Uncle Bill described how a neighbour staying over one night had heard footsteps in the room where my grandpa used to spend most of his time. Although I was happy to be in my uncle's company, I found the recounting of this incident, especially its conclusion – that the neighbour encountered Ghost Grandpa – awkward. I grew up with these tales of translucent human visions. Sometimes they strolled around the streets because they weren't aware they were dead, or sometimes they appeared abruptly and stared without speaking, a sign for something you had to inconveniently figure out. Hearing the story was like listening to something that used to hold sway over me, but had become distant and discredited – sort of like an ex. By then, my intellect seldom dealt with anything supernatural, and a venture towards this was considered a misstep into the irrational. Knowledge, as it was impressed upon me, was gained through rigorous research on the observable. Modern thought insisted that it was evolved, estranged from ponderings about the unmeasurable mind and soul. To be trained in the scientific method was to consider only the facts, derived from following a systematic process of careful observation and documentation. That it could be applied to human behaviour to accurately explain ourselves has its critics, but studying us scientifically was to protect the integrity of acquired knowledge against ourselves, creating a sense of certainty about us.

*

In early 2020, online obituaries appeared for the criminologist and psychiatrist Donald West. I knew of him but knew very little about him – I used to pass by his framed portrait when a Ph.D. student, thinking he had a kind expression. In criminology lineage, I am his intellectual descendant, as he had trained and mentored my Ph.D. supervisor during work on the Cambridge Study in Delinquent Development. West was born in 1924 in Liverpool, near the docks, and was later raised in Crosby. Although his home life lacked intellectual and cultural stimulation, his parents adamantly believed in the importance of education, and West was able to study medicine at the University of Liverpool. His oldest research interest, however, seemed to be in the ability to communicate with spirits, and he first indulged this curiosity by attending séances in Liverpool.

In one of his earliest works, *Psychical Research Today* (1954), he recounted the challenges of providing solid evidence that mediumship was real. In one séance, he exposed a fraudulent medium by smearing his hands with red ink and touching the supposed spirit that moved about in the dark. Sure enough, when the lights came on, the red ink also appeared on the medium. But instead of everyone in attendance being angry at the medium for fooling them, they kicked out West, claiming that a bad spirit must have possessed him and that the red ink on the medium was actually remnants of ectoplasm – a gauze-like substance that a spirit can appear in. Research into the existence of spirit communication proved to be difficult, as West detailed, particularly because the people involved really wanted to believe, and their biases distorted their perceptions and interpretations, rendering completely different observations to one another.

By way of example, West described the experiments of S. J. Davey, who replicated the tricks popularly used by mediums at that time. Davey and a colleague had rehearsed what they were going to do during their séance: pretend to lock the door, and while their music box chimed away in the dark room of the unwitting sitters, his colleague would slip through the unlocked door and pull out their props, hidden in a cupboard, and imitate a spirit, illuminating his face with glow-in-the-dark pages from a book. After, they compared what their audience members thought they saw during the séance and what actually occurred: the participants vehemently believed they had encountered spirits. Even when Davey admitted the séance was a hoax, a leading spiritualist refused to believe him. This strong bias towards the existence of spirits led to West's dismissal from the Society for Psychical Research, where he was a researcher. Considered a sceptic among members of the Society, first formed by a group of intellectual influencers of the day, he actually was simply frustrated by the lack of results and by other members who readily assumed the existence of the supernatural and rejected any findings that challenged their beliefs.

West was adamant that the careful design and implementation of scientific experiments was the best bet in reaching a more truthful understanding of this paranormal phenomenon. His research on mediumship suggested that this mystery was capable of being deciphered, that it was not beyond human comprehension. It was his death early in the year that provoked my curiosity towards his thorough psychical research, and it was Uncle Bill's sudden death late that same year that prompted a revisit to old possibilities.

*

Up until late that year, I accepted that death was the end, and there would be nothing more, just like my pre-existence where I had known no better. For whatever reason we were here, so better make the most of it; but, also, perhaps we were an accident in a careless universe full of chance. Yet the night following Uncle Bill's passing, my mind kept returning to what he had said about my grandpa; and so, absurdly, I hid under the covers. It didn't help that the week before I had binge-watched the latest season of *Unsolved Mysteries* and there had been an episode about the surviving residents from the Tōhoku region, the area of Japan hit by the 2011 tsunami, in which more than 15,500 died and nearly 2,600 were still reported missing as of 2015 by the National Police Agency. I remember the earthquake that caused the tsunami. I had been working on some of my research in Kyoto when it struck, but as I was more than five hundred kilometres away, I mistook the slight shifting of my building walls as a sign for a break. A sight that has never left me came from live aerial footage from the news that day: a silent mass of darkness creeping steadily along, blithely devouring buildings and roads and vehicles. Miles ahead appeared a lone car, moving away. It kept going as the dark wave trailed behind, determined to outrun it. But then it slowed, tried to veer left, then right. It was so little, that car, and whoever was in it must have thought it futile to try to escape, so the car turned to face the tsunami and waited. Following the disaster, many residents reported seeing apparitions, soaked and lost.

Some of the research on which the episode was based came from the *Times* journalist Richard Lloyd Parry, who described encounters from the likes of cab drivers whose passengers would disappear by the time their destination was reached, and a group of temporary housing occupants, startled to see their dead neighbour come by for a cuppa while drenching the cushion on which she sat with seawater. Those who were unable to locate missing loved ones had even sought the help of mediums. Parry noted that a 'cult of the ancestors' seemed to make the immense collective grief more profound because the dead were then unable to be adequately provided and cared for – proper burials were impossible following the destruction; ancestral altars were lost or destroyed; sweeping familial lines abruptly ended. 'In such circumstances,' he remarked, 'how can there fail to be a swarm of ghosts?'

Whether people believed in ghosts or whether ghosts were real was beside the point in the *Unsolved Mysteries* episode. Yes, the episode scared me, so that, days after, I was hesitant to even walk down my own corridor alone, but it lingered because it was so deeply sad: a mother left out her son's toys so he could come back to play with them; a dead girl had promised to hold on to her little brother's hand and was pained for letting go when the wave hit them; a man finally found the body of his baby daughter under the debris and had to wipe her muddy face to confirm it. Isn't communicating with the dead a way of knowing if they're okay? When I found out that Uncle Bill had only a few days left to live, I rushed to fly back to Seattle. I found my hurry, though, completely nonsensical, and I couldn't explain exactly why it was pressing for me to see my uncle one last time. Even though I would later learn he had died by the time I caught the second leg of my flight, I came to understand that my urgency was a hope of reassuring him, a show of love. And following his death, I began to think how lonely Uncle Bill would be in a cemetery full of strange others and Jimi Hendrix.

*

'Love never ends,' Marilynne Robinson writes. 'Projected forward it is hope.' Love itself doesn't die the moment someone we love does. When they go, hope is the only action we have left in expressing our love for that person: I hope you left loved and in peace, I hope you're okay. In

Uncle Bill's bundles of news, he had let me know that I wasn't alone, wherever I was, even over the Atlantic, but distance seemed trivial among a family history of recurrent migration. In asking whether I had eaten and if I was healthy, he was hoping that I was okay. So-called modern thinking may scoff at these sentiments about mere corpses and the inevitable, seeing these as a kind of bias towards meaning or 'wish-fulfilment' in a universe that in actuality is empty, but Robinson, again, provides an alternative: 'Or we might call it a vision of Being that is large and rich enough to accommodate the experience of human love and grief.' This is a way of saying that we are more than we have purported to discover.

In his final book, a memoir written towards the end of his life, Donald West provides a similar stance. His lifelong research interest in the paranormal is apparent throughout, and the last substantial section just before the brief ending is an overview of the latest in parapsychology. Unfortunately, no strong evidence has been reported to date, but West maintained he was never a complete disbeliever, as he understood there was something there in a few of the astonishing historic cases of psychics and experiments on telepathy. His dedication to psychical research was born out of love: at the University of Liverpool, he had fallen for a fellow student named Richard whose friendship and interest in the paranormal provided encouragement to pursue the subject further. Life as a gay man, when it was a crime and then when it was not, informed many of West's intellectual curiosities. He found the received wisdom of his youth on what was then known as homosexuality suspect, so, in university, began reading books on spiritualism and psychical research. A lifetime of research on the paranormal, though, yielded no certainty for him, no grand findings or firm conclusions, but he was fine with this. As someone who was used to being an outcast, he seemed confident that psychical research had philosophical and social importance despite its dismissal by mainstream science.

*

Whatever happens after death isn't certain. But it is love after loss that now makes the notion of emptiness and a lack of wonder, while alive and afterwards, a dreary and unworthy prospect for Uncle Bill. There are two lines from the fourteenth-century West Midlands poem 'Pearl', about grief and loss, that I hope for him:

My soul by grace of God has fared
Adventuring where marvels be...

I became acquainted with these lines because of Marilynne Robinson's essay collection *What Are We Doing Here?*, its title taken from her 2015 public lecture at Liverpool Hope University. Two lines that make me breathe easier, like the world suddenly expanded and became vast, capable of accommodating the knowable and unknowable about us – a place able to appreciate my uncle in all his complexity.

On my way to the prayer service, I briefly registered a woman speaking to my eldest uncle and a couple of other relatives off to the side of the funeral home's main entrance.

'Good morning, Vietnam!'

I stopped and looked up. It was her voice, but I heard my Uncle Bill. The woman was gesticulating, and I realised it was part of her story as she continued her conversation with my family. I hadn't heard the greeting in such a long while that the sound was a jolt of joy shot out from somewhere dormant and nearly forgotten. A door opened, a haste of beloved familiarity appeared: Uncle Bill calling by in a white dress shirt and wide tie, a head full of dense black hair, tucking away his earpiece, asking if I had already eaten. I first came to Seattle because of him, and he had welcomed me at the airport. As we drove in his car, untidy from a full life of family, he told me all about the aunts and uncles and cousins who lived nearby, their names, ages and what they were up to.

CUCKOO

DÉSIRÉE REYNOLDS

He could tell by the way the air hung around her head that she wasn't sleeping. He pretended to stretch and yawn and rolled on top of her. Afterwards the same air dried her eyes.

Niomi raised herself up and lit the rest of last night's spliff; she lay back down, trying not to disturb that same talkative air. She felt between her legs, still wet. Years ago that would've made her feel loved and warm, safe and cared for, but now it made her feel wrung out and tired. She caught her breath on the roach and choked a little. Shit. She got up.

'Wha? What's happening? Where, where you goin, Niomi?'

'To have a wee, is dat okay wid you?'

'Galang den, chuu, what's wrong wid you? Skip it, don't care.'

She crept around the room, found knickers on the floor and put them on. She got fully dressed, even though she only wanted to wash.

'Go and fine him.'

'He'll still be sleeping.'

'I said go an fine him!'

She didn't want to bump into him now. Last night was intentional, they'd been watching him for weeks. He shuffled under the dark yellow street light and turned when she said hello. The flat was tiny, every door faced another door. The bathroom had once been nice but the orange blossom was covered with mildew, and wetness streaked down from somewhere on the ceiling, making small puddles she had to step around on the floor. It smelt of old water, musty and desperate. She'd been in bathrooms like this before: only barely serving its function, more there to witness its own lack of use. She cleaned herself with cold water and the sleeve of her jumper and listened. She thought she heard something: shuffling movement, that wheezy cough; fat feet in fat slippers slapping against the lino.

She listened at the door; she felt him pressed against it too, listening for her. She moved back and sat on the toilet, waiting.

'Shit.'

She waited until she didn't hear anything, grabbed her stuff and opened the door a crack.

There he was.

He had been there all that time, a cup of tea in a white cup with tiny rivers of brown fractures running down it. Pink flowers on it, on a mismatched saucer. He held it out to her and his hands shook, his eyes fixed on the floor. His nose remembering the smell of a woman.

'I mek dis fi you.'

'Oh, er, right, thanks, Mordacai.'

She took it from him and he waited. She held it and her clothes and willed him to go away. He didn't.

'Don't mek it get cold.'

'Oh, right.'

She dropped her stuff on the floor and they both stared at the toothbrush, T-shirt and knickers. She quickly took a sip and fought back the urge to vomit. It was cold and sweet. He'd made it with evaporated milk, like her gran used to make it.

'Lovely, thank you.'

She didn't know what to do. She could feel her hair making her top wet. The damp sleeve made her shiver. She drank it all and handed the cup back to him, picked up her clothes and stepped past him back into the bedroom.

Jay was sitting up now, smoking a spliff and switching channels on the TV.

'Was dat him?'

'What do you think?'

'Easy, what's wrong wid you?'

She stared at him, thinking her hatred could pour out of her, tepid and sweet like Mordacai's syrupy tea, and cover everything. And he would never know it was her. She saw him sink down into the liquid, it coming burning out of his nose, him screaming for help. The thought made her smile. She sat with her back to him on the edge of the bed. He threw a paper at her, made her jump, and suddenly she remembered what they were going to do.

'Shit! Can't we jus get out of here, you know, jus go. He gives me the creeps.' She didn't hear as he slid down and kicked her off the bed.

'God, Jay! What did you do dat for?'

'Can't see the TV.'

She got up. He was smiling as he held out the spliff to her. She took it because she didn't know what else to do.

'You know what? You're looking old. You need to sort yourself out. Can't keep doing this if you lose your looks. No one wants pensioner pussy.' He smiled happily up at her, not registering the pain in her body or the hurt in her eyes. She sat on the windowsill.

'So, what's happening today, Jay?'

She blew the smoke out the window and watched it curl up into the spitting sky. Sky hemmed in by the estate, blocked off by high-rises, a small patch of grey-blue in the middle. She listened to the music around her. The dripping tap beat out a rhythm in the bathroom with the pipes knocking and the boys spitting lyrics under a stairwell, dog barks and sirens. She took the end of the spliff and held it close to her leg. The smoke trickled out the top, caressing her thigh, snaking close to the fabric of her denim skirt. It seemed to her it was looking for a way in. A tiny, marshy grey cloud dancing with the material, stretched over and tied her up, hypnotising her and the cloth. While she was watching the smoke, she could block out everything.

Her eyes felt heavy, maybe she could sleep? Right here. The smoke trying to get her to sleep. She smiled down at it. It meant everything. She finally tore her eyes away from her leg and looked at Jay. She never realised how ugly he was. The shape his mouth made when he was angry, the way his eyes would dare her to breathe, and she wasn't sure, but wasn't it her right to breathe? How most of the time he never asked her how she was, what was she thinking, feeling, never gave her anything, but could take until she was empty. Who was he anyway? Why was he? All this in a moment. What was he saying?

'Whadjou mean? Man's comin over tonight, everyting curry, yuh get me? Everyting's hooked up. What's wrong wid you? You fraid?'

'No, jus has it got to be today? Feelin kinda funny, yano.'

'Save me from your fuckeries dis morning.'

'It's half one.'

'Wah?'

'Nutin.'

'What did you say?'

'Nutin, it's jus not morning.'

'You see! Dat's what I'm talking about! I've nuff fi do widout you stressing out my head top.'

'It's jus that it's afternoon, is all.'

Jay got to her before she could turn away and grabbed her by her face. He pressed her head against the window, her forced-out breath frosted the glass.

'Don't you get it, the pressure dat I'm under? Dis is it, we're doin it today, now move your fat arse and go and fine him and tell him the coo. Alright?'

She couldn't speak. He squeezed a little harder so he could see the blood pumping around her eyes. And then he let go. He started to look for clothes.

'Fuck, you're getting fluffy, your batty looks big, man. Gonna have to lose some weight, starting to look like my grandma. Go and keep him sweet.'

The smoke had moved from her lungs to her head and took movement away from her arms and legs. She didn't feel like doing anything.

'Move!'

Jay's shouting snapped the light in her head. She

shuffled to the door and was about to open it when she said, 'I think he likes me.'

'For fuck sake, dat's the point. Allow dat.'

She grabbed the weed, Rizla and cigarettes off the bedside table.

He was sitting on the sofa staring at the TV. He turned to look at her, struggled to get up, and she thought she heard his knees.

'No, no, it's alright, don't get up.' She sat in the armchair opposite and tried to pull her skirt down. She started to skin up. It was the only thing that was keeping her from running.

'What you watching? Oh, it's not on.'

'Don't need it, pictures all in here.' He took one of his short, stubby fingers and tapped his head. They were the shortest, fattest fingers she had ever seen, with thick grey-brown nails at the thumb. Just the shortest and fattest ever.

'You've got very strong hands.' She was transfixed by them. Imagined them twisting a chicken neck, swinging a bat, beating a drum or squeezing a woman's throat. That was the talk on the estate, that he'd killed his wife. He found her with another man, and while she was still naked and warm, he squeezed all the breath out of her. He spent twenty-nine years in prison. He'd slept rough for years, until he was given this place. That was the talk.

'Steady as a rock.' He held up a hand but a tremor started, so he used it to rub his head. Brown meeting black and grey.

'Oh yeah,' she humoured him. He knew it, she knew he knew – all a part of the game.

He looked at her long fingers, curling the papers over the tobacco and weed, her tongue, small and pink, licking the edge of it. She put it in her mouth and lit it, catching his gaze as she looked up.

'Want some?' She held it out to him. Maybe he wasn't so stiff after all.

'Me? Oh no, no, dat ting will mess you up dat will.'

She chuckled. 'That's the point.'

'I don't know why people need it.'

Her eyes darted across the room; she was looking for the spotlight, she suddenly felt under.

'What, you've never done it?'

'No.' He was proud, actually proud.

'What never, ever? Big man like you? What's dat about?'

'I didn't mean to ...' He rubbed his head. 'Sorry.'

'It's alright you know, I'm alright.'

'Sorry.'

'Stop saying sorry!'

'Sorry.'

'No, I'm sorry. I don't know why ...' She let her voice drift away from her, too tired to catch it back.

'Why what?'

'Why I do it. I don't know, it makes me happy.'

'Happy?'

'Yeh, you know. Like nothing matters, everyting cool, you know.'

'Everyting matters.'

'Yeh, but it's nice to feel like it doesn't.'

'Did your man tell you dat?'

'What do you mean?'

'Dat nutin matters? Everyting matters. And when you

know dat you can live straight.'

'Like to live widout killin people?' She felt misjudged, who was he anyway? She looked at him and saw shame.

'Anyway,' he continued, and fought the silence that fell between them, 'it's bad for you.'

'I don't do it cossa Jay.'

'Bad for you health.'

'Every thing bad for you if you do it too much.'

'And he don't mind?'

'Who, Jay? Fuck no!'

'I'd mind.' He stared at his slippers.

'You what?'

'If, you know, if I cared about you, I'd mind.'

She didn't know what to say. Words gathered in her mouth and rested there.

'Is ... is he up?'

'Who? Oh yeah, he's up. Jus getting dressed. Er, um. Thank you for putting us up, we didn't have anywhere else to go.'

'Is alright.'

'Really, thank you, we're very grateful.'

'I'll put on di kekkle.'

'No, let me.' She floated up out the door towards the kitchen.

'I mean it, Mordacai, you've given us your bed and everything. Thank you. I don't know what we would've done if we hadn't met you. Is that your local shop, then? They were nice. Couldn't go back to the last place, too many scopers, yuh get me? So, you live by yourself then?'

She didn't know why she kept this up. Everybody knew he had no one. That's why they were there, cos he had no one. No one should have no one, she thought, everyone should have someone. She felt tired, small and stupid. Why was she here? Why wasn't she at home? But they wouldn't let her stay by herself. They wouldn't let her stay in the hospital with her mum, either. They grabbed her in front of Niomi, still in her school uniform. She couldn't go with her then and she cried, cried longer than she had been alive, she cried so much she felt like all her water done. She thought maybe she would never cry again but she did. She cried in all the homes she stayed in, she cried when her last foster parents wanted her out, she cried when a boy first kissed her and then slapped her, she cried when she had her first abortion. That was when she stopped crying. She looked over. Mordacai was staring at her.

She was talking too much but the weed was making her tongue loose. She shut her mouth. She put the kettle on, it was one of those old-fashioned ones with a whistle. She was still holding her neck. Her own hand made her jump. When she looked up he was standing in the doorway. Smiling, at least she thought he was smiling. He was showing her his teeth. Yellow and crooked. She wondered if he did like her, the way he scoped her all the time. She wondered if she wanted him, the thought of his naked, short, spongy body made her drop her cup.

He eyed her suspiciously, as if he knew what she was thinking. 'Lucky it didn't break.'

'Yeah, lucky.'

She thought she could poke her finger through the lines under his eyes, that the skin would just envelop her. All that time on the streets. He was probably younger than he looked.

'How did you wash?' She couldn't help thinking about him, on a corner, in a doorway, cold, wet, spat on, *Big Issue* people looking down on him.

'What do you mean?'

'When you lived rough. How did you ...?'

'Oh, well. Soap is cheap, me moder always seh, an I could go into public loos or MacD's or ...' He stopped, the image of his mother, dark brown, ample, flat-footed, cherry and almond smelling, waving a bar of soap under his nose. Soap cheap. She could tell he wasn't there.

'Mordacai?'

'What?'

'Oh, er, nuffin.'

He went to sit down, she brought him tea.

'Dis rain won't stop, will it?'

He looked out the windows that took up half the wall. He wished they weren't so big. They were letting the world in. All life under him, all death on top. She wanted to know what he was thinking.

'Mordacai, I ...'

'What?'

'Listen to me, you should leave.'

'Leave what?'

'L—'

'Mornin, all.' Jay breezed in, pulling on his trousers, shirt in his hand. He kissed Niomi on the cheek and stared into her eyes. 'Who's leavin?'

'I was telling him to leave his tea, I'm crap at making it.'

'You're not fuckin wrong there.' He stood over them.

She looked like she had been electrocuted. Her eyes wide, her mouth slightly open. She looked up at Jay, he winked, she recognised the fake laughter. How could he just not care at all? Mordacai looked puzzled.

'Wah gwan, Mordacai, you want piece?' Jay pointed at Niomi and then slapped Mordacai on the back. Mordacai started to tremble and stutter. 'Cos if you want it, it can be arranged, you get me?'

'Jay!'

'What? I'm joking. What's up wid you two. Somebody dead?'

'Me don't tink so, but me haven't been out as yet so me don't know.'

They both looked at him.

'How are you dis morning, Mordacai, you feeling good?'

'It's nearly two.'

In the silence her laughter ran in and settled between them all like another person.

'Yeh, well, anyway.' Jay looked at Niomi and told her with his eyes that she was going to get a box.

'Mordacai, we did tell you we're having some friends over tonight?'

'Well, I don't know about that.' The look of worry increased the lines and made his eyes wide. She was looking at a child.

'You mean ah party?'

'Yes.'

'A real one?' The excitement was building in his voice. 'But, but, what will we do?'

'Bout what?'

'Eeer food an music.'

'Well, that's it.' Jay sat next to him and put his arm around him and shook him every time he spoke.

'So, check it, Mordacai, we goin to have a nice time. But you're on it, we do need food an that. You an my girl go out and get some stuff, then we good. That cashpoint in that shop still works.'

'I don't go in dere.'

'But we need cash, you got some innit? Take some out and we'll pay you back tomorrow. Not much. Take her wid you.'

Mordacai looked at her and she looked at him, and the rain whispered against the window. Mordacai was trying not to look at Jay, who was sitting closer to him than anyone had done in a long time. Their noses almost touched.

'You're going to get some money out, innit Mordacai?'

'Y ... y ... yes.'

'Good, that's good times. I knew you would. Tell you what. Take out enough for tonight and maybe tomorrow? Eh? We could go on a little trip, dat nice park, and on the way back we can get you your money.' She watched him pretend to ask, like she had so many times before.

'I not sure.'

'Is nutin, you worry too much. I need to bus a piss.' They heard him in the bathroom. 'And get some toilet paper too!'

She felt it in her soul, the look Mordacai had on his face, and she tried not to let him see the guilt in hers.

'Shall we go then, rain looks like it's eased a bit.'

'Go?' Mordacai hadn't moved. It was as if Jay was still there, his arm around his shoulder.

'Yeh.'

'I ...'

'Just a minute.'

She rushed to the bedroom and stuffed her things in a plastic bag. When she came back he still hadn't moved.

'Come on.'

'Yo! Did you hear what I said? Paper, don't figet paper!'

'We won't!'

She went over and took Mordacai's arm.

'Where's your coat?'

He didn't answer, and she went out into the hall and found it on the floor and came back.

'Come on.'

'We goin?'

'Yes, we goin.'

THE POSSIBLE PARABLE OF CAROLINE CARLTON

ROBERT WILLIAMS

Each morning as Caroline Carlton rode her bike to work, she was filled with dread at the thought of the people she would meet during the day. Some mornings she would be required to stop at a pedestrian crossing on the busy road beneath the low green trees, and the people crossing might wave or nod thanks to her. On lush summer mornings, on snapping blue winter mornings, they were liable to call out, 'Lovely day!' or, 'Beautiful morning!'

Caroline, feet poised on pedals, ready to push forward, would reply, sometimes, with the smallest of nods.

People wore Caroline out. There were so many of them. And because each and every one was different there was no single position to assume, no multi-person approach guaranteed to work; you always had to be alert, ready to switch tactics. It was exhausting. For example, people could be impatient or jolly or lazy or needy or friendly or sad or sulky or whiny or loud or smelly or helpful or moody or anxious or delighted or satisfied or grieving or in love or bored or playful or witty or gormless or smug or arrogant or kind.

Everyone was always something.

But that wasn't even the half of it. People could be more than one thing at a time. A person could be ill *and* angry, for instance. Caroline once met a woman who was tired, happy, mischievous and impatient all at once. Where do you start with *that*?

Every day, all day, she longed for the moment when she would sink into the cold-at-first water of the council swimming pool. All day, every day, she was sustained by the thought of those first seconds underneath the water when she would hear nobody, see nobody, sink slowly, deeply down. And then, when her lungs could take no more, just before they imploded, she would kick back to the surface, take a few deep breaths and start on the first of her fifty daily lengths. By the end of her time in the water, Caroline would feel strong enough to see the day out. She would survive the few remaining inevitable encounters before resting her head on her pillow and sleeping until the next morning, when it would all begin again. If I couldn't swim, I'd rather be dead, thought Caroline every night.

And then, of course, disaster struck.

Caroline was riding her bike to work, dreading the day ahead. A new colleague had been assigned the desk next to hers, and he talked, this man. He wanted to make Caroline drinks, he wanted to know if Caroline had had a good night, a good weekend, a good whatever he could think of next. What was her favourite colour, he wondered. Her favourite country, month, biscuit, animal, programme, book, tree, band, her favourite song ... He sucked so much from Caroline that by the time she finally plunged into the water at the end of the day, she was nearly empty, almost unable to sink to the void at the bottom of the pool.

And so, it was not inconceivable that on the morning of the disaster, Caroline was more preoccupied than usual when she nearly rode her bike into the bouncy little girl on the pedestrian crossing. Seeing the danger at the last moment, Caroline swerved sharply and only squashed the toes of the girl's left foot. But the girl cried out in pain and hopped in a circle wildly before falling to the ground and writhing in the exuberant manner only a healthy, unharmed child could. As the crowd gathered around the whirling, vigorous little thing, Caroline pulled herself up, holding one useless arm in the other scraped and bloody arm. It was two hours before she was shown the clean break on the X-ray, a thin black line spearing the bone like a shot arrow. She was discharged from hospital with her arm in a cast, two boxes of painkillers, her nose bloody, her right cheek a grazed, gory mess. Six weeks, they said. Six weeks before she would be mended, six weeks before she could swim again. A disaster.

Life became intolerable.

Work informed her they would send a taxi in the mornings and a woman from HR would drop her back home at the end of each day. It was no trouble, Caroline was told when she protested, when she said she would prefer to walk – they had an account with the taxi firm and the woman from HR would be passing her house on the way to visit her mother.

So began Caroline's nightmare.

First thing in the morning, a chatty taxi driver. 'What happened to you? You look like you've been in the wars. How's the arm today? Any better? Does it itch? You want to get a knitting needle down there.'

And then work and the fake concern of colleagues she didn't like, colleagues who didn't like her. Then the final torture: stuck with the woman from HR in heavy traffic on the way home, slowly passing the blue, blue pool, trying not to listen as she was told her about the mother's descent into dementia. 'She doesn't even know who I am anymore,' the woman said sadly. Caroline felt a twinge of jealousy.

On the fourth night she could take no more. She waited impatiently for the bath to fill. When the water was to the brim she removed her dressing gown and lowered herself. And then, after a second of anticipation, she plunged her head under, the white-plastered arm held aloft, a mini lighthouse in a tiny sea. But it was no good, the water wasn't deep enough, and she could still hear the chatter of the taxi driver, the nattering of her colleague, the squeal of the little girl as she ran over her toe, the sad and lonely voice of the woman from HR with the demented mother.

*

The next six weeks were the most miserable six weeks of Caroline's life. Weeks filled with people and no swimming. Finally, the day arrived to have the plaster removed. Caroline had booked the day off work and went straight from hospital to the pool, staying there until she was asked to leave. In the water, for the first time in weeks, she felt relief, a deep peace settling inside her. Before she fell asleep that night, Caroline remembered the previous six weeks with a shudder.

*

And so, for the rest of her life, Caroline made sure she was careful whenever she rode her bike, whenever she crossed a road, whenever she left the house. She made sure that she wasn't preoccupied, that she didn't let hatred of people get in the way of safe progress through the world. Caroline enjoyed another seventeen years of swimming before she died. A brain tumour. Something vital snapped in her head and she was gone before there was time to sink to the bottom of the pool. Happily, the last five years of Caroline's life had been her best. She enjoyed retirement, swimming twice a day, and avoiding most people most of the time.

The church was almost empty on the day of her funeral, but not quite as empty as Caroline would have liked. On the fifth pew back, on the left-hand side, sat the talking man from the desk next to Caroline's. 'What's your favourite hymn?' he asked, turning to the vicar.

The vicar spoke quickly and rattled through the essentials in a pleasingly brusque manner, and Caroline was

141

buried, unmourned, with the warm sun beating down on her coffin, not a drop of rain in the sky, not a drop of water on the ground that day. But it didn't matter. Caroline was gone. Caroline had swum.

HOW YOU FIND YOURSELF

SARA SHERWOOD

I. **Y**ou decide, at thirteen, you like 'bad boys done good' because you overhear the phrase in a conversation between your mother and your Auntie Tina. That, and you have a crush on Jamie Mitchell off *EastEnders*. At your high school in Batley, the closest to this you can get is Stephen Dooley.

   a. Stephen Dooley has a shaved head and a fake diamond stud in his right ear. He holds your hand at Bradford ice-skating rink one Saturday in November.

   b. The same day, Stephen Dooley kisses you, your first kiss, with sloppy lips and a tongue which still tastes of bacon-flavoured crisps, at Bradford Interchange bus station.

   c. As your relationship develops, one of your regular arguments becomes whether *EastEnders* or *Coronation Street* is the better soap.

   d. You will, throughout university, work and beyond, have this argument with many other people. You will always gun for *EastEnders*.

2. Due to your notorious snogging sessions with Stephen Dooley in the Year 9 common area, you become irresistible to other boys in your year group. Most notably:

    a. Mohammed Nassar in Year 10 (October to March).

       i. The highlight of your relationship is when he fingers you on the sofa to the sounds of canned laughter in *Ant and Dec's Saturday Night Takeaway* when your mum is out at Auntie Tina's.

    b. Kieran Luther in Year 10 (March to July).

       i. You go out with Kieran for four months until he kisses Aleena Ahmad at the end-of-term disco. From here, you will always associate Usher's 'Burn' with the gut-punch of heartache.

    c. Harry McDonald in Year 11 (September to June).

       i. Harry McDonald is in Sixth Form.

       ii. You get drunk for the first time with Harry McDonald.

       iii. You lose your virginity to Harry McDonald at his brother's flat in Huddersfield.

       iv. You tell all your friends how romantic it was, but all you remember is a dusty spider web which spanned from the ceiling to the naked light bulb.

3. At sixteen, you tell your friends that you have outgrown rough-talking boys; you now like boys who are into the Ramones, books by Jack Kerouac and vinyl

records. This is mainly because you stumble across a repeat of *The OC* over the summer holiday and decide that you prefer Seth Cohen over Ryan Atwood.

a. Your school's equivalent to Seth Cohen is Sohail Sheikh. He's the older brother of your friend Khadijah Sheikh.

b. Sohail is at college in Leeds, but you see him at parties.

c. Sohail writes poems – funny poems – about TV and craving cigarettes during Ramadan.

d. You spend your two years of Sixth Form devoted to Sohail. You change your Myspace profile picture to something poutier and more filtered in black-and-white to get his attention.

e. It never works.

4. As part of your devotion to Sohail, you develop an all-encompassing crush on the host of *Big Brother's Big Mouth*, Russell Brand.

a. You create a LiveJournal devoted to Russell Brand. You find pictures on the internet and use Paint to draw hearts around his backcombed hair.

b. You stumble across FanFiction.net. You write long messages to your fellow writers on the strengths and weaknesses of their stories which revolve around Russell's madcap adventures through London with a female sidekick (with whom, of course, he eventually falls in love).

c. You develop friendships with these online girls. They're much more interesting than your friends at school: they live in happy-sounding places like Guildford and Hereford.

d. Over the course of Year 12, you write a 90,000-word romantic comedy fanfiction in which Russell Brand is forced to pretend you are his girlfriend as part of an undercover operation.

i. You win Best Overall Fic at the online awards on LiveJournal.

ii. Your Head of Sixth Form says you cannot put this on your UCAS form.

5. When you finally kiss Sohail, at a Year 13's birthday party at Ackroyd Street Working Mens' Club in Morley, his tongue feels small in your mouth. You remember walking away from him, to the smirks of your friends, the soles of your shoes coming unstuck from the beer-stained floor.

a. Your crush melts and flutters into the air like confetti. You try to catch it. You force yourself in his bed, in your bed, in someone's parents' bed while a cruel house party rages on beyond the bedroom door, to like him – to want him – again.

b. You become his girlfriend.

c. You realise Sohail is deeply boring; you develop a furious dislike of the Beat poets and listen to Beyoncé loudly, obnoxiously and with joy.

d. Your break-up is triggered by an argument about the ethics of reading novels by William S. Burroughs.

    i. He calls you inauthentic.

    ii. You call him a knobhead.

e. You find comfort in assuming the identity of a grieving ex-girlfriend (you've been told you look pretty when you cry) but really you feel like a failure, like you've been scrubbed clean and found to be less than.

f. When Sohail leaves for university, you're relieved, but you are unmoored without your hobby of the crush.

6. At university – York, where you study English Literature – you meet Jasmine. She has long blonde hair and hardy thighs; she's used to riding horses, sloshing through mud in Hunter wellies and eating her breakfast – porridge, with blueberries – in a flag-stoned Shropshire kitchen. You're surrounded by girls like these on your course, in your halls, on the student newspaper, but Jasmine ... Jasmine is magical.

    a. You bond by watching *Gossip Girl* on ITV2.

        i. Jasmine has blonde hair which makes her the Serena van der Woodsen to your Blair Waldorf.

        ii. You both agree that Chuck Bass, rather than Dan Humphrey, is the romantic lead of the series. This is mainly because of Chuck Bass's hair which, unlike that of many of the boys in your seminars, is parted at the side and swept romantically across his forehead.

iii. The subject of your daydreams, which was previously a man in skinny jeans with riotous hair, morphs into a suave New York hotelier with a transatlantic accent and a bottomless bank account.

7. In your second year at York you meet Ben. You both review albums and books for the university newspaper. He's from Sheffield, and his accent – harsh and deep – sends electric sparks down your spine and into your knickers. Ben likes *Peep Show*, coffee and Modest Mouse.

   a. You quickly school yourself on all three.

   b. When he catches you scrolling through *Oh No They Didn't*, your favourite celebrity gossip website, in the library, he uses this as an example of your shallowness.

      i. This becomes a running joke throughout your relationship.

8. You allow Ben to fuck you – and your heart – and mock your love of celebrity stories for two years.

   a. In the run-up to your final exams, you walk out of a seven-hour stretch in the library to get a coffee and KitKat Chunky with Jasmine and see Ben kissing Charlotte, his housemate, outside a cafe on campus.

   b. When he changes his Facebook status to 'In a relationship' two days after your final exam, you delete him from your Facebook and cry for three days.

c. On the night you get your final results (a First despite the fact you spent your exam worrying more about Ben than Patrick Hamilton), you text him a topless selfie from the pub toilets. He doesn't respond.

9. You move back home and are unemployed. Batley has always been depressing, but now it's even more so. You hate it. You wish you didn't have the lazy vowels of the West Riding cursing your voice. You wish you were Jasmine, who is staying with her godparents in Barnet and has just scored her third unpaid internship at a fashion website.

   a. You're not jealous of Jasmine.

   b. You direct your anger at your mother, who has kept you stuck in a two-bedroom terraced house on the outskirts of three useless cities.

   c. You wish you had:

      i. Rich godparents.

      ii. A successful aunt.

      iii. A cousin who works at *The Telegraph*.

10. In February, after months of endless applications, London beckons you with a graduate scheme at a multinational marketing firm which offers career progression and a pension, and you oblige.

    a. You find a flat in Clapham on SpareRoom.

    i. You choose Clapham because Jasmine's brother lives there and he's the only person you know who lives in London.

b. You gradually get rid of your New Look mini-skirts and stained Primark knickers and, with your new money, buy minimal dresses and structured blazers from Whistles, Hobbs and Jaeger.

c. You tie your hair in a severe bun. At first it hurts; you feel like your hair is being twisted away from your scalp.

d. You attend a training session for women in leadership where you learn not to talk about what you watched on the TV last night or apologise for your mistakes.

e. You start saying things like 'Why don't you just find a better job?' when your mum complains about her ongoing pay freeze.

    i. You roll your eyes when she tries to explain that there aren't any better jobs around there for her, and besides, she likes her friends at the school, likes the summer holidays, the pension. Why would she sacrifice that for a couple of pounds more at the end of the month?

II. You start to construct a narrative about yourself, about your past.

a. You were born into an ambitionless household.

b. You are the product of social mobility.

c. You try to scrub away all the automatic references your brain makes to *EastEnders* and *Gossip Girl* and *Big Brother*.

d. The new identity fits over you, like armour.

e. You do battle in it every day.

12. You're twenty-five. You're at a networking event in a bar in Canary Wharf and you meet Andrew. He's tall. He's handsome. He's a perfect fit for you, the new and shiny you. Everyone says so.

a. At first you tell Jasmine that you think Andrew speaks like he's got a cock in his mouth. Eventually you forget you ever said it.

b. You meet his friends, his parents, his granny – a woman so unlike your own chain-smoking Nana – in Winchester.

c. He comes to Batley to meet your mum.

i. He tells you that he's never been in a house where you step straight off the pavement and into the living room.

13. When you're six months into your relationship, you and Andrew go on a bank holiday trip to Whitstable.

a. You have oysters for the first time on the seafront.

b. Across the table, you run your fingers along his cheek and let his day-old stubble scratch under your fingernails. You can't stop touching him. He can't stop touching you.

c. Back at the hotel, you fill the deep, wide bath with Neal's Yard bubble bath.

> i. You both get it. He smiles across the bath at you, his two front teeth resting on his sea-salt lips.
>
> ii. You tell him that when you were small you would fill the bath up to the top, clamp your legs together and wiggle about, pretending that you were a mermaid.
>
> iii. You tell him how lonely you were as a child.
>
> iv. With no brothers or sisters, you would read or watch the telly so your imagination could explode with stories to keep you company.
>
> > 1. You were a lost princess trapped in a boarding school.
> >
> > 2. You were an orphan sent from India to live in Yorkshire.
> >
> > 3. You were a mermaid who longed to live on the land.
> >
> > 4. You were the secret daughter of spies.
> >
> > 5. You were a lion running away from the death of her father.
>
> v. 'I've never told anyone that,' you say.
>
> vi. 'I love you,' he says.

14. You and Andrew have been together for two years. You suspect something is wrong.

   a. You only have sex once a month.

      i. Once every three months.

   b. He rolls away from you in bed.

   c. He spends more time at the gym.

      i. You suggest you go together – you normally go to Spin on a Saturday morning with Jasmine, but you're desperate enough to forgo this to save Andrew.

      ii. He bats the suggestion away with a scrunched-up mouth like a punch to the chest.

   d. You try to resist but you end up going through his phone. You find what you're looking for: flirty messages from a woman – Polly – who he works with.

      i. Of course it would be a fucking Polly.

      ii. You find her LinkedIn and feel smug when you find what you're looking for: a nursery-to-Sixth Form private education in the south of England and a First Class BA (Hons) in Classical Civilisation from Christ Church, Oxford.

      iii. Of course, Andrew would leave you for a Polly. Someone who wouldn't need to be taught how to pronounce Diptyque and whose family also has a bolthole in Norfolk.

         1. 'What the *fuck* is a bolthole, anyway?' you rage at Jasmine.

e. Days later, when you confront him, Andrew tells you it's nothing, but he wishes that he didn't feel so stifled by your relationship.

   i. And, by extension, you.

   ii. He suggests some time out.

   iii. You suggest getting engaged.

15. You find a flat. You pack up your life (half a life, because who are you without him?) into boxes. You cry into the pillow on your first night in your new flat in Stoke Newington. Quietly, so your new flatmates – Sophia and Beth – don't hear.

   a. When you wake up on Saturday morning, you reach for him but there's nobody there.

   b. The bed smells of nothing.

   c. Food tastes of nothing.

   d. You are nothing.

      i. Just another girl whose voice melted away into a regionless blur, whose only true interests are Kylie Jenner's Instagram Stories and the new series of *Gilmore Girls* on Netflix.

      ii. You wish other people didn't have so much when you feel like you have so little.

      iii. Basic bitch.

      iv. Working class.

      v. Shallow cunt.

vi. Boy-obsessed.

vii. Stupid twat.

viii. Ex-girlfriend.

16. Time passes slowly.

a. You learn what loneliness is.

b. You stand in front of a Jackson Pollock painting and feel … nothing. It's just red and black.

c. You sleep in the middle of the bed.

d. You give yourself to Netflix at the weekend.

e. You start watching *EastEnders* again because there's nothing else to do in the evening.

f. You download Tinder.

g. You stare at the ceiling while a Durham-educated civil engineer, with a body like a mountain, fucks you.

i. He invites you to watch him play rugby and to meet his friends.

ii. You ghost him.

h. You learn that Sundays are the worst.

i. And bank holidays.

ii. And weddings.

iii. And hen parties where everyone seems to think that squealing 'He put a ring on it!' is an acceptable form of congratulations in 2016.

17. On 16 June 2016, you see your phone ringing in front of you on your desk. 'Mum' flashes on the screen. She hangs up. She rings again, and again, and again. You ignore it.

    a. There's breaking news on the BBC. The alert interrupts your stream of WhatsApps. The name of your home town, Batley, makes you pay attention.

    b. Your MP, the MP at home – proper home – has been stabbed in the town centre. She is being airlifted to hospital.

    c. You call your mum back. She's crying. You can hear shouts in the background – you imagine Janice and Michelle, your mum's office mates, are having panicked conversations with their husbands and children.

    d. 'Have you seen what they've done to her?' your mum manages to choke out.

18. She was murdered outside the library where you used to borrow books and videotapes.

19. That weekend, after watching a repeat of *Mamma Mia!* with Jasmine, you book two weeks off work and a return flight to Greece. You've had a bottle of wine and three double gin and tonics, but you've never been on holiday on your own. You're feeling reckless, and you never feel reckless.

    a. You wonder if you'll get bored of yourself.

    b. You wonder who you'll talk to.

c. On the plane, you wonder if this is self-care or self-destruction.

d. Reading *Heat* magazine makes you forget your inevitable death for twenty minutes.

20. You're desperately lonely in Athens. You thought you were lonely before, but it turned out that was just the origin story of your loneliness.

    a. You write a poem about it, go to bed and fall asleep scrolling through Twitter.

    b. The poem is so horrifyingly bad that when you read it back in the morning, you laugh at your self-pity.

        i. Weirdly, this seems to help snap you out of it and you visit the Acropolis.

21. You stumble across a free night-time city tour on TripAdvisor while eating your tea in a cafe. On the walk, you make friends with an American woman around your age: Rita from Ohio. She's just finished her MFA in Creative Writing at Evergreen State College and is travelling around Europe for the summer, writing as she goes. She tells you that after Athens she is planning to travel up to Berlin, stopping at Thessaloniki, Sofia, Belgrade and Budapest on the way.

    a. At first Rita asks you about Brexit, and you ask her about Trump. You both repeat things you've read in the *Guardian* and the *New York Times*.

b. You and Rita then find common ground in Katy Perry's documentary *Part of Me*, especially the bit where she's mourning the breakdown of her relationship with Russell Brand.

> i. 'I used to write fanfiction about Russell Brand,' you say, feeling brave, after two Greek beers. The only other person you have ever told about that is Jasmine.

> ii. 'Really?' Rita says, delighted. 'That's awesome. Do you still write?'

> iii. 'Just Tinder messages,' you say.

> iv. Rita laughs. 'That's still writing.'

c. You and Rita go to the open-air cinema in Athens and watch the midnight screening of *Mamma Mia!*, drink more Greek beer and eat nachos.

22. You stop wearing your hair in a severe bun. People at work tell you that you look younger with your hair down.

> a. You let the soft vowels of West Yorkshire, of Kimberley Walsh, Jarvis Cocker and Jane McDonald, curl back over your tongue. It relaxes you. Some days you think it feels right, whereas at other times, you feel like you're impersonating an older version of your former self.

> > i. You wonder if that's appropriation.

> b. You hear clients talking about last night's episode of *Love Island* as you're walking out of a meeting. Before you can stop yourself, you're giving your

opinion on if you think an islander is overreacting to another islander's betrayal in Casa Amour.

c. You find that they – Katie, Sarah and Rhys – smile at you across the meeting room table when you see them again.

i. You start speaking more in meetings.

23. You spend the entirety of Easter bank holiday with Jasmine rewatching *Gossip Girl* season two, which you both agree is the show's imperial phase. You wonder why you didn't realise that Chuck Bass and Blair Waldorf's relationship was toxic at the time.

a. You open the bottle of Champagne you got for a good performance at work and discuss with Jasmine until her Uber arrives.

b. You pace around your room and feel something close to an epiphany about your relationships with men, identity, romance, society and expectations.

c. Open your MacBook.

d. Close your MacBook.

e. No, fuck it, open your MacBook again.

f. Register for a Wordpress.

g. Call it *Gossip Hurl*.

h. Finish the Champagne.

i. Write.

j. Write.

k. Write.

24. You never thought writing was hard – it came so easily when you were writing for the university news-paper, or your university essays, or your work reports, or your Russell Brand fanfiction, or your shopping lists, or to-do lists – but *fuck* is it hard.

   a. But you keep doing it.

   b. Time seems to glide when you're writing.

   c. You write about *Gossip Girl* and *The OC* and *Love Island* and *Riverdale* and last night's episode of *Coronation Street*.

   d. Jasmine is the only person who is allowed to read your blog.

      i. But you suspect that she's sending it to other people because you keep getting more hits.

25. In November, you book a week off work and a return ticket to Batley. Your mum takes you to visit the new shopping centre in the middle of Bradford. After lunch at Pizza Express, you wander around the exhib-ition on the history of TV at the National Media Museum.

   a. You wonder if growing up in a single-parent household where the TV was your babysitter, best friend and father has made you more respectful and reverent of TV.

      i. You may have needed to be taught how to pronounce Diptyque but you can talk about the significance of Danny Dyer's pink dressing gown in *EastEnders* and what it says about contemporary masculinity.

b. You have your photo taken next to a Dalek in the entrance of the National Media Museum.

i. You caption it: 'Exterminate me, Daddy.'

ii. It gets 372 likes on Instagram, your most popular post yet.

iii. One of the likes is Sohail, Khadijah's brother, who you wasted your Sixth Form years on.

iv. You click on his profile. You didn't even realise he was following you, and see that he is now an accountant, not a poet.

26. That evening, your mum invites Auntie Tina around to watch *Strictly Come Dancing*. Your mum has made her own glitter paddles out of cardboard, which you hold up at the end of each performance. At the end of the show, all three of you cast your votes on your phones.

a. At 11 p.m., when you get up to go to bed, your mum kisses you on the forehead.

b. You open your laptop.

c. Your mum pauses by the door.

i. 'Are you going to write one of your blogs?'

ii. 'How did you know about those?'

iii. 'Your friend Jasmine emails them on to me. They're always interesting.'

iv. You don't know what to say.

v. 'You probably don't remember, but when you were little you would leave these little stories, these lists about the telly, for me to read. "Reasons Why I Should Be Allowed To Stay Up To Watch *EastEnders*." Always made me and Tina crack up.'

vi. You don't look at your mum. You look at the picture of you on the mantelpiece. It had been fancy dress day at your primary school for *Children in Need*. You and your mum had taken a cardboard box and made it into a TV, covered in tinfoil, with an aerial made out of bright-pink pipe-cleaners. You'd worn it as a headdress and won second prize in assembly for best costume. Your smile is joyous, straining your cheeks.

i. It sits next to your graduation photo. Both you and your mum look stiff, too formal, out of place.

d. Your mum kisses you on the head and closes the door behind her.

e. You turn back to your laptop and start filling up the blank space.

THE COORIE

CARMEN MARCUS

We're never to walk the same way twice, we mustn't lay down paths, our tracks must fall light so they can be blown away by sand or snow-forgetting. I told you that but you're like Mammy, you don't listen. Mammy walks her own way above the high-tide mark, her feet crusted in red muck as she churns a path straight to the Burn House. She cannot steady herself as she needs both hands to carry you. I walk ahead so's anyone watching would see I wasn't on her side. I spook a little crowd of plovers.

—Get up. Get gone.

I don't want to see their dippy heads today. They clatter up.

—This would be easier by road, Mammy says, but the island hasn't got any.

—We don't need roads here.

She knows that. She knows we're supposed to follow the shuls: the deer paths; the rabbit paths – their dotty tracks. She knows that she's not supposed to be wearing that lace dress that dips below her coat like sea-foam, asking for a finger to knot in it. She knows she wasn't supposed to get all fat and have you at all. The whole island staring at your pebble roundness, like you were a bad winter they wanted to warm between their hands.

And worst of all Mr Berengar coming round to our Coorie, right up over the yellow line, to tell Mammy off. Least she carries the box, least she knows that. She carries it high on her hip the way she used to carry you, your legs hooked tight round her and the islanders trying to find something else to stare at in the blank grey sky.

I wait for her as she climbs the dune. Her feet crack the thin frost that flours the sand. Even though I hold out both hands she won't let me carry the box. I run ahead; there are no clouds between me and the cold, and all I have to feel is the good numb the first dip into winter brings. I tread up and up to the Burn House door and Mammy shouts for me to knock. The damp wood eats the sound but Brak opens it before we can step back behind the line. He was watching for us.

I like Brak. He's maybe the biggest person on the island. I like the way he leans down to talk to me, like a cormorant when it dives. Brak has a way of making me feel held without ever touching, like leaning into the wind. You can say anything to the wind and it never tells. Brak never told about the feather.

Mammy tries to put the box down on the cold table but Brak takes it from her without waiting to put his gloves on. He takes you from Mammy and she lets him, holding on until she's sure he has the weight.

*

I wasn't supposed to hold you when you first came but Mammy said she couldn't do it all on her own. It was true, her eyes had sunk deep into her head and she was all hollows. She said I'd have to give you a bath and not to worry because the rules weren't for babies. You were the only baby on the island, so I supposed she was right. I scrubbed and scrubbed until the marble path of my scald opened, and Mammy said —Stop, for god's sake, stop, and then she handed you to me and went to find some sleep. I cleaned a guillemot once, at school, dug the soap deep into its feathers and scraped the oil off and the whole time it was going for my eye with its spear beak. It didn't get sick just because I'd touched it. Nothing I ever touched before wanted to be held.

I took a hold of you by your head and bottom above the water and your eyes crinkled shut and you went so slack inside your body. Not like a bird. Birds are muscle smoothed around light that bobs and fights. Then you bucked and arched your back, your eyes and mouth popped open. I thought you could read it in my skin – the fear that tripped on the briar path of my scar. I shoved my whole hand under you to stop the water swallowing you down. I dabbed you, head to foot, with my fingers. One of your feet was curled up to your shin, it was smaller than the other. My hands knew what to do. I rubbed your soft bones straight. You took a hold of my thumb with your tiny purple hand and you didn't mind one bit about my scald. I always bathed you after that.

*

Brak doesn't say goodbye. He says —You mustn't write his name, not on a tree, not on sand; not even a mark on your body. I had never thought of doing anything so mad as that and it was easy to promise not to.

—Go home, nothing more to be done now. Brak closes the door on Mammy and me before the heat of the burner can reach our faces. I can see our Coorie from up here. It looks just like a bump in the ground where the snow can't settle for the warmth. Mammy dug it out of the dirt like a den, a cup of muddy hands to hold us in our beds. She called it our Coorie. We're not to tell because naming things is the same as leaving a mark or making a track, names mean something, they leave something behind. Coorie means to hold. Mammy means the same. When we lie deep inside it, no one looking from above would believe we were even there at all. We can't go back there yet, not with all your stones and feathers and sticks all over the place. We can't go back and clear a space that you won't fill again.

I hear the Burn House roar, the tall chimney sucking in cold air to feed the fire. It breathes out white ash. When a fox takes an eider duck: I've seen this. When the first snow comes in: I've seen this. The warm ash-down falls in Mammy's hair and my hair, it settles on our eyelashes and smears our hands. I want this mark to stay. I want to cut it into bark, to score it in sand, I want it to splinter under my skin so that it will stay with me and hurt every time I touch something that isn't you. But all I feel is the slow pinch of winter. I step on feathers and trip on stones all the way home. Mammy dumps our over-clothes into the scald-water by the door and it turns white like shock.

*

At school Mr Berengar says —Do your best to get back to usual, in his good-job-gold-star voice. —Those sad feelings will go. —Like snow, I said and he said —That's right, Hura, just like snow. But he's not Brak. He doesn't promise. Brak doesn't have much to say about teachings, he doesn't worry whether I keep the rules, he only worries if I'm hungry. Brak is solid as a nut and Mr Berengar is wind-seed, spiky as a thistle and as hard to please. He said that he won't think less of me for Mammy's selfishness. He meant you.

You didn't get big enough to go to school. School is not like our Coorie, it is above ground, built over the marsh, there are no walls, there are only wooden roofs and wooden walkways. There is Mr Berengar's station in the centre and the children's stations jut out from his on their own islands like the toothy rocks that surround our island. The other children don't ask where I've been or if I was sick, even though we always ask about illness: how much phlegm got coughed up; was there blood in it or just green gob? It makes our own bodies tingle, to know that we've all felt the same thing – even if it was a fever or the lung-punch of a cough – because we cannot reach a hand out to read someone else's skin across our yellow-lined stations. We know what bodies do. We learn it all, but we never touch. The more we know about how our bodies work and stop working, the less there is to fear. We must be good at dying. So Mr Berengar says, and he is good at making us not scared, not because of what he says but because of the special voice he uses. It's a loud and sleepy sound all at once, like the sea sucking itself back through stones.

Mr Berengar starts every day talking about the Earth. He says we are the Earth, meaning the whole planet not dirt, and we, meaning our bodies, our heads and fingers and feet. We are full of bits of the Earth – iron, oxygen, water, carbon. Even inside our bones. He says that when we die, we go back to being the Earth again and in this we way we can finally touch. And he says this in that special voice, so that growing back into mud and stints and marram grass sounds like it might feel like a feather being drawn across my skin, not like being burned to pieces.

Aran, he's the oldest boy, he says even the dirt wouldn't want to touch me. He knows that it's only sickness on the inside that matters, but he still looks and I can see his eyes following the raw dips and creases of my winter-hand. Lucky it can't feel him, lucky it's always cold. He looks and looks but those lines won't take him anywhere by looking, I've tried.

Mr Berengar doesn't hear him. He's too busy because it's Log Day and the islanders who are well enough have already started to take their places in the queue. They've all walked down from their shelters, stepped careful over rough, uneasy ground, hoping they haven't walked that way before. We don't know about direction but we know about distance and how to keep it. No one is still as they drift to keep the gap between each other even. They grip their Logs, little square books filled with little squares that are only big enough to hold what is relevant, accurate and true about our bodies: pains; fevers; if we have touched someone; who and when and where.

You didn't have a Log. Mammy had to make space for you in hers. Mammy wrote about you when you were new, before you could walk even. She wrote 'dark blue grey dusk' in and around the tiny square for eye colour.

She wrote that you would only go to sleep on her tummy, turning until you fitted snug under her collarbone. She wrote that there was no more day- and night-time: only feed-time, sleep-time; that your tongue was a clock and that she was as thin as the moon when it shows up in the day-blue sky. She wrote how your mouth was the first thing to wake up, popping for a feed, and if she waited till you cried, her boobies would cry milk back at you. Mr Berengar read her Log, tugging at his spiky gold hair and rubbing his red beard, scrit-scratch, rubbing her words away. He crinkled his grey eyes at Mammy and shook out a breath. He said —None of this is relevant. Mammy laughed with just her body so she didn't wake you. She can do that. An angry shaking laugh that could easily be mistaken for a fever. Mammy said he didn't want her to write anything about you because you scared him.

I stand in Mammy's place in the queue. She is not here today but I hold her space for her. The woman who goes in the place behind us shouts.

—Is your Mammy sick?

—No.

—Is she late?

—No.

—Grief is a luxury we can't afford. We all know why we're here.

She doesn't shout this but breathes it into the space I left for Mammy.

I open my book for Mr Berengar and he checks my yeses and noes, and I watch to see if I can tell when he reads about my bleeding stopping because of the pills he gave me. I can't. I don't write about the ash-snow and the marks it made on me. He closes my Log, swabs my throat and gives me a 'Well done' smile when I gag.

—Why don't you take Kora and go tracking today?

*

It is my job to look for winter, I have a winter-book. I tell it when all the birds arrive and when they go, I copy down their marks.

On the west beach the wind rushes at the side of the cliff, bringing a gust of spray with it, all salt and alive. My winter-hand prickles with splinters. This is a change but I don't log it. All that's relevant here is when will the winter come; how long will it stay; how many will get sick and leave no marks behind.

—Is it always this cold? Are these curlew tracks?

Kora never shuts up, so all the birds get scared away.

—There are no curlews, they're summer birds.

Everyone knows she's only allowed to measure rainfall because she can't draw, even though Mr Berengar says it's because she's the best measurer. I can draw, that's why winter is my job. —Star, star, star, Mr Berengar says about my tracks. The trick is not to draw the shape of feet, because they have already gone, but the pressure of touch on mud and snow-crust.

You were good at being quiet, even when I tied you to my back when your legs got tired. And when I got tired, I'd set you down in the deep grass, like the deer-mammy does, so I could keep following bird signs for Mr Berengar's gold stars. I won't tie Kora to my back even if she cries to be carried. I'm not her deer-mammy.

—Are these curlew tracks?

—Husht.

I want to shout at Kora. I want to dig my hands into her puffy cheeks until the splinters stop hurting but I don't, not because it's a rule, but because it's not her fault and the splinters aren't real. They're just the cold eating my burned fingers.

—You need to look at the ground.

—I am. What are these? Shall I draw them?

—They're black-headed gulls' tracks.

—They're rubbish. I'm not drawing them. Why were you off yesterday?

—None of yours.

—I saw the Burn House lights.

—Shut up.

—Was it your brother? Did he get the fever? Was there something wrong with him before? Is that why he died? Lena was only seventeen and there was nothing wrong with her before.

—There was no Lena.

—Yeah, okay, *there was no Lena*. But, all I mean is, she was just like us.

Kora's sliding, she's not paying attention to the slush ice. I go faster. I want to see her fall.

—It's better for you and your mammy he's gone. He wasn't supposed to have been born anyway. Who would take care of him when – you know?

I hold what I want to say on my tongue like burning meat. Kora is a pain but she's not wicked. Not that wicked. She says it like she's been told it. So I hold the cruel thing I want to say until it's cold enough to swallow.

I can't laugh with anger-fever the way Mammy does so I look for the little dents bird-feet have made in the numb ground. There is a small pad shape in the snow, almost as big as a snowshoe hare's mark. Next to it a bigger pad with five circle toes. There are no forefeet tracks, just two hind-feet, one bigger than the other. Kora sees them too.

—Is that a curlew? Will I get gold stars if I draw it right?

Poor Kora, I send her onto the worm-flats after the oystercatchers.

I draw until the splinters in my hands dig into hurt-less bone. I keep drawing until I feel you wriggle in my fingers as I rub your small foot straight. What would Mr Berengar say in his special voice? Would he say that all the heat-torn pieces of the universe wanted to make themselves back to you?

*

Mr Berengar slowly tears the drawing out of my Log, careful not to leave a raggedy edge sticking out from the spine.

—Do you miss your brother?

—I have no brother.

—Alright, Hura, I just want to know where you think he's gone?

—Back to the Earth.

I'm right but his face doesn't say so.

—I've spoken with Kora. What I want to know is why you didn't come to me with this yourself?

This is not his gold-star voice. He gives me stars because I draw exactly what I see. Accurate. True. But stars don't really have pointy fingers, like a small hand reaching for a feather, the way that Mr Berengar draws them. I could draw them better if he let me.

—What was it you were tracking?

—Hard to tell, the snow was soft.

He holds up the torn page. Two feet, one bigger than the other. It's drawn perfectly accurate and true.

—What is this, Hura? Did you make this up?

I drew them with my pencil and then traced over them again with the fine black pen so it couldn't be undrawn. They look like islands now.

—Your job is to record accurate, observable facts.

He opens Kora's book on the desk next to mine. A gold star next to her clumsy forks of oystercatcher feet.

—Kora didn't log this, so why did you?

—Kora can't draw.

—That's unkind, Hura. So ... what do you think these tracks belonged to?

—A young hare?

—They're nothing like a hare's prints.

—My hands were cold.

He won't look at my winter-hand, he keeps his eyes on the tracks.

—You're usually so good at this sort of thing. This cold will surely kill a leveret born so early. I doubt you'll see it again.

I worry for the babba-hare digging in the hard ground for a green shoot even though it's a lie.

He crumples up the page and puts it in his stove where a little sea-coal burns; it takes awhile for the paper to light. I don't wait to see it blacken.

*

At home Mammy wears her wool and cloud colours and her belly has sunk in as if it's forgotten the shape of you there. I don't know whether to tell her what I drew. I don't know if I say it out loud – will she blow away like ash-down?

*

It was me who first knew you were sick. I got in from school and before I could drop my clothes into the scald-water, you held up your hands for a carry, fretting with the wait. I could feel the heat coming off you. I didn't trust my winter-hand to tell me the truth, so I pulled up your jumper and kissed your belly and rolled my cheek over your skin. I stuck to your hot tummy. —Mammy, I said and she did the same. I watched the little drum of your belly blow up and down. I watched the gooseflesh bloom. I noted the winter as it settled into you, next to the redwing sighting; they can't hide their bloody ribs in the snow. There is a lot to attend to in watching.

Mammy said:

—Go to Berengar and get paracetamol.

—But we can't stop it. Mammy knew that.

—He can, Mammy said. —Go and tell him it's for your brother.

—What's paracetamol? She wrote it down next to your name.

*

I gave Mr Berengar the paper. And he told me to come in, I stepped over the yellow line and tried not to breathe too deeply. He went to a metal cupboard in his wall. There were small bottles and boxes, the kind we found washed up and cut out of the bellies of fish. There were the pills he gave me to stop my bleeds. He pushed them aside and took out a feather; it flickered a dun and mucky gold.

—You can have the pills if you can tell me what bird this is from?

He held it by the quill and stroked the smooth vane through his fingers. I couldn't name what bird the feather came from and I know all the birds on the island: their tracks; their wingspan; their nesting places. I could still feel your heat on my cheek. Then Mr Berengar said it didn't matter what the bird was called because they were all gone.

—What about the paracetamol?

He took my hand and put the feather inside, folding my fingers over it, and I felt the itch of the need to clean my hands.

—Do you want this or not?

*

I showed the feather to Mammy and you saw it and did that little grabbing star with your hand. You made the noise, that high gurgling cry when you saw something you wanted to touch. We rubbed your tummy, we tried to give you a stone to hold. But it didn't stop the noise and you held your open hand out to us. You gave it all the fight you had left in your body to get that feather but

Mammy said —No. We passed you between us, from one hush story to the other, all the time the noise scalding us, until you threw yourself into a kicky sleep.

When you took cold I climbed into Mammy's bed and we curled up, cooried you between us, like deer-mammys do, all in a snug. Being hidden in the earth didn't feel like we were being held anymore. I wanted someone to see us. See that we weren't already dirt.

I rubbed your hands and feet. Held them in my mouth. We just couldn't get you warm. Mammy said your name over and over. Names are for places that you're from or have left behind. I asked if you were Earth again and Mammy said that was a load of shite. And she held you because that's what Mammy means.

*

I tell Mammy. I tell her about the tracks and draw them again in the ground. Mammy packs me up a bag full of things this island doesn't need. Her dress. Maps to a place that has roads and names. I cut her hair because I won't be there to comb it and as I cut the splintering in my raw fingers comes again, like a thaw, and for the first time I am afraid of winter.

*

Once, before you, I woke to a soft padding against my window. The rain was a new sound in the thaw – something less mad than the constant creaking and tutting. It was skin-hunger – for something that wasn't rough wool or the numb nuzzle of cold – that made me go out. I opened my hands and the rain, fearless, fell into them – burrowing deep inside the creases. It wasn't enough. I unbuttoned my parka; when it hit my skin the rain mapped me, finding places that wanted names and wanted me to say them. Mammy must have seen me like that, seen the unbuttoning and my mouth open for words I did not know. —What the hell are you doing? she shouted. —You'll make yourself sick. So I plunged my hand into the scald-water, clean and safe and screamless. She went to touch me then pulled her hand back, remembering the rule, and let the rain hold me. Mammy doesn't always mean to hold. By the time I'd healed to numbness, I had the patience to watch for winter.

*

Snow falls like feathers after a kill. Bright and sudden. I'm making a path and someone is following close.

—Show me, Mr Berengar says. So I point to the ground and he gets onto his knees to look.

—Here?

He walks his fingers across the snow in case they can see what he can't. But you've gone. It's only winter lying there.

—It was a corncrake.

I don't understand. Crake is your name.

—The bird the feather came from. I wanted to name him. Ask your mother? he said, like it was her who let you die. Like he'd written it down that way so many times it was true and accurate.

*

The night before we took you to the Burn House, Brak
came. He said I should put something in the box with you
and he wouldn't tell. —What something? I asked him and
he said —Like a flower or something he liked. So, I put
the feather in your starfish hand and closed your fingers
round it. Brak tied the box shut then and said I mustn't
say anything to anyone about putting something in the
box because that was worse than making a path.

I tell Mr Berengar —I put your feather in Crake's box.
This marks a path right through him. He says it over and
over – the bird's name and your name.

*

In the place with roads, it is my job to take people's
names when they come into this building, I write their
names and give them a badge. The people here are afraid
of distance the way we were afraid of losing it. Some of
them want me to give them my name in return – so I tell
them the one Mammy gave me, the one she dug out of
the earth, the one that's marked me with where I'm from
and what I've left behind – and they hold out their hands
to take it.

—Hura Coorie.

—Coorie? What does that mean?

—It means to hold.

Their hands are all different, in the same way their
names are different, sometimes cool like sea-fret when it
comes in the morning after a hot day, sometimes warm

and heavy as a stone. Winter is not quick or cold enough to leave a mark here, so it cannot find its way back into the scald. There is only the hollow in my palm where your foot fitted perfectly inside that never gets tired of taking their hands.

THE MARY HOUSE

CRISTA ERMIYA

I wanted to be an only child, and I almost was. My sister Abigail was born with a hole in her diaphragm: her intestines pushed up through the gap to wrap themselves around her heart, dragging it to the wrong side. Abi's life was saved by an operation when she was only a few weeks old, and she has a scar to prove it, a long thin line along her front torso, from left to right. Lift her blouse and it looks like her stomach is grinning.

Thirteen months younger than me, Abi could run faster, skip rope longer and hold her breath underwater a full minute more than I could. Most bitter of all, although we shared the same Pinoy features – dark hair, dark eyes, our mam's flat cheekbones – things don't look quite right in my asymmetrical face, whereas anyone who met my sister agreed: Abigail was a pretty girl.

Dad loved her. Miranda, our stepmam, loved her. I won't say I hated my sister, but if someone tells you they have a sister who is younger and smarter and prettier, you don't need to be told much else.

*

We didn't hang out much but Abi hassled me to go out with her sometimes at the weekend: dire parties at friends of friends, or, when we were a little older, some dodgy club where she always claimed to know a sister of the cousin of the doorman who would let us in. I was invisible at such gatherings. Boys and girls would lock on to Abi, who chatted and danced while I sat unwanted in the kitchen, or at a tiny table surrounded by underage drinkers in a darkened corner of the club. I'd go home alone and cover up for her with Dad and Miranda, who believed she was staying over at a friend's house to study. She always got A* grades anyway. I did too, but I had to work for them.

That summer I was seventeen and heading for the last year of my A levels. Abi was sixteen and waiting for GCSE results. We were at that stage in August when teenagers get bored enough to miss school when Abi suggested: 'Let's break into the Mary House.'

St Mary of Gaunt – everyone we knew called it the Mary House – was a tiny convent and seminary built in Northumberland in the early 1800s, near the small town where we live. It was an anomaly even then, built by a wealthy, largely absent landowner shortly after the English discovered their new-found tolerance for Roman Catholics. The convent and the main seminary closed in the early 1960s, but the junior seminary stayed open as a secondary school, until finally closing twelve years ago. Dad went to school there and even considered going on to Ushaw to train as a priest. If he had, Abi and I would never have been born.

Dad's not into religion much now, we're not even Roman Catholic. He left the Church shortly before I was born, and only had me baptised Church of England so I could get into the local primary school. Abi wasn't baptised, because they usually let you into the school if you've already got a sibling there. But it's always been a fascination for Abi, Dad's counterfactual life without us. People break into the Mary House all the time anyway, and post the photos to social media. Sometimes security tightens up, but then the diocese runs into cash-flow problems and it goes back to an unmonitored CCTV system. There is a high fence around the perimeter with barbed wire at the top but there are gaps in it, if you know where to look. Abi did.

'How many times have you been here?' I asked.

Abi shrugged, and said nothing.

*

The buildings were constructed in the Gothic revival style, all crenellations and gargoyles, but at a weirdly small scale, low-rise like almshouses. The north wing housed the convent, the south wing housed the seminary, and the kitchens and chapel were shared. The walls were covered in ivy, red edging the shape of each new dark green leaf. I thought it was beautiful.

'Hideous, isn't it?' Abi wrinkled her perfect nose. 'I hate to think of the women stuck here their whole lives.'

'They chose to be here,' I said.

Abi was incredulous. 'You know why most of them came here, don't you?'

*

The story of the Mary House is this: in the old days, all the novices are unmarried mothers, who arrive when they are close to labour. Some die in childbirth. Those who live stay on to become nuns. No one ever sees the babies. Locals say the boys are kept hidden, until they're sent to the seminary at the appropriate age. They say that the girls, those not still-born, are smothered before the cord is cut. That is the kindest version. The other version is that the babies are buried alive, smothered in soil, a dry-drowning of earth and worms.

*

'That's just anti-Catholic propaganda,' I protested. 'People love to slag off nuns and priests.'

Abi smirked. 'Where do you think they buried the babies?' she asked.

'Piss off.'

'Don't be so worthy,' she said. 'They must have buried them somewhere. Unless they ate them.'

The main doors were boarded over with heavy iron-mongery and the windows had bars.

'Come on,' Abi said. She pulled on my hand. I pulled away.

She sighed. 'This way.'

We entered through a modern extension that turned out to be a toilet block. We climbed through a collapsed wall until we could stand upright on the tiled floor. The cubicles were painted a very pale sky-blue, or perhaps they had only grown pale from exposure to the sun. Part of the roof had fallen in – thieves had stolen some of the materials and made it unstable – so that the August sunlight filtered down. Ivy grew across the floor and up through smashed sinks. It trailed from toilet bowls and hung down from the gaping roof, curling over the high-mounted cisterns and down along the pull-chains. The palmate leaves of the ivy, their delicate stems, the sunlight on the pale blue wood and the dusty porcelain, were an Insta-worthy composition. However, as soon as we walked through to the next room, the idyll of reclaimed nature transfigured into a choking mess of dust, damaged floorboards and tufts of probably asbestos-infused insulation that drifted through the vandalised building like tumbleweed.

The smell of damp was partially suppressed by the dryness of late summer. Our voices sounded thin in the space. I had been hoping for something more ... well, Gothic. But where I had wanted to find wooden beams and cloisters, instead poky offices and corridors made up the derelict interior. People had broken in over the years to loot wood or metal or anything else they thought might be of use or sellable. August sunlight knifed through fractures in the walls and through the bars on the empty windows, casting shadow-cages onto the floors. We could hear the scratching of small creatures moving around inside the walls and the echo of pigeons from the roof. The ivy had got in here, too, and was carefully making its way across any foothold, navigating crumbling plasterwork. Some of the walls had been graffitied, mostly tags or profanities, and we came across the occasional discarded spray can. On one wall, someone had sprayed a huge heart and the names 'Sam and Justin'. On another, a directive to 'Fuck the Mags', the black cat stencil underneath indicating it was put there by a Sunderland fan.

Tucked away on one corridor was a door with a small sign labelled 'Administration'. The roof and walls were undamaged here, and even with the summer light slanting in from one end of the corridor, it was easy to miss the door. I would have walked past but Abi stopped me.

'In here,' she gestured.

It was small inside, more like an unusually spacious cupboard. The ceiling was intact, the room surprisingly dry. The walls were solid, one of the few places in the building where the wiring hadn't been stripped out. A frosted window on the far side was unbroken and large enough to let light in, but small enough that no one looking in from the outside would be too interested. Inside were beige filing cabinets and, incredibly, stacks of largely undamaged files were both inside the cabinets and on top, piled halfway up to the ceiling. A few scrapes on the floor showed there had been some desultory attempts to move the cabinets, but I guess whoever had done so couldn't be bothered to empty them first, and they were too heavy to lift otherwise.

'What are all these files?' I wondered.

'Student records,' Abi said. 'Can you believe these were left behind? There's a couple of other offices dotted around, with all sorts of shite in them – tenders for building contracts, stuff like that.'

I wasn't that surprised. There hadn't been much of an exit strategy when the junior seminary finally closed. Apparently it was a minor scandal at the time. There were grumbles even now by people who thought the diocese was negligent in safeguarding the fabric of the building. A new 'youth centre' had been built by Hexham &

Newcastle, used by schools for summer retreats for Years 7, 8 and 9, and it was always around this time you would hear the most complaints, accompanied by little waves of nostalgia for the junior seminary. Not from our dad, though, it must be said.

'Wouldn't it be amazing if we found Dad's record?' Abi asked.

I stared at her. 'Do you think it's here?'

'I imagine so. I haven't found it, though.'

'You've been looking for it?'

'Yes, of course. Aren't you curious, Leah? He never talks about it.'

A section of the room had been disturbed; some files on top of the cabinets looked like they'd been moved recently.

'Priest or Dad, he was always going to be a pisshead,' I said.

'Something must have made him that way. Why doesn't he love us, Leah?' Her voice was matter-of-fact, as if she were asking if it was raining out, or what the time was.

I snorted. 'He loves you, Abi. It's me he has a problem with. Or are you going for the "nobody loves me" strategy?' It's something she used to say when we were small, to escape punishment. Anytime she was told off, she'd start wailing 'nobody loves me' and Dad or Miranda would instantly melt into giving her hugs. I never dared try.

I had a sudden thought. 'Is this about Dad, or about our mam?'

We hardly ever spoke about our mam. Neither of us could remember her, although we'd seen pictures. She came to the UK from the Philippines as a nurse, recruited to help plug the shortage of British nurses, and was dumped in the arse-end of Northumberland on the geriatric ward of the local hospital, with patients who asked if they could have someone local instead. Dad met her at the hospital when he was volunteering on the ward, reading to patients. He was eighteen, she was ten years older.

'I don't care about Mam,' Abi said. Yeah, sure.

Mam had left the day after Abi turned one. I didn't feel like there was any great mystery to Dad's bitterness. It was all in plain sight, not hiding in a filing cabinet in an abandoned building.

'You know everybody loves you, Abi.'

'Do you?' she asked.

'You're my sister,' I said.

*

We left the admin office and Abi led me through a corridor to the chapel.

The destruction was magnified here and made worse by the fact that I could still see it must have been beautiful once. Paint peeled off the surfaces in a mildewed riot of blue, red and gold. The pews had been ripped from the floor and, instead of being taken for the wood, wantonly discarded. Gothic doors weighed heavily on the floor like fallen gravestones. A statue of Our Lady with the baby Jesus had been desecrated, obscenities spray-painted over the Virgin's dress, and genitals carved into the baby Jesus's forehead. It must have been recent: not that long ago I'd seen photos of the statue from an Urbex account, without the graffiti.

'This is horrible,' I said.

The small tabernacle door set into the wall of the sanctuary had been ripped away, probably for its metal, and someone had squashed a beer can and an empty crisp packet into the space where the reserved sacrament would have been kept.

Abi pointed to the window. 'That's quite pretty,' she said.

Rainbow light filtered through an incongruously intact stained-glass window behind the altar, illuminating the sacrilege.

There was more graffiti on the table altar. Someone had taken red spray paint and scrawled across it: 'Luke 17:36'.

Abi came and stood next to me. 'That was here last time. I looked it up,' she said. '"Two men will be in the field. One will be taken and the other will be left."'

'That's a bit cryptic,' I said. There was something very familiar about the loop of the letters. The '7' had a horizontal line through the downward stroke, exactly the way Abi writes her sevens.

'Yeah, no doubt the product of a disturbed mind,' she said.

My mouth was dry. 'Abi, what are we doing here?'

'I just thought we could hang out, Leah. A bit of quality sister-bonding time.' She clapped her hands. 'Do you want to see the swimming pool?'

*

The swimming pool was a 1950s addition, dug into the basement a few years before the main seminary and convent closed down. We needed to descend a narrow staircase, and because there were no windows, for the first time we had to use the torches on our phones. Abi's phone lit her face at odd angles. We were hidden from the sunlight, which I suppose is why it was blisteringly cold down there. It was quiet, too. Until we reached the basement, there had been a steady background noise of birdsong through the gaps in the walls and windows, but there were no cracks for birdsong or light to enter here.

'Can you imagine anyone swimming down here? It's so creepy,' Abi said cheerfully. The pool had been drained long ago but a thick layer of mud had mysteriously built up at the bottom, as if it were a river that had silted. I almost expected to see a shopping trolley embedded in it.

'There's nothing here,' I said. It wasn't quite true. I felt something. It felt wrong, even more wrong than the destroyed chapel. At least in the chapel I could see the decay. Here, in the dark, the decay was atmospheric pressure, pushing down on us. I could hear our breathing, strangely laboured, even though neither of us had exerted ourselves. I shivered.

'Let's go,' I said.

But Abi had gone over to the far end of the pool, where she sat on the edge, banging her legs against the side.

'It's always so strange down here,' she said, her voice sounding thinner in the space. 'Can you hear that wind?'

'What wind? It's dead quiet.' But then, suddenly, there it was.

'It makes me think of crying babies,' she said, sounding far away.

'Fuck off,' I said, but it did sound a little like babies crying.

'Let's go,' I repeated. 'It's freezing in here.'

My sister sat where she was, humming slightly to herself.

I called out sharply, 'Abi!'

'Okay,' she said, in her normal voice, and swung her legs back up.

When we reached the top of the staircase, back in the broken sunlight of the building, I asked her, 'Why do you come here? No one would just "hang out" in a place like this.'

Abi pulled at some ivy clinging to a wall, startling a fat spider that had been hiding there. It scuttled under the cover of nearby leaves. Abi didn't reply to that. Instead, she asked, 'Do you know what Abigail means?'

I did.

'My father's joy,' she said, and laughed.

'Sounds right,' I said.

Abi frowned into the ivy.

'You think everything's so perfect for me, Leah. You don't know what it's like.'

If she gives me the Imposter Syndrome speech, I'll kill her, I thought.

'No. Shall I tell you what it's like, Abi?'

I had been ten when Dad's bitterness spilled out of him one Christmas, drunk in the kitchen. 'We'd been watching some crappy Christmas film about orphans and Santa Claus. Suddenly you asked, "Dad, did you want us?" It would've been a weird question, right? But it was a big deal in the film, how the children weren't wanted.' I paused.

Abi gave me a strange look. 'I remember.'

'Do you?' I was sceptical. 'Well, later, after dinner, Dad and Miranda were both drunk. I'd gone into the kitchen and Dad followed me. And all of a sudden he said, "It was your mam." I didn't know what he was talking about. But he went on and on about how he was going out with Mam but he'd tried to break it off, because he wanted to become a priest. And Mam told him she was pregnant, and that she was going to have an abortion. And he persuaded her not to, saying he'd stay with her and all that.'

I'd gone back to the front room and watched the relentless cycle of Christmas television, stony-eyed. 'I don't think Dad even remembered that he'd told me later, when he was sober.'

Abi stared at me. 'Well.' She let out a breath, and when she spoke again her voice had an edge to it I couldn't decipher. 'At least you know Dad made a definite decision to keep you.'

'That's one way of looking at it,' I said.

'And Mam ...' Her voice trailed off. 'She stayed for you, Leah. She didn't stay for me. Do you want to know the real reason I come here? It's a place for the unwanted.' She looked at me. 'That's how the world divides, Leah: into the wanted and the unwanted.'

She was talking out of her backside. There was no one more wanted than my sister. Our dad and stepmam both loved her, her teachers adored her, the boys wanted her, and her girlfriends wanted to be her. *I* wanted to be her.

'I dream about this place, you know,' she said. 'It's always the same dream. I'm down by the swimming pool and the ivy has got in. It climbs up to my heart and drags me into the mud.'

Her full lips trembled and she had to wipe away a perfectly executed teardrop on the lashes framing her mournful eyes. Only the good-looking get away with this kind of rubbish. Everyone else gets told to pull themselves together. 'Time to go,' I said. It really was. I grabbed her hand and pulled her along, like we were two small kids again and I was leading her round the supermarket; through room after room, dust floating in the cracked light, over gaping holes while ivy curved beneath the soles of our trainers, and beetles and rats scratched in the walls; past the graffiti and any number of ruined doors until we were back at the toilet block. The chains hanging from the cisterns clinked gently against the damaged porcelain, making a slightly demented sound like off-key wind chimes. I let go of Abi's hand to clamber out, and stood in the open. I turned and waited for her.

'What're you doing?' I called, after a while. 'Hurry up.'

The only sound was the woodpigeons somewhere off in the trees beyond.

'Stop pissing about, Abi.'

I went back in. She wasn't in the toilets. I retraced our steps. I thought I'd catch up with her soon enough. I called out as I went along, but my voice disappeared into the brickwork. I reached the room with the filing cabinets and peered in, but she wasn't there. I tried her phone. I walked all the way through until I was back at the chapel and its desecrated altar. *One will be taken and the other will be left.* I shivered. And then the swimming pool was the only place left to look.

*

I meant to look, but I lost my nerve at the top of the stairs and went home alone. I don't even remember anything between the staircase and arriving home. The police believed me, eventually.

*

Abi's disappearance made the national news. The police took away my phone, and both my and Abi's laptops. They never found her phone. Later, they took away computers and phones from some of the boys she knew, but eventually everything was given back. The diocese was criticised for lax security at the site, and after a few months they sold the buildings and land to a developer for a pound. When the news came that the Mary House had been sold, Dad said, 'It should have been burned down and the ground sown with salt.' Other people were more scandalised by the sale than by Abi's disappearance, and pressure was exerted once more for the diocese to merge with Hexham & Newcastle. It might even happen this time. Abi's picture was everywhere, but after a time people started to say she had likely run away, and how she'd always had a bit of the wild in her, for all that she had seemed a good lass; like the mother. They moved on to other topics.

I was sent to counselling, but I never had anything to say, and as it was voluntary I stopped going. Dad and Miranda still go to their counselling. I assume they find things to talk about there; they barely speak to me. They blame me, of course. I thought they were going to throw me out, but they haven't yet.

What is there to say about the tedious aftermath? I abandoned my A levels and got a job at a call centre in North Tyneside. It suits me. I like the distance imposed between me and my surroundings by the headphones. I don't talk much to my co-workers and they leave me alone for the most part. I should have enough saved for a rental deposit and a month's rent soon. It would be good to move away.

Abi's room is kept for her, in case she returns. Miranda tidied it up a bit, but otherwise it's pretty much as it was when she disappeared. I don't go in there. I don't even like going past the door. I do see her sometimes. It's always the same dream. Ivy twists around Abi's body and drags her away. I reach out to pull her back but a hand that is not my sister's grabs hold of me; a soft, tiny hand that curls around my fingers. I can feel its grip exerting pressure. A baby cries out to be comforted, but when I wake up, it's only ever the wind, and all the tears are my own.

DOORSTEP PICTURES

J. A. MENSAH

Cambois was a place that had no signs pointing towards it until you were on the road that led only to Cambois. It was as if the people who made the road signs thought that no one who had anywhere else to go would be headed there. Once they were sure that was where you wanted to be, they felt you deserved to know you were travelling in the right direction. Anna Harbottle had lived in Cambois her entire life. All fifty-something years of it. She knew everyone and they all knew her. She had learned to drive on its narrow streets and learned to swim at the beach beyond her front gate. She'd spent summer nights waiting for the sky to turn black, knowing full well that at that time of the year, in her part of the world, the night would never fully arrive. It would be twilight all evening until the sun rose again.

For decades she had looked at the village's only venue – the working men's social club – and wondered what lay beyond its dark wood doors. As the name implied, the club was only for men. But lately, a girl from the council had got the men to agree that women and children should be allowed to go in, once a month, for a special event – a film night. It was on account of there being nothing much to do in Cambois. There were no pubs or cafes, not even a butchers, a grocers or a post office. And certainly no pictures – just houses, the sea and the working men's club. The one bus that served Cambois stopped at 5 p.m. After that, if you didn't have a car, you were stuck. Anna had one, but she had nowhere to go and no desire to drive. She didn't mind staying put, it was the young ones she felt for: now, with the internet and all that, they could see the lives of others and it made Cambois feel a bit more like suffocating. Both of Anna's children had left as soon as they could. Ryan went to Newcastle and Katy to Glasgow. Big cities where you could fade into the crowd. They came home once or twice a year. Each time Anna had promised that the next time, she would visit them. But Billy wasn't a traveller, and she couldn't go and leave Billy by himself.

*

Anna Harbottle did her make-up in the bedroom mirror, preparing for her first night out at the working men's club. The foundation was too pale and the lipstick too bright for her too-full lips. She rubbed the lot off with a wet wipe, frustrated. Then she spotted them – perhaps Billy had left them out for her. She picked them up and slipped the small dangly jewels into her earlobes. A little touch of sparkle was what the occasion called for – not too much, but not too little. Billy had bought them for her for their twenty-first wedding anniversary, and she'd never got much wear out of them. Tonight was the perfect night to show them off. There was a little flutter of excitement in her stomach as she looked at her reflection. She didn't look at all like a film star, but there was definitely a glow about her.

She still couldn't quite believe this was happening, but it had all been agreed and no one could turn back on it now. Once a month the women and children would have access to the social club to watch a new film on a big screen with a projector. The council had it all arranged – it would be like having the pictures on your doorstep, the lass from the council had said that. She wasn't from Cambois, you could tell. She was probably from some-where like Blyth or Whitley Bay; she had the air of the outside about her. She'd managed to win them all round, but when it came to the final meeting, she hadn't turned up. That was the problem with the council types and their community development ideas – none of them were from around here, and every six months you had a new face telling you what the neighbourhood needed, but no bugger hung around long enough to finish the thing they'd started. For that final meeting, the council had sent another lass. Anna thought it had been a mistake: the new girl looked even more out of place than the first one. Her difference wasn't just an air about her, it was a physical thing. It made Anna's skin tingle. Anna had wondered if that was why Billy had joined the meeting that day: he saw the new lass and was nervous that things might kick off. He was never interested in the council's community development projects, but he came to this meeting – sat at the picnic table along with everyone else, and he watched and listened, and pretended to care.

The new girl didn't seem aware of her difference – or maybe she was pretending. She talked to Si, who ran the social club, in the same loud voice the other lass had. Anna wondered whether the council taught them that in a training session when they gave them the job. *Speak loudly and confidently like you have all the answers.* The girl looked younger than Si, but you couldn't tell by the tone of voice she used when she spoke to him. When it had all been agreed, the lass made a comment about holding the next meeting inside the club instead of in the car park, then she laughed and touched Si's upper arm as though they were friends. Anna held her breath and waited for Si's reaction. He smiled. He said next she'll be asking him to put out a spread of drinks and sandwiches, and they laughed together like they were in on the same joke. Anna still didn't breathe out, waiting for it to build. She felt Billy tense up beside her. Si shook his head and said it was a pleasure to be involved in this project, and in fact they had been talking for a while between themselves about how the social club needed to become more – he paused to search for the word – *progressive.* That word was like a giant jellyfish that jumped out of his mouth and landed on top of the picnic bench. If Anna had tried to go near it, she'd get stung. She tried not to look, in case she drew attention to it or herself.

'I bet the council's giving him money for this – fixing up the club or something,' Billy whispered to her.

Si and the lass were still laughing between themselves. Then the lass seemed to grow aware of them – Anna and Billy, the only community members that hadn't spoken during the meeting. She moved towards them and opened her mouth to speak. Anna's throat caught a sudden heat. She gave Billy a nudge and fled towards their house without checking if he was following behind her.

*

Anna Harbottle slipped her feet into her brown leather loafers. They weren't the most glamorous footwear, but they were comfortable, and she felt the tassels at the top were an appropriate nod to the occasion. She thought back to that final community meeting: it had been rude the way she'd run away when the new lass had tried to talk to her. She was hoping the lass would be there tonight, for their Doorstep Pictures premiere event. Anna would speak to her this time. She'd ask her where she was from – her accent sounded English, as though she was from somewhere down south, but she could even have been American, or from somewhere else in the world completely. Anna would ask her how she'd ended up working in Cambois. She'd make polite chat and show that she wasn't uncivilised. Billy popped his head into the room and asked if she was ready. She nodded, her earrings swung a little; it felt nice.

Inside, the social club was not what she'd expected. The dark wood of its outside doors was continued in the bar and furniture, but with so much of it under a low ceiling, it felt more oppressive than opulent. Elsewhere there were burgundy curtains that were turning brown; a mustard carpet that was threadbare and soiled; and heavily patterned lampshades clouding the glow of weak light bulbs. Anna felt silly in her sparkly earrings and tasselled shoes. She was glad she hadn't bothered with lipstick and foundation, it really would have been too much. She slipped the earrings off and into her bag while Billy was at the bar. She made her way to the screen and got seats for them both near the front. The new lass from the council was there already – the sight of her caused Anna's skin to prickle into gooseflesh. The lass was busy setting up the projector and a man, another one of the council types, was helping her. Anna would wait until they had finished and then she'd go up to the girl and say something. The start of the film would provide a natural end to their conversation, so there would be no long, awkward silences. But if they'd had a friendly chat, then they could start up again at the end of the film. It would be easy enough: Anna could ask what the girl thought of the film. It would be the most natural thing. Billy slipped in next to her and handed her half a cider; she gave him a peck on the cheek. After a few moments, the opening sequence of the film began. The new lass slipped out of the social club without even a goodbye. Anna lost the chance to speak to her.

The film was *WALL-E*. The kiddies liked it. Anna did too, although she was disappointed that the girl had left so early. *WALL-E* had been out in the cinemas last year; one of the families a couple of doors down had the DVD. Billy had borrowed it, and they'd already watched it at home together a few months ago. Anna supposed that it was nice to see it on a bigger screen, but this still wasn't the same as having the pictures on your doorstep.

After the film, they stayed for one more drink and then Billy was ready for bed. Anna led him home and then walked out to the beach like she sometimes did. Sitting on the sand, she thought of the social club. She remembered old pictures she'd seen of it as a child. It looked like a place celebrities might visit, with its velvet curtains and all that dark wood. To see what it had become hurt more than never having seen it in real life at all. She'd wanted to believe that somewhere a brilliant kind of joy existed, untarnished, and if she could only get access to it, she would enjoy it too. All those years Billy had spent his nights in that social club, she'd been angry and jealous of him; was the place already starting to look so sad back then? She used to put the bairns to bed, do the dishes, then come out here to watch the horizon. In July you could come out at 10 p.m. or even midnight, and it would never be dark – it was dusk and then dawn with no midnight in between. She would imagine the other lives she might have, somewhere beyond the horizon. She would picture herself swimming towards the skyline, coming out of the water on the other side; on a different continent, as a different person. She would sometimes imagine herself here, allowed to go into the club, drinking whisky and ginger and dancing until 3 a.m. Billy would tell her it was time to go home, and she'd say she wasn't done yet. Everyone would cheer her on, and the lads would tell Billy how lucky he was to have her.

*

Anna dusted the sand off her dress and walked towards home. The little Corsa was parked out front, as it always was. Her son, Ryan, had bought it for them. Billy knew how to drive, but said he had no need for it now there was no work. Everything he needed, he had right there in Cambois. Anything that wasn't there he could get with a bus trip to North Blyth, which was cheaper than petrol. Ryan gave up on his dad, and instead taught her to drive. When she passed her test he thought she'd make use of it – maybe drive down to visit him in Newcastle sometimes. It wasn't that far, he'd tried to convince her, maybe forty-five minutes if she kept to the speed limit and didn't go too slowly. Anna didn't know why she even bothered with the test; she knew she'd never drive. Perhaps she got caught up in Ryan's excitement. She liked being doted on by her son; being mothered by her little boy as he attentively taught her something new. He navigated her carefully through the streets of Cambois and slightly beyond.

Anna looked at the car, touched the door handle; gave it a gentle tug. It opened easily in her grip. The key was where it always was – in the glove compartment. There wasn't the need for much security in their part of world – no one had anything worth stealing, or that they wouldn't lend you if you asked. She got in, turned the key in the ignition and tried to pull away. The car stalled. She nearly got out. But then she stopped herself and tried again. This time, the car hummed and gently rolled forward as she eased her foot off the clutch and applied more pressure to the accelerator.

When you drive out of Cambois, the road signs start early. They show you all the possible directions you might take – Newbiggin-by-the-Sea, Whitley Bay, Berwick-upon-Tweed, Newcastle, Edinburgh, The South. But when Ryan was teaching her to drive, and she'd be trying to find home, it wouldn't be until she got to that one road that led to nowhere else but Cambois that she'd find a road sign telling her that this place even existed.

*

Anna sat in her car, facing the beach at Newbiggin-by-the Sea. It was a nice, but it was nothing compared to the beach she had back home. In the distance, on a plinth out at sea, a couple stood looking to the horizon. They had their backs to the coast. They could have been anyone: a famous power couple hiding from the media by holidaying in a small, northern seaside town. That could be me and Billy, she thought. Back when we were young and looking in the same direction, with our backs to everyone in the village. Standing on a plinth in the sky and looking out at the world together. She liked that; the thought of the time before. She turned the key in the ignition and drove on.

Anna thought she was heading home. She'd had her little adventure, her drive out to Newbiggin, and now it was time for bed. Then she found herself wondering about that new lass from the council. Where would she live? Not somewhere like Cambois, or even Newbiggin. Maybe she lived somewhere like Newcastle or Glasgow, where there would be other people whose families came from different places. Probably Newcastle, she thought. Definitely Newcastle.

That night, Anna was not like herself at all, but like the heroine in a film; she found herself making impetuous decisions. She put her sparkly earrings back on and

DOORSTEP PICTURES

started to drive to Newcastle. If she drove carefully it might take an hour, but she was going to do it. What would she say to the lass when she found her? *I'm like you – more like you than I am like them. You might not be able to tell, but I am not really all white. My husband is the only one that knows for sure.*

Anna's mam had told her that her dad had been a prince from the other side of the world. She'd said one day his people would come and take her to be a princess in their home country. She was far too old to believe in fairy tales, but the appearance of the girl, and Si and the men allowing women into the social club for Doorstep Pictures, suddenly made everything feel possible.

When Billy asked to marry her, Anna's mother said yes for her. She said that none of the other lads from the village would ever marry her because there were rumours she was different – which she was, but no one knew for sure. She went too dark in the sun sometimes and her hair curled a bit too much when there was moisture in the air, which was always when you lived by the sea. That was why she developed her signature style – hair tied back in a plait, where no one can see what it's up to. She liked the way the new lass wore her hair, it hung like a cloud around her face – all out in the open with no apology.

*

The little Corsa sped down the A19 and Anna thought of all the things she might say if she met the girl. If it's meant to be, she would find her, that's how it happens in the films. She would pull her car up on a street in Newcastle, it didn't matter which one. The girl would be coming out of a nightclub, pissed with her friends, or having a fag and a coffee in a trendy cafe that is open until two in the morning, listening to people read poetry. She'd stumble past Anna's car and lean on it to support herself, and when she happened to look inside the window, she'd see Anna and recognise her straight away.

'Are you stalking me?' she might say, with a teasing smile. Or, 'I knew you'd come.' Or maybe, 'I came for you.'

Anna would step out of the car and look at her. Anna would realise that the girl was probably not much older than her own kids – Anna could be her mother. But as she looked at her, Anna would feel the urge for this lass, this young woman, to mother her. In the middle of the night, in Newcastle, as the girl is coming out of a club or cafe, Anna would look at her properly, not avoiding her gaze this time. And no matter what the girl had just said, she would look back at Anna, and they'd realise they had the same eyes, the same full lips, it'd be obvious – to them and to everyone else watching. They'd both know at once, they won't need to say anything, they'll know. She'll invite Anna back to hers and they'll sit in her kitchen drinking gin, because she'll be all out of tea. The girl will tell Anna about her dad, she'll call him *our* dad. She'll tell Anna where they're from, what life is like back in the place they call home – maybe it'll be Kenya or London or the Bronx or Brighton. She'll tell Anna that their father never stopped trying to find her – but there are no road signs leading to Cambois unless you're on the road that leads only there. It'll be evident to both of them that the council sent the girl to Cambois because of

Anna, because the things that connect them were leading them to each other and always had been. Anna had
been waiting to be found. Ever since her mam died, and
before. Definitely after the kids had been born. Katy had
been okay, but Ryan came out too dark, and there was
talk about whether she'd had an affair. Back then, things
kicked off daily. Billy was constantly in fights with neighbours, people who had been his friends. They called her
names and said unkind things about Ryan. It was only
after he turned two, when his features had completely
lightened, and he clearly had Billy's eyes and Billy's ears,
and Billy's hyperventilating laugh, that the accusations
and the name-calling stopped. But then the village had
a realisation, a confirmation, and other whispers started
again. It took years for Billy to get back in with his mates,
and for her – well, she'd never had many mates to begin
with, so maybe she never had as much to lose. From then,
Billy spent his nights in the social club – proving he was
one of the lads. She spent her evenings on the beach waiting for the dark to come, except for those months when
it never arrived properly. Those months felt the most like
real life. The girl will nod and understand. She won't need
elaborate explanations, and Anna will be at peace.

*

Anna drives around Newcastle, staring into the crowds
that loiter outside bars and clubs. In the films you find
what you're looking for, or it finds you, or you realise
that perhaps you never needed it. None of these things
happened to Anna that night, because life isn't a film. Her

car crept along the road, trying to avoid the drunk people who fell into her path. Anna parked the car and waited for the girl to appear, like she would have done if this had been anything other than Anna's life.

It wasn't completely dark yet, but Anna knew the sun was already preparing to rise. Billy would be up soon. She started the car and followed the road to a roundabout. She went all the way round, returning through the exit she originally came from. There would be no road signs to guide her home, but maybe there never are.

INFLUENCER

LARA WILLIAMS

The restaurant was painted serenity blue and cheerleader pink. It was as if it had been determined by algorithm, unseen by human eyes until too late, prompting a bone-deep vertigo that was to be endured alongside the uninventive small plates and mostly okay orange wine. Bella identified a corner dense with macramé plant holders and snapped a photograph of it on her phone. 'Dreamy restaurant corners,' she captioned, before posting to her Instagram account, @littledarling, where she had 221,000 followers. She took the opportunity to check her email, requests filtered through her manager: a chain of juice bars wanting to collaborate on a smoothie, a wellness summit in Palm Springs. She asked how much they were offering before checking on her numbers, the new photo already in the high thousands. 'What nobody realises,' she said, to no one in particular, 'is that we are content curators, digital marketers, creative consultants and small business owners.' But what nobody did realise was that Bella was leaking out of virtually every orifice, and had been for some time.

The leak began in her nose: a golden, viscous drip that was at once beautiful and upsetting. She caught it in a tissue and studied it beneath the clinical light of her brand-new bathroom. It had an iridescence, microscopic flecks which sparkled when they moved: the kind of thing she might rub into the skin around her eyes to stimulate collagen production. She was loath to toss it away but of course she had to: she had been living with her boyfriend, Michael, for only one month and strange bathroom habits had to be kept in check. She flushed then joined him on the sofa.

'What were you doing in there?' Michael said.

'That's a...' Bella stuttered. 'That's a very personal question.'

The pain at that point was minimal: the flex of a comma or half an ant convulsing deep within her nasal passage. She removed a blister packet of paracetamol from her handbag, knocking back two with her tea. She mostly forgot about it until the following morning, when she felt something moving in her ear. An investigatory finger came out slick with the same glittering slime. Her pillow, she noticed, was stained. Her hair was a little crusty, too. She watched the rise and fall of Michael's giant chest. She imagined explaining to him what was happening, but there was no telling where that might lead. Would she sneeze into his mouth? Would she pull down her knickers and take a dump in his lap? She would not. Instead, Bella called her mother from the bathroom.

'I think I have a sinus infection,' she hissed.

'A what?' her mother replied.

'A sinus infection. Or possibly it's something to do with my ears.'

'You should go to straight to the hospital,' her mother said, after a pause. 'One of these days you're going to give me a heart attack.'

She did not go to the hospital but she did go to the pharmacy, and was offered a nasal spray by a pharmacist with razor burn and bloodshot eyes.

'Any changes?' the pharmacist enquired. 'In your normal routine.'

'I moved in with my boyfriend,' Bella offered. 'Could that be it?'

'Everything's connected,' he said, waving his hands in front of his face. 'Moving. Nose. Mouth. Ears. It's all connected.'

She used the nasal spray, which seemed to dry things up, and thought about what the pharmacist had told her. Bella *had* met Michael just six months earlier. They'd met on a press trip in Dubai: he was coming out of a long-term partnership with a dental supplement and she was just getting going in her new grid girl career. She had only 70,000 followers at that point, a fact that made her feel like an imposter at the poolside mixer. But when Michael introduced himself to her, his head cocked like a shy sixth-former at the end-of-term dance, she understood she belonged. That night they went back to his hotel room for firm, efficient sex, Michael flipping her over like an ornament he was angrily varnishing. They agreed to move in together a couple of months later. It made sense because Bella was still living at home, where things between her and her sister had escalated to what her mother described as an 'atmosphere'. Plus, it was good brand synergy.

On moving in they were gifted the grey velvet sofa on which they now spent most of their time, pretend-eating slices of pepperoni-studded pizza. Michael had lots of good ideas on how her content could be more 'raw' and 'real'. And since they'd met her follower count had skyrocketed, and soon she was being offered five figures to get veneers or wear face-shaped earrings. She discussed these offers with her manager, Rachel, who she met once a month at a gym, where they took it in turns to toss a large rubber tyre from one side of the exercise studio to the other. They then sat in the gym cafe, hydrating and talking strategy.

It was during one of these meetings that Bella felt the first stab of pain somewhere around her pelvis. She pressed her hand to her lower stomach, excused herself and made her way to the bathroom. The pain increased steadily in volume until Bella lay curled around the foot of the toilet, riding out tides of agony, her hands clutching her crotch which was soaked and doughy. It lasted no more than ten minutes, subsiding as quickly as it had come on. She rolled down her workout tights and heaved herself onto the toilet, wrapping lengths of toilet paper around her hand before going in to assess the damage. It was the same golden substance; more jelly-like in texture this time, or in fact more like little lumps of jelly marooned in a thin, glistening liquid. She wiped herself down and waited: girls knew what to do when other girls had been too long in the toilet.

*

Rachel arrived a few minutes later and Bella told her she'd had some menstrual problems, asking whether she wouldn't mind fetching her clothes and also a tampon or sanitary towel from the locker room. In the cubicle she changed and plugged herself up, though the leaking had mostly stopped. Outside the gym she rang her mum.

'Bella,' her mother said. 'Bella, is everything okay?'

'I'm fine,' Bella replied. 'It's just ... I have a discharge.'

'Go straight back to the hospital,' her mother said. 'And you let me know what they say.'

Bella went back to the pharmacist. His eyes were still blood-shot; his razor burn replaced with a patchy grey beard.

'I need something for ... a discharge,' she said.

'From where?' he enquired.

'From my ...' Bella whispered, '... vagina.'

'Vagina?' he said. 'Makes sense.'

She was given a suppository. At home, she pushed the cream capsule into herself, curled over like a cat licking itself clean. Then she switched on the TV, spread out across the grey velvet sofa and waited for the suppository to do its job. She stared at her stomach: nut-brown and flat as a pancake, impossible to reconcile with the large wooden bowl of pain she had felt earlier. Rolling over, she closed her eyes. When she woke Michael had slipped in behind her, his arm resting heavily across hers. They brushed their teeth side by side in the bathroom, before taking it in turns to urinate, both solemnly pushing the door shut and allowing the other their privacy. When it was her turn, she had a quick check, moving some things around, and flakes like dried egg white fell into the bowl, but the leak had dried up. She flushed and went out to where Michael waited in the bed.

'Do you want to?' he said.

'Yeah,' she replied, climbing on top of him.

She woke a few hours later, feeling a wetness between her legs and more pain in her lower back. The leak again already or, she wondered hopefully, possibly just stray semen? She had a little probe but couldn't feel anything other than the everyday wetness. On moving her hand further back, she identified the real source: her anus. Now this was a worry. Strange things were always coming out of vaginas – more than a couple of times she had found purple clots in the bath – but anal seepage was something very different. Cancer, probably. She crept to the bathroom to call her mother.

'Mum?' she whispered, hearing the click of the receiver.

'No,' a voice came back. 'What do you want?'

It was her twin sister, and she sounded annoyed. She always sounded annoyed.

'Is Mum not there?' Bella asked. 'This is a situation for Mum.'

'Is this your sinus infection?' her sister replied. 'Why don't you just ask your stupid boyfriend about it?'

Her sister and her boyfriend did not get along.

'Can you tell her to call me back?' Bella said.

'No,' her sister said, and then she hung up.

*

Things between her and her sister had always been strained. Bella charted this back to what she now recognised as a peculiar choice on the part of her mother, who had told Bella, when she was seven years old, that she had a Guardian Angel. Bella had been involved in a car accident which she had survived and her father had not. Lying in her hospital bed, her body a waterpark of colourful wires and drips, Bella's mother clung to her hand and told her all about her Guardian Angel: the leviathan span of his white-feathered wings, rolling waves of straw-coloured hair. She brought him up with semi-regularity throughout the years that followed, especially during moments when, say, Bella tore open the last layer of wrapping paper during a round of pass the parcel, or when everyone in her year, including her sister, had their scalps colonised by lice, except for her. 'That's your Guardian Angel,' her mother would say, and Bella would be ravenous for details. What was his name? What did he smell like? When did he watch over her? 'Always,' her mother told her. 'He is always watching over you.'

A few years after the passing of their father and the manifesting of the Guardian Angel, Bella's sister had an accident at school. She was racing her friend in the school playground, tripped over and ripped open the skin above her eye: an injury requiring three butterfly stitches. That night Bella lay in the top bunk, listening to her mother soothe her sister. 'Mummy,' her sister said, in the smallest, most miniscule voice she had ever heard. 'Do I have a Guardian Angel?' Her mother paused for a while. 'No,' she replied. 'Just your sister.'

217

*

Bella thought about her sister as she eased herself into bed beside Michael. They were non-identical but they looked the same, like the Olsens. Bella often thought about the Olsens: how thin and sad-looking they were, how they both preferred clothes that drowned them. Bella wished she and her sister had something to orient their relationship around, like oversized outerwear or holidays. She looked at Michael, lying face-down, the sculpted dunes of his body. Often, he felt more like her twin, or even the exact same person: like how she'd learned to paint butterflies at school, folding the paper down the middle and daubing one half with a body and a single wing, then squishing both sides together. Though he also felt a little like her Guardian Angel: the person who'd whisked her away. She snuggled up close to him, glad to have found someone the same. Falling asleep, she was struck by a violent fantasy in which Michael sucked the leaks right out of her, continuing until only her skin remained, a popped balloon on the floor of a birthday party.

The next morning she wondered again whether to tell Michael about the leaking. Sometimes they would collaborate, drawing attention to issues they both felt strongly about, like global warming or mental health. Those posts performed very well. But bodily rupture did not feel like the right kind of project to collaborate on. She went back to the chemist instead. He looked even more dishevelled, his eyes more alarmingly bloodshot, than the last time she had seen him. Was the whole world falling apart, she wondered? Is that what was happening now?

'How can I help you today?' he said.

'It's that leaking,' she replied. 'Except this time, it's from ... my, uh, bottom.'

'Have you been under any mental strain?' he asked.

'I've been a little tired,' she replied. 'With work.'

'I see,' he said. 'Connected. The bottom and the brain.'

'What?' she replied.

'The bottom and brain,' he repeated. 'You don't think the bottom and brain are connected?'

He gave her an herbal supplement and told her she needed to get more sleep.

A few days later she got an email from Rachel: a last minute invitation to Paris to learn about a new Dior lip palette. She moved her hand to her crotch before replying – moving her hand to her crotch had become an instinctive gesture, like how she used to fuss with her hair when someone mentioned a boy she liked. Rachel didn't like it when she said no to things.

There was a cocktail reception at the hotel on arrival. She knew all the other bloggers and influencers in attendance. They sipped cucumber-garnished drinks and talked about brands. 'Oh they're a great brand,' an influencer said, about a line of lambskin apothecary bags. 'So cute,' another coquettishly agreed. Bella shifted her weight, feeling the beginning of a trickle. There were moments when she could conceive of the leaking as less painful, not necessarily unpleasurable. She smiled and nodded along, an ultra-absorbent sanitary towel doing its worst.

*

Her room was beautiful. A garland of white lilies greeted her, along with a handwritten note: *We're so grateful to take you on our journey!* She took a photograph of it, uploading it with the hashtag #spoiled. There followed a whirlwind of singularly exceptional experiences: a lip-art tutorial on the riverbanks of the Seine; a personal consultation with a runway make-up artist; a lavish four-course dinner. Every now and then she was interrupted by intrusive memories, one in which she recalled overhearing Michael tell two friends about some pornography he had recently viewed, which allowed you to see 'inside the nipple hole'. And periodically she needed to excuse herself, to swap out the soaked maxi pad from her underwear, or to plug her ears with cotton wool. But other than that, she smiled through it all: she was a professional.

On the flight home she scrolled through Instagram. She browsed some of her friends' grids: their overstuffed living rooms, hippy hats and avocado-based brunch. She checked briefly on Michael: an old photo of him in Brooklyn captioned #TakeMeBack. Finally, she looked up her sister's account, something she did rarely. Her sister had three photographs in total: two of their mother and one of the front garden. She also had a video of five baby otters, definitely stolen from someone else's feed. The otters stood on what appeared to be a wood-effect plastic floor, a single chair leg breaking the edge of the frame: an ordinary person's home. The otters made hysterical chirruping sounds, like chickens made mad by a fox in the coop. They pawed at each other and at the floor with extreme desperation, throwing their fur-covered bodies around. They squeaked, it seemed, because they wanted to understand, but also because they wanted to be understood. Whenever the video ended, Bella replayed it, every time feeling more like she was trapped inside the video alongside the otters, and no one was getting to leave, ever.

After watching the video for perhaps the thirtieth time, Bella found herself crying, desperate and hysterical, just like the otters. But her tears were interrupted by a bump – first a small one, then another, much bigger, this one lifting her momentarily out of her seat, enough to provoke a small yelp from the woman next to her. She looked around the fuselage: the hangovers and lethargy had been replaced by a grey, shivering panic. The seat-belt sign pinged back on and the air hostesses or cabin crew or whatever they were called, marched back to their seats, impossible to scrutinise.

The bumping continued and all around her people were murmuring, though at the same time sitting extremely still, aware of how the smallest movements might throw the plane off-balance once and for all. Bella had a strong urge to disrobe: to be unburdened and able to think straight. She started breathing very quickly, the liquid pouring from her nose and ears. She squeezed her eyes shut and covered her face, thinking about her Guardian Angel. When did he watch over her? Always. He was always watching over her.

The plane lurched once more then settled. A loosening bled through the cabin. Ashen and exhausted, the passengers paused, waiting for permission to carry on as before. They had experienced something significant together but also something undeniably routine: briefly united in their endeavour and already faintly embarrassed by that union. Bella looked at the woman next to her, who looked back, their faces both streaked with leakage. When the plane eventually landed, there was a round of applause, which Bella joined in with, though more than anything she just wanted to go to sleep.

Bella got an Uber home. The pain had returned, behind her eyes and in her stomach. She'd thought about touching the option that meant the driver wasn't allowed to talk to you, but then she thought talking might be quite a good distraction.

'How's your shift going?' she said.

'It's fine,' he replied.

He had a vaguely Eastern European accent.

'How about you?' he asked.

She was struck by a vision of the car crashing, its metal shell crumpling like pleated lamé, not unbeautiful. Though watching the traffic move sluggishly along, she knew it wouldn't happen.

'I'm not very well,' she said. 'I don't think.'

'Oh really,' the driver said, turning around. 'You should get yourself to a hospital.'

'Yeah,' she replied. 'I probably will.'

Michael was by the front door when she got back, holding a love-heart-shaped balloon. He started making a video on his phone as soon as she walked through the door, lifting her in the air and spinning her around, finally pressing his thumb to the screen, stating dryly: 'We got that.' He'd cooked dinner: grilled chicken, steamed vegetables and boiled rice. Before they sat down for dinner, he took her hand and led her through to the middle room, where he had stacked the various boxes and packages she had received in her absence.

'It's a good haul,' he said, still holding the balloon.

Bella began unpacking: a silk bralette and thong; organic linen wrap dress; semi-translucent setting powder; English rose and black pepper perfume; oversized cotton blouse; woodsmoke scented candle; silver seashell necklace; Italian small dishes recipe book. She stopped about midway through, and Michael took over, diligently unboxing and setting aside. Bella looked around the room: the boxes half-opened and tissue paper thrown everywhere; the rose gold homeware and identical slim-cut jeans. Her hand went back to her crotch: not exactly dry but not exactly damp either. Next door the grilled chicken was getting cold, a nauseating thought.

After dinner they watched a film starring Amy Poehler and Paul Rudd. Bella wondered which parts she was supposed to laugh at and which parts were supposed to make her feel sad, or whatever the next thing along from sad was. She intermittently looked at her phone. Her Paris posts were doing well; Elizabeth Olsen was still the only Olsen on Instagram. After the film, they fucked on the grey sofa. There was something excitingly desperate about it: two people conversant they will never make themselves a single whole though nonetheless persevering.

*

She went to the bathroom after they'd finished. The sex had shifted something and the leaking was worse than usual. She sat on the toilet, letting it drip into the bowl. She looked around the tiled space, lined with all the toners and exfoliators and moisturisers she had been gifted. Between her legs the leaking continued. After a while it started up in her nose again, then in her eyes and ears, too. Finally, droplets sprouted from her breasts. She thought about overhearing Michael talking to his friend. The grave seriousness with which he'd said 'nipple hole'. Outside the bathroom door he called to ask her if she was okay.

'I'm fine,' she replied, sniffling. 'I'll be out in a bit.'

NOT MY USUAL PRACTICE

TRICIA CRESSWELL

I t is slack water time and the log barely moves, debris pooling round it, mermaid's hair. The sun is up, midsummer early, but the world is still sleeping. I know this time well now, in my new life here, high above the Tyne.

The log rolls and something white moves outwards; the mermaid has an arm. I look away from foolishness. It is not a body and I will not look at it again, but when I do the whiteness is clear in the strengthening daylight. The previous owner left binoculars: a present, he said, when I moved here last year. Just a cheap pair, for looking at the cormorants and kittiwakes, he said, certainly not strong enough to see into the windows of the flats on the far bank. Strong enough, though, for me to see the naked torso, the face half covered in tangled hair, the arm outstretched on the oily water.

My eyes water as I squeeze them tight shut, then open them again, and look through the binoculars, again. I do not think I am mad, not now. I can see a body, and the tide is turning. My pulse starts to race and I feel the heat rise up my neck and the cold sweat begin to run. The mantra: do not think ahead; do not rehearse what happens; do not think about the questions, the police, the media. Do not hyperventilate. Do not.

Keys and phone and yesterday's jeans over my pyjamas and then I run out of the flat and down the stairs and down again to the quayside path.

The body is still there but moving a little now, bobbing in the water as, to the east, the sea ebbs. Not a woman but a man, his long beard and hair twisting slowly across his face and naked chest. His legs are covered, trousers or no, are they wrapped together? How strange to feel curious. Then the head rolls towards me and the wide-open, glaucous eyes look at me. Soon he will be gone, hard to find as the river takes him away to the sea. I press 999.

There is an initial slight pause from the call handler as I describe the body but I use my no-longer title to make her take me seriously. I am joined by a jogger as I wait for the police. He is young and looks sick when he realises why I am there, what he is looking at, and I find myself using the voice, reaching out and patting his arm. He smiles weakly at me, as a son to his mother, a patient to his doctor.

*

The police station is new and shiny, a metal and glass kit-building with the required grey-blue carpet tiles and display screen: the strapline scrolls across, 'Proud to Serve Our Community'. An obese blonde woman, not in uniform, makes chatty conversation as she escorts me to the interview room, seemingly unbothered by my too-brief replies. She has marked xanthelasma around both eyes and I wonder what her cholesterol and lipid levels are, which takes me upstairs to a heavy blue door which she leans hard on to open, the blue cardigan straining over her shoulders.

I am expecting a uniformed PC in a tiny office with chairs placed cross-corner so our knees are too close as she, or he, slowly turns my words into hackneyed statement-speak. But this is a formal interview room with a man and woman sitting at the far side of the wide table with an empty chair facing them. I stop in the doorway, pulse beating in my ears, but my voice is measured and calm.

'I was asked to come in and make a statement, which of course I am happy to do. But?' I end with a clear interrogatory lift to my voice and raise my left eyebrow.

The man stands up and leans across the table with some sort of smile.

'Hello. I'm Detective Constable Milburn and this is Detective Sergeant Taylor. Thank you for coming into the station to make your statement.' He is very young and the words are rehearsed.

'I was expecting a uniformed officer, as on the quayside.'

'This is now a murder inquiry. Your statement, as the person who found the body, the deceased, is very important.' He puts out his hand and I move into the room and shake it quickly; the handshake is firm but his hand is sweaty. The detective sergeant's handshake is brisk and cool and dry.

I smile and adopt the parent-to-child voice, slow and clear, and keep my eyes on the boy's.

'In that case, with the two of you in the room, I prefer to have my solicitor present. Can we agree a time to meet later today?'

He starts to speak but she cuts across him.

'Yes, of course. That will be fine, Dr Jamieson,' she says.

'*Ms* Jamieson.'

'Why did you do it, Ms Jamieson?'

'Do what?'

'Why did you call us?'

'Because the tide was turning. The body may have been swept out to sea.'

'A good citizen,' she says.

We are both expressionless. I nod and leave.

*

Charles Dixon was my solicitor last time and, after initial incredulity, is forthright on the phone. He swears just once and then pauses, time to think, and I wait, trusting him.

'You should've ignored it,' he says.

'Really? Would you have said that if I'd called you then?'

'No. No, not really. Two o'clock in the car park. Wait for me. Do not go in without me. We'll have a talk and then go in. Tell them two-fifteen. Smart clothes, not black.'

Charles is still good looking in that overweight, former rugby-blue way and I know he is both charming and uxorious, devoted to his very clever barrister wife and two excessively attractive daughters. He has given me very good legal advice, for which I paid a lot, but he was also kind, which cost me nothing extra, so I can forgive his plenty. Although hearing him again is still painful.

Two-fifteen and the police station again but with him beside me. The memories are swelling in my head as we go up the stairs. The air thickens and I have to pull it in through my nose as I count between the breaths. My lips are clamped shut: I will not have a panic attack. Not here. Not now.

'You okay?' Charles's voice is calm as he takes my elbow.

The elbow: no doubt one of the safe places for a lawyerly touch, far away from buttocks and far enough from breasts, difficult to misinterpret. The thought helps as I sit down in the chair he pulls out for me. He is beside me, solid and real, as the introductions are completed.

'For the record,' he says, 'my client has come in voluntarily to the station to assist the police by making a statement.'

'Of course. Thank you, Ms Jamieson,' DS Taylor says. Her accent is northern but flat, not quite Geordie.

I nod, matching her blank expression. I know how to do this.

'So could you tell us what happened this morning?' DC Milburn now.

I describe exactly what happened from when I first saw the apparent log until I called 999. I speak slowly and fluently. They all listen without interruption, Charles and DC Milburn taking notes, DS Taylor looking down. I stop and watch the DC look quickly at the DS. He has already given me too much time. She nods and the questions start.

'So you were looking out of the window at,' he pauses theatrically, 'five a.m. this morning?'

'I was sitting by the full-length glass balcony doors looking down at the river,' I say. Only repeat what you have already said. Give no new information that is not in your statement: do not try to explain. A lesson hard learned.

'Are you usually looking out of your glass doors at five a.m.?' he says.

The DS intervenes as Charles raises his eyebrows just a little.

'It is important for us to know if you had been disturbed, perhaps by a noise outside,' she says.

'I am often awake with the light. It is my usual practice to sit by the balcony doors and watch the river at that time.'

I hear Charles's very slight intake of breath at 'my usual practice'. Just words. I am too damaged for words to wound me anymore.

The questions go on and my answers are brief, calm, consistent. Another mantra. There are no surprises until the DS, having thanked me politely, stands up, a signal for us to leave, but Charles remains seated.

'You are aware, of course, of the appalling harassment to which my client was subjected previously. It is essential—' He pauses, '—*essential* that she is not identified to the media. I seek assurance on this.'

The DS looks at me, not him, and her trained gaze is level.

'Of course. We wouldn't release witness ID at this stage of an investigation.'

'Not your usual practice to do so,' I say.

Charles is motionless, a message.

*

We stop by his car.

'There should be nothing more. You, a good citizen, have done your civic duty.'

'And when it leaks you'll release the statement you are rushing back to the office to prepare.' I manage a smile.

He nods.

'I want to go to the press now,' I say.

'No.'

'It will leak. Why not get my version in first?'

'You mean the truth.'

I shrug. 'Whatever,' I say.

'No, not yet. Leave this with me. Please.'

*

This time Charles is wrong: they are already there, reporters with microphones but no TV cameras yet, a gaggle at the high outside gate, watched by the concierge in his glass office.

'Dr Jamieson, Dr Jamieson.'

I pause politely, smart in my one remaining blue suit, expensive scarf, hair and face in place.

'Dr Jamieson, is it true you found the body?'

Never say 'no comment': another hard lesson.

'Yes. I've just given a statement to the police. DS Taylor is in charge of the investigation and you will need to contact her. I saw a body in the river and called the police, as anyone would.'

They are strangely silent, the pack, and they step back to let me walk through and the concierge shuts the gate behind me. He is excited, keen to be seen as my protector, for now at least, but there is still that flicker of uncertainty, the dropping of his eyes, as I walk past him.

I go upstairs and shower and put on clean clothes, smart clothes again, and then I sit and watch the river, waiting.

*

I didn't know that Prof. Wallace had left me anything at all. I knew she was lonely and dying slowly and that her death would be a long-awaited release. In all the years I was her GP, there was never any sign of her spending money on the decrepit but beautiful Georgian house, or on clothes or travel, but the house alone was way beyond any academic salary. She understood her illness intellectually and we talked, always briefly and on her terms, about what would happen as the disease progressed, about being immobile, unable to shop or to cook or to feed herself, about incontinence. She refused any discussion, though, about care, about family, about hospices. She grudgingly gave me her next-of-kin details, her solicitor's card.

I was asked in court if I had liked her, a question cleverly phrased by the prosecution barrister, an immaculate woman.

'She was my patient. I cared for her as her doctor,' I said.

'So you felt nothing for her. You feel nothing for your patients?'

'That is not what I said.'

Charles had prepared me well for this line of questioning. This was not going to be a car crash like the GMC hearing, he had said. There, unprepared, I had answered openly with too much detail, a doctor explaining. And had been ruined.

In truth, I hadn't liked Prof. Wallace: she was autocratic and selfish and demanding, a difficult patient. I admired her, though: she faced her future unflinching and unbending. When she asked me to help her die, she was well prepared; her argument was phrased academically, evidence quoted, as was my response. The response we are trained to give: the end-of-life care plan, the living will, the need to involve family and friends, the support available.

'You had to say that,' Prof. Wallace said, her voice already weakened, almost a whisper. 'All I want from you is the drugs. I'll take them. It needs to be soon, while I can still—' She paused and almost smiled, '—self-administer. But I need to be certain that it will work. Here, this is what I need.' She handed me a printed sheet complete with headings and bullet points.

I refused of course, at first. But she was implacable. In the end, because she was alone, because there was no one to help her, no one to love her, I gave her a series of prescriptions for drugs to alleviate her symptoms, enough to make a lethal cocktail. She, in return, took the drugs when she knew I was away in Ireland at a conference, and it was Jane, my colleague and friend, who certified the death. That should have been the end. An expected death in a woman with an incurable and now rapidly progressing disease.

She left everything to me: a house worth over a million, jewellery and paintings worth much more. Her solicitor asked to see me the day I arrived back from Ireland, about the will, she said. She was very insistent and agreed to come to the practice, and I saw her in my room. She told me that Prof. Wallace had made a new will twelve months before her death, replacing a huge bequest to the university with a huge bequest to me. All of it.

I sat in my usual chair, at my desk, and looked at this non-patient.

'I didn't know. I don't want it,' I said.

She nodded but her eyes slipped away from mine. She suggested I sought advice.

I went straight to Jane.

'I'll just give it away. Give it to the university,' I said.

'Yes, of course. But there'll be probate and stuff. Phone the Medical Insurance Group. Get advice. It's what we pay them for.'

We looked at each other. She stood by me almost to the end.

*

The university immediately contested the will and complained to the GMC. The GMC decided that I had had too many deaths, way above average. I explained that it was because I was the oldest partner, had the highest proportion of patients over sixty-five, led on terminal care, had previously covered the hospice. I made it worse. After that, I can barely remember the sequence of events, it all happened so fast. The GMC suspended me. The GMC referred me to the police. The media called me the second Dr Shipman. I was struck off by the GMC. I was arrested.

I was tried for murder.

In court, Jane, stoic in my defence, told the truth. That she knew Prof. Wallace had asked for help to die, that I had given proper advice, that we had discussed this as colleagues should. But when asked about why she hadn't recorded the conversation, why I hadn't, she fell apart. Lost in explaining too much, she made all the mistakes I had made at the GMC hearing.

This time, though, I was clear and explicit. Yes, I had prescribed the drugs. Yes, I had told her what the lethal combination would be. Yes, I had given her the means.

'Let me summarise, Ms Jamieson. You admit that all these are your prescriptions and that you had informed Professor Wallace that these drugs in overdose, and particularly in combination, are lethal,' my defence barrister's calm and measured voice, repeating what the prosecution had already stated.

'Yes. As does any doctor who prescribes certain drugs. Our duty of care requires us to explain the risks, fully and in detail.'

'Did you know she wanted to take her own life?'

'Yes. But I advised her not to.'

'But did you gave her the means to take her own life?'

'Yes. And advised her not to.'

'Is it the case that without the drugs she could not have taken her own life?'

'Yes. Because she no longer had the choice, the physical capacity, to hang herself or jump from a high building or run her car into a wall. I gave her back the means to make her own choice. I gave her back the power to make her own decision.' My voice started to catch and I could feel the tears so I stopped.

The silence carried on. I looked at the jury and they were all watching me, motionless.

'I was Prof. Wallace's GP for twenty years. All I could do for her in the end was give her that power, that decision. Give her back to herself.'

I was acquitted. Set free to live alone, here, in my high tower.

*

The river is running slow again, the gulls barely moving on the water. The first of the end-of-work runners go by, then the boot camp teams, stopping to do kerb press-ups and star jumps on the broad path. I can just hear the shouted instructions. I remember Jane, never in favour of exercise requiring sweat, dismissing a personal trainer on the grounds that she was not paying some boy to shout at her. I can see her, imperious, then laughing. My friend, before they all ebbed away.

I watch the kittiwakes take off from the ledges on the Baltic. I sit, waiting.

AND THEY SAY IT'S WHERE YOUR HEART IS

REBECCA HILL

She helps him unload the truck, laying saws and sledge-hammers on the grass and propping the strimmer against the wall, and he watches her turn a claw hammer over before peeling the plastic covering off the head.

'Didn't know what we'd need, so I brought a bit of everything.'

She hums and throws the hammer in the toolbox before ripping open a double pack of eye protectors. He takes the other pair when she offers, and for a moment he's back in GCSE chemistry, just inches from Bunsen-burnt fingers and nitrate-stained arms, but his eyes won't leave the way her hair curls almost perfectly around her ear, pressed smooth against the wire of her glasses, until she shoves the plastic goggles on.

Then it's just a mess. But it's nice to know she still looks ridiculous in them, and he's willing to bet she'll still be happy to tell him he looks better in a welding mask, even if she won't look him in the eye.

'We don't need to demolish it,' he says, pulling on a dust mask. 'But I thought you might like to gut it.'

She doesn't answer, just stands back and looks up over his head at the roof, speckled with missing tiles and the dips of broken beams, little pockets of hollow space where it's falling in on itself. Some of the windows are already broken, cavities of smashed glass and splintered frames dark against the Georgian white stucco, the sunlight no longer bouncing off the walls to blind them.

He watches her, dragging his eyes down her throat the way she drags her own down the side of the house, and he wishes he didn't notice the subtle loss of definition in her arms or the small lines of tension in her legs as she bends to pick up a sledgehammer.

He weighs up a hammer of his own and gives it an experimental swing. 'Still working out?'

'Still running,' she offers. She collects a saw and examines a power drill before heading towards the door. 'Come on.'

But she shoulders the tool bag without much effort, and leaves him standing in the shadow of the house, his skin prickling in the shade.

He collects what he thinks he needs and jogs after her.

*

The kitchen falls more easily than expected.

They work on opposite walls, hacking at plasterboard and brick, insulation spilling out around their feet until they're left with nothing but two windows and a sliver of exterior wall, dull but for three or four patches of crisp white paint where the sideboards had been.

There are fist-sized openings already, uneven channels where someone has stripped the copper from the wires and left the empty coloured casing hanging from the cavities. Cobwebs drape over detached pipes like shawls, and the mildew rises up the wall in ever fainter bands until it disappears just below the red pen line of *Kieran, age 8*. The edges of his notch are worn smooth and dark, blunted to an old, ridged scar in the stained wood of the door frame, above *Jack, age 4*.

For a moment she stills, one hand half-reaching towards the frame a few inches below Jack's name, as if expecting something else to be cut into the wood there. It's hard for him not to stare too, not to go down that same track and press his fingers to the wood where he can picture the top of another child's head so clearly, the curls that could have been his shade of brown or her shade of burnt caramel.

Instead he coughs quietly, taking in the mildew on the lone supporting wall. It's as blackened and damaged as the exterior, with parts spilling out into the garden, brick dust streaking the grass like chalk lines on slate. With most of the wall down the July air comes in stagnant and heavy, warming quickly through the rubble, the promise of true heat pressing against his shoulders as he nudges some clumps of bricks around.

He turns to find her still there, chipping away at one small corner almost too carefully.

'Hey,' he says, watching as she slowly pulls herself back to him. 'You need a hand with that?'

She takes one last long look at the wall, eyes grazing over the faded paint and the mix of crayon colours amid the water stains, the history slipping between the cracks, and pulls herself up straighter, hefting the sledgehammer in both hands.

'Nah, I'm good.'

She doesn't stop swinging until the whole wall is down.

*

Upstairs the air seems to brace itself, and he's not sure if it's the way the ceiling threatens to fall or the way her shoulders refuse to, her posture tight and tense and completely foreign on her. He wants to reach out, to press his thumbs against her spine and push his fingers into the knot of muscle at her neck, but he just flips his hammer and lays down his saw instead, knocking on a wall to check if it's hollow.

The guest bedroom door is closed and stiff, and he has to take a chip off the frame to get it open. She wanders in behind him a few minutes later, her eyes scanning the joins and corners where they meet the floorboards. From the looks of it, she's aligning the floor joists from down-stairs, and he leaves her be for the moment. She stops beside him, just past the doorway, and whistles low and soft as she looks around.

'Wow.'

The ceiling has pretty much gone and the floor angles sharply away towards the trunk of an invading tree, the exterior wall little more than flaking paint scattered at their feet. Water stains obscure the scuffs and paint lines left by furniture, and only his memory allows him to fit their bed into the space below the bulging ceiling where shattered boards have given way to thin branches and leaves. Above them he spots the outline of the water tank, and a few other pipes poke through the gap left by the collapsing gable end.

She kicks at a small piece of plaster, listening to it roll across the floor and crash down through the branches. Neither of them hears it hit the bottom.

The roof creaks.

'I think we'd better leave this one,' he murmurs, moving aside to let her edge out of the door.

She nods, adjusting her goggles as she heads towards the master bedroom, allowing him to take one last look before he shuts the door and follows.

The main room is dull and humid, the old sash window clogged with vines and wallflowers, small white blooms peeking from the cracks in the sill. The facade is still crumbling; the wallpaper peels crisp and crooked in patches where it hasn't slipped off in the rain, and plaster flakes dust one corner where the sockets had been ripped out and filled in as an afterthought.

Even small, faint strands of pastel cotton still cling to the wall, trapped under the tiny roots that cover the smoke-yellowed patch beside the window where she'd made him *take that shit outside; if she's born with asthma it's your fault.*

He cocks his head at the back wall.

'Ladies first,' he offers, the corners of his mouth turning upward as she scoffs and nudges his feet back with the hammer head.

She splits the ceiling with the first swing, a surprised little bark sharp in her throat.

'We're better at this than we thought, huh?'

It's too much of a murmur to be directed at him. Her breath doesn't even disturb the air or the loose flecks of wallpaper, and she smooths a hand over the crack in the wall before she begins to chip away at it, pulling the cladding away from the timber frame.

He watches the thin trickle of sweat roll down her neck, as she scoops out more insulation and clumps of broken board. She used to sweat like that during hockey practice, chaos theory playing out across her skin, pooling briefly in the dips of her vertebrae before disappearing beneath her vest. Her hair is looser now, no longer straining and curling against her bobble but still drawing thin wet lines over the back of her shirt as she moves.

He misses those days.

One knotted chunk of plaster gets stuck between the unbroken part and the frame, and as she tries to lever it out, one of the support beams cracks and groans above her head. She doesn't notice, too absorbed in grinding the plaster down to dust, too busy to look anywhere else even when he throws his hammer down and creaks across the floor.

'Careful,' he calls, watching a beam inch closer to her head, but she just grunts with the effort, swearing at the way the edges of the cladding turn to dust every time she manages to grab hold.

'Whoa, hey—' He stumbles across to grab the splintered beam before it can fall. 'Got it, go on.'

She gives the block another yank before it falls loose, and steps away to let him lower the lintel to the floor, wiping her forehead with the back of her hand.

'Teamwork,' he grins, though his voice is uncertain and small, one hand hovering dusty and awkward in front of his shoulder. She looks at it, then at him, and some of the dust has settled before she slaps her hand against his in a high-five.

'Teamwork,' she agrees, before striding off to the opposite wall.

His palm tingles, even after he wipes it on his jeans.

*

There's a pharmacy receipt scrunched up behind the bathroom sink, the paper yellow and mottled with damp, the ink pale and greying just like the pair of them. It's probably just as worthless as the rest of the crap, probably just another reminder of his many attempts to quit smoking, but something tells him to open it. He does, and he stares at the date, at the product code, at the small but clear title still visible despite the creases.

He stills, quiet.

'What's that?' she asks, when she finally notices.

'Daisy.'

She stops, the last chink of breaking cistern ringing loud off the walls.

'What?'

He brushes his thumb over the date before handing it to her.

'Your pregnancy test. For Daisy.'

There's little more than a quiet *thunk* as she lowers her hammer, the paper not even rustling as she takes it gently, carefully, like she expects it to fall apart at her touch.

It's almost difficult to look at her, how still she stands there, gathering more than the right words in the dust. He shifts his weight uncomfortably then turns away, pretending to look for more receipts behind the pipes. His fingers and eyes begin to itch as he remains crouching.

He wonders if he should confront it, if he should just swing for it like it's another section of partition wall, if they'd be better for it crumbling between them at their feet, pressing sharp and bloody into their soles.

'We never really—' he starts, pushing himself up to standing.

'None of that,' she warns, eyes back on the crumbling wall. The receipt seems to have disappeared from her hand, and it's not until she turns away and hefts up her hammer that he spots the neatly folded edge sticking out of her back pocket.

She carries on swinging, though her rhythm's a little off.

He watches the rise and fall of her shoulders for a moment, the pull and stretch of tendons, before he hums and turns back to his own wall, listening to the awkward whine of rusted pipes under the stiff angle of her wrist, the joints and bolts not what they used to be.

'None of that,' he agrees, and starts to chip at the sink, pulling the panelling from the side of the bathtub to pile up in an ever-growing bonfire of oak-effect pine and broken tiles, the scrunched-up balls of mottled wallpaper scattered as kindling.

When they're done they pause to wipe their eyes and faces, pulling their shirts up over their noses because the insides are the only clean bits left. On the landing, they ignore the one other closed door down the hall, dappled from stickers and pockmarked where Blu Tack has pulled off the paint. They find themselves looking at each other again, and hesitate.

He pushes his hair out of his eyes and she watches his hand, something cautious and concerned on her face. He thinks of the band still on his wedding finger, the lack of one on hers, and tucks it away inside a pocket, pretending to look for screws and trying not to clear his throat as he palms it off.

'Do you want to take a break?' he manages, twisting the elastic of his mask between two fingers.

'We only have the garden left,' she says, muffled by the bobble between her teeth as she gathers her hair to retie it. 'We could push on.'

'Surely we can take five minutes, though.'

She shakes her new ponytail experimentally, the loose curls untucking themselves from behind her ears, and shifts her weight. The floor whines beneath her, high and tired, and the sound seems to echo throughout the shell of the house, slipping past the door they've left unopened. Eventually she nods, resting the hammer against the remains of the wall.

'Yeah, we can take five minutes.'

If it feels like fleeing as they head back downstairs, well, at least they flee together.

*

He takes a spade to the sapling ash and a strimmer to the lawn and hedges, razing the years of neglect to stumps and clumps of grass. Across the gravel she dismantles the

shed, laying each panel and windowpane out on the deck-
ing until every flat-packed piece is accounted for; a splintered, rusting inventory of woodworm and mould on the
upturned lawn. He offers to do the same for the summer
house but she talks him out of it, tying bent nails together
with garden twine and leaving them in his empty mug as
a bouquet.

It was never more than a kitchen garden, just a splash
of green and some broken pebbles on which to build,
and it takes them less time than he expects, the end in
sight right from the beginning. He wraps the last of the
strimmer's wire around the handle and walks over to her,
laying it in the truck as he passes.

She stands and stretches, tilting her head back into
the sun, and he dumps his tools and stretches too, an
awkward pull of limbs before he sits down, the metal
frame of the chair cool on his skin through his shirt.

'We're done,' he sighs, tipping his head back and closing his eyes. He opens them again to find her looking,
really looking, something resigned but not unhappy in
the set of her jaw, and a lightness in her eyes, a looseness
in the fall of her shoulders.

'Yeah, we're done.'

7.43

SHARON TELFER

It's not until some days later that I realise the woman on the bridge must be a ghost. Weeks even. I lose track.

I don't remember seeing her before. Before I started walking, that is. I don't know how I missed her. She doesn't shift: same place, same position, one foot on the lower bar, elbows on the handrail, hands cupping her chin, a shadow in the first smudge of day.

I can't avoid her. I have to go past her if I want to get across.

'Morning,' I say. As you do. That'd be the third day. Or was it the fourth? She doesn't reply, doesn't even nod; eyes fixed out to sea steady as the red warning lights on the tower overhead.

There's a tanker on the horizon. It must be massive up close. From here, I can sink it with the tip of my finger. I can't see it move, not as such, but still it inches further along that unreachable line.

Is that what she's glued to? That infinitesimal snail crawl?

*

It takes an age to cross the bridge on foot.

I have to set the alarm earlier to be sure I'm not late for work. The street lamps are fading, the air's strained as weak tea.

I'm not sure how long it does take, actually. It would be seven minutes on the bike, on a good day. Quicker with a tailwind, fifteen when it's against you. Which is pretty much every day. It's prevailing, that headwind. I allowed twenty-five. On the bike. You need to leave a bit in reserve, a margin for error, for the worst-case scenario.

I keep meaning to time it, the walk, exactly. I'd do it now but my watch has stopped. I check it, over and over, can't break the habit. I forget, quick glance, straight away, bang, there it is: 7.43. Idiot. Not budged. I'd use my phone but I can't find it. I've searched every pocket, more than once. I've left it at home. Again. Draining down on the kitchen top, the odd judder whenever Robin tries to get in touch.

Robin's forever telling me off for leaving it behind.

—*What if there's an emergency? How'll I get hold of you?*

You're meant to stay connected these days. Not supposed to go off-grid. I don't say it. I feel a freak even thinking it. Truth is, I prefer it. Disconnection. No expectations. No pressure to reply. No ties, no tethers. No satellite stalking you from one end of the bridge to the other, monitoring those two chill miles, plotting your position; a red dot slowly blinking its way over the grey depths.

*

I mumbled hello to her again the next day and the day after. The woman. Made *me* feel better. Still nothing back, mind. Rude, I call it. What am I? Made of mist?

Then, of course, it gets awkward after that, doesn't it? Wish I'd never started. I've considered switching sides. I could use the other footpath, the one that faces upstream, inland towards the nature reserve, away from the sea and the city, from the ships and the docks and the towering aquarium biting into the sky. There are sharks there, you know, real ones, swimming over your head, over your head with their gurning great teeth close enough to part your hair. And you gaze up at those pale bellies and wonder just how thick that glass above you is; what would happen if it cracked, under the weight of the water, and the menace, everything spilling out in shards and salt and sharpness; those jagged teeth chomping you apart, limb by limb, blood swirling up in hopeless smoke signals from the deep?

I used to do it that way, on the bike. The upstream side. It's strange, looking upriver, against the flow. Made me feel more peaceful. You'd think it would be the other way round.

But every morning, now that I'm walking, without thinking I find myself taking this path, exposed to the sea, scuttling past a silent woman with my eyes on the pavement and my crabby pincers raised.

All I want to do is get to the other side.

*

I thought I should say something to her. Something more.

*

People do jump. Every now and then.
    Quite often, really.

*

7.43.

*

You do notice that much more when you're on foot.
Those dead bees, for instance. No way I'd have seen them
if I'd still been on the bike. Curled brown and gold like
Sugar Puffs spilt right across the pavement by the entry
barrier. Then little clusters scattered here and there all
along the bridge.
    I got to forty-two before I gave up counting. I can't
imagine what killed them. I mean, what were they even
doing up here, buzzing round all this asphalt and steel, so
high above the water, so far from any green? I don't know:
they lost their way one morning and gave up, simply
dropped from the sky. That's all I can think of.
    And the noises change, too. You're going too fast
on a bike to hear anything but the air whistling as you
whizz along. Now it's all those other wheels turning.
Right by your head, the way the level of the footpath runs
below the road. Right in your earhole. Wheesh, wheesh,
wheesh. Incessant. Tyres hiss, the whine in the wires,

gulls screaming, the rumble and rattle, the beat, beat, beat of your heart as it battles against the wind.

Even if you block all that out, even if you could, that shiver's inescapable. Along every bone, through every cavity. Yes, of course, I know, it's the weight of the traffic, the lorries and the buses and the cars full of people, going about their business. It's not going to collapse, the bridge. But it feels as if it's you, each step, setting it trembling like a tightrope, all those tonnes of concrete and metal, every careful step threatening to bring it all down.

Maybe that's what makes it take so much longer. The noticing.

*

It was the dead bees made me think of it, the ghost thing. I should have clocked it earlier. Stupid of me. I mean, it's obvious, really.

Because she seems the same, the woman. Sort of desiccated. Dropped. It's the wind in my eyes, maybe, watering, but I can see through her. She's not all there. Only the veins of her, the skeleton of a leaf.

*

Your mind wanders, when you're walking.

*

The next morning I stop. She doesn't turn, doesn't seem to notice. I rest on the handrail beside her. Metal's all cold and gritty from years of easterlies hurling onshore. We stand side by side, me and her, that same vibration chording between us. Beneath us, the currents swell and pull like the belly of a snake.

*

I did see something, now I think. Yes, it's coming back to me. When I was cycling. About halfway across, round about here, where we're stood, me and the woman.

I'd had to get off, adjust my helmet. Something's wrong with it. Don't know what. Dodgy clip, Robin says, it's not safe, I should buy a new one. When I get the chance, I say.

That's when I spotted the roses, the fancy, fraudulent kind, forced heads drooping the very next day. Garage carnations, too. Loads of those. And a toy rabbit, lashed to the railing, a tiny pink witch strapped to the stake.

I don't remember seeing her then. The woman. The *ghost*. Perhaps she was there. Perhaps not. Honestly, I couldn't tell you.

Anyway, I had to get on. I had a meeting at ten. Another heart-numbing session. Beige hours in a beige room making beige decisions that mysteriously unravel only to reappear unmade, as if by magic, a few days later. I'd rehearsed my list of bullet points all night, for all the good it would do, the street light striping the ceiling through a slit in the curtains, Robin snoring on the opposite side of the bed. Long, deep breaths in out, in out, in out; the soft waves of a sleeper who doesn't fear waking.

*

Not a cool name, you have to admit. Robin makes a joke of it. Bob, bob, bobbing. Riding through the glen. Holy Cliff-hangers, Batman! Holy Fate Worse than Death!

Sounds pathetic, when you say it out loud. Out of *context*. But it makes us laugh. Some things you can't explain to other people. Private jokes, dreams, nightmares. Doesn't mean they don't matter. You have to be there. You have to be there to really get it.

*

I couldn't shake it off, that rabbit, the image of it – popping up all the time during that endless meeting – pink fur stiff and spiky – popping into my head in some mental game – whack, whack a, whack a – no, that's moles, isn't it? – a rabbit, a creepy rabbit version of that – the slides flicked by and we broke for dry sandwiches and the talk droned on and on and on and the hands of the clock on the wall barely moved at all.

*

7.43.

*

I should jog really, while my bike's off the road. Be quicker, better for me. I'd lose some weight, feel fitter. I'll start tomorrow. After I've found the right trainers. I'll do it then.

No one else seems to cross on foot. Runners and cyclists blur past, the suck of them picking at my clothes.

I must have had that energy once, to spin the wheels so fast. Keep them spinning. I must have done. My head's full of ache I can't shake off. Sea fret. It clings. The trudge of it.

*

They're still there, the flowers. Crinkly brown and shuddering. There's these notes taped to each bunch, handwritten mostly, a few typed – why would you do that, though? Type a remembrance note? – all wrinkled, already disintegrating. Some've had the sense to wrap their card in cling film, but that hasn't kept the damp out. The messages weep like streaked marble.

There's a name, I can tell that much. Begins with C. Hard to make out – Cathie? Callie? Carrie possibly? And clouds of felt-tip hearts, all bleeding in the rain.

*

You can see the bridge for miles from land or water. Not that I've been out on the open sea, but that's what they say. Even at night, it's a line of light threading the dark.

Seems to have been here forever. Weird to think I've been around longer than it has. Ferry, that was the only way over before. One of those dodgy-looking ones, an open deck with room for a couple of cars. Down there, near where the reed bed is. Didn't run in bad weather. Couldn't. Miles to drive round. We used to come down to the foreshore to watch when we were kids. Cranes hoisting each section from the tugs as though they were weaving webs in the air.

I've no idea how it stays up. Something to do with suspense, with tension? Robin would know, could explain. Holy High-Wire, Batman!

The red lights glare at the top of each tower, to show you it's there, in the dark, if you're up that high. Or that low, I suppose. Whatever. You wouldn't think it, but they're hollow, the towers, enormous organ pipes sinking into the seabed. Put your ear to one you'll catch the echoes of the waves, howling quietly.

They say it won't ever be paid for, the bridge. Just the interest piling up year after year after year, an impossible, irredeemable debt.

There is a toll, one way. You have to pay to drive out of the city. No charge for pedestrians. If you walk across, the bridge causes more wear and tear on you than you do on the bridge.

*

I've taken to stopping by her every day. I don't bother saying anything anymore. I lean and stare, as she does. It's easier. Comfortable, almost. Companionable, like. It's such an effort to keep moving. I could stay here all day.

On the bank, the home side, the reeds bend and lift, bend and lift, dark then light. We had a cat, when I was little. The softest, silkiest creature. Puts me in mind of her fur, those reeds. Didn't come in for breakfast one morning. And that was that. She became an absence. Not there, but not gone either, not properly, if you get my drift. We never did find out what happened. Feared the worst. I cried for days. Inconsolable. I still catch her, sometimes, slinking, in the corner of my eye.

I stand and watch the reed bed moving. I hold my breath, try really hard to hear. But the sound can't carry over the traffic and the wind and the thrum in the wires. If I could, if I could hear it, touch it, stroke it, I fancy it might be purring.

*

There's been an accident. Right next to us. Traffic cones, tattered red-and-white tape flick-flacking, blocking the way, the pavement glittering blood red. Crunch and crackle under my feet. A smashed bike light. It does get slippery sometimes, treacherous. Patches of black ice where condensation's dripped from the cables.

Care. You must take care. Constant care. A split second, that's all it takes. You don't have to jump. It's easy enough to fall. Let yourself keep falling.

*

When she does turn towards me, her hair's webbing her face so I can't see her eyes.

She's got one of those name necklaces. Gold squirling across her throat. Callie? Yes, Callie, not Cathie or Carrie.

They're for her, the flowers. In memory of her. She's gone. She must have gone. Still, here we are. Me and her, stuck halfway across the bridge, above the deep, blank, unreflecting sea. Me and my ghost.

*

The cables hum overhead. *Hmm. Hmmmm.*
Ready to snap.

*

I had a puppet when I was little. The screws fixing the strings would swivel undone. Ever so slowly. Then the strings'd get all knotted up, arms and legs sticking out at weird angles. Devil's own job to untangle it all.
My body's coming loose.
Look, this is me, trying to lift my hand, but it just hangs there.

*

I've always been here, on the bridge, suspended between bank and bank.

*

We could step out onto that vast shimmer, me and Callie, stride right out east, right out straight, all the way to where the sea meets the sky.
What happens if you reach it? The horizon. Topple clean off the edge? Slam into a brick wall, the back of the stage?
Nothing. That's my guess. Nothing at all. *Nada. Nichts.* Nowt. Nothing.

*

The wind cuts right through you this high. It bites, really bites. Like a shark.

Sometimes I wonder if it's the only thing holding me up.

*

There's a gap in the traffic.

The road's empty.

Some incident somewhere.

Can't hear it anymore, can't feel it, that rush, can't feel it inside me, the speed, the vibrations, the motion.

*

7.43.

How long's it been flickering like that? The light? That warning light at the top of the tower?

*

7.43

*

Callie's climbed onto the railing. She's holding out her hand.

*

... and the waters roar and rise and crack and gape and curve and wall and tunnel and away the seabed stretches disclosing all that was once and is lost the plastic the plastic the dumped bycatch torn nets rusted hulls the skulls of sailors the ribs of whales the broken rudder rotting timbers dragon prow fallen warhammer home abandoned stone axe the broken pot smothered fire drowned bones of mammoths stumps of uncountable forests the petrified footprints the melted ice the huge jaws the giant claws the spiralling shells the spiralling the bed the bottom and the waste and the nothingness of the world ...

*

Callie walks out onto the seabed, into the tunnel of water. Her footprints tremble behind her, before the sand lifts to fill them, sucks them away.

*

... the waste and the nothingness ...

*

Waving.

*

A kittiwake screeches, arcs away and out to sea.

*

Waving.

*

I don't mean to look back. I don't want to. I can't see the point.

*

Movement. Down on the foreshore. That's what's caught my eye. Someone waving. Someone small.

A child?

No, not so tiny. Just so very distant. All I see is what they're wearing, that dab of brightness.

*

They all look back, don't they? In the old stories. No matter how much they've been warned, how many times. Like me checking my watch when I know it's broken. You don't mean to. Don't want to. You can't help yourself. It's habit. Instinct.

*

A scarlet parka.

Same as the one I gave Robin last Christmas.

It made us laugh.

The colour, you see, with the name?

It's what we do. We make jokes together. Proper bad jokes, that nobody else would get. We laugh. We have laughed.

*

I've lost sight of Callie.

There's too much, too much stuff. It's just, just.

I can't see her anymore. However hard I blink, my eyes won't clear.

*

Fierce bird, a robin. Cool. Keeps singing all winter. Most birds don't.

When the north wind doth blow. And we shall have snow. And what will the robin do then, poor thing?

Robin sings loudly every morning, in the shower. A terrible, out-of-tune, new-day happy song.

*

I'm on my own out here.

*

If you woke and the life you expected to find wasn't there? Only absence? Could you keep singing? Would you keep singing then, poor thing?

*

Buzz!

*

The walls of water crest, and break.

*

Buzz! Buzz!

*

My cheeks are stinging. The tops of my ears are burning with cold.

*

Buzz! Buzz! Buzzzzzzzz!
  Holy Tintinnabulation, Batman!

*

The surface of the sea settles back, smooth, concealing.

*

What *is* that? That buzzing?
  Bees. The dead bees lifting, rising around my head, crowding as if I'm sweet with honey!
  No. No. Don't be daft. There. It's been there all along, I just couldn't put my hand on it. In my pocket.
  My phone.

*

—*You're back. Thank God, you're back.*

*

I've not been paying attention. That tanker's moved. It's almost disappeared now.

*

7.44.

*

The second hand on my watch swoops, like a compass seeking north.

*

It's hard work, changing direction, turning away from the middle of the bridge. Heavy-going. The jam must have cleared, the traffic's picked up again. A constant stream. I'm facing into it this way, towards the further side, towards home.

The wind's shifted. Coming off the land. Still blowing, mind, a right buffeting.

I put my hood up. Through the thick cloth, over the engines, under the hum of the wires, somehow, somewhere, soft as a lullaby, I can hear the rustling of reeds. I hunch my shoulders, brace, start walking.

LICKED CLEAN

SAMMY WRIGHT

He had a group of friends, male friends, and they would walk through town in neat shirts and sheepish bravado, carefully laughing at anything serious. He liked them, but he also didn't like them. He sometimes wondered if they all felt the same way. Occasionally, he would find himself with just one of them, and the conversation stuttered awkwardly. Somehow, their friendship worked as a group, but individually, they had little to say to each other.

On their nights out, they would talk about women. They would egg each other on to approach women at bars, but rarely did so. There were certain women on their course, and in their halls, and in their wider circle, who they agreed were fit. They would talk about them with crude bluntness, undercut by fear.

When he kissed her, in the union bar, he knew he was transgressing in some way. He didn't call her. He held off for a week. One night, after a few drinks with the boys, he walked home along the canal. The night was warm, and the weedy bank of foliage smelt rich and green and seedy. He texted her.

When she spoke about him, she often started with a criticism, proprietary, fond, qualified at the end with, 'but

I do love him'. When he was with the boys, he tried to avoid discussing her, but when he did, his face went red. Sometimes, at night, when they lay in bed face to face, he felt himself dissolve into her. He found it hard to believe in both parts of his life at the same time – the days of unease and banter, the nights of quiet, overwhelming intimacy.

After university, he stayed in contact with the boys, but their friendship fell into a specific pattern. Once in a while they would all meet, for an occasion, or just an agreed night out. They would greet each other with loud cries. They would hug, backslapping. They would drink, and talk in mockery and reminiscence. Through the evening, he would sway from a deep glow of acceptance into an awkward sense of dislocation. When they parted, with more hugs, he had the sense of fulfilment after a difficult task completed with no injury.

Most of his life was with her. They constructed it together. A house, bought with a mortgage and a loan from her parents. Furniture, discussed, bought, admired, looked after. A shared calendar. He loved the quiet embrace of routine, and it seemed to both of them that what was between them was real.

At night, he dreamed of women he saw on the street, women with long legs and bright hair that tumbled on bare shoulders.

When he proposed to her, he did so with a deep seriousness. He cried. He felt that barely discernible doubleness, that he was both entirely in the moment, and also aware of how he would remember this moment. He knew they would both say how he had cried when they told the story, and they both did.

He cried again at the wedding. He believed in their life together. He believed he had made a good choice, and that she gave him what he lacked. He believed they were a good team. Deeper than that, he knew she gave him safety from having to pretend to be something he was not.

When he remembered his stag night, he shuddered.

*

They took three years before consulting a doctor. In that time their life had settled firmly into shape. They went on adventurous holidays, carefully planned. They upgraded things in their house. There was a scale of stuff, like a pay scale, that they felt impelled to move up. IKEA was at the bottom, followed by branded stuff bought at John Lewis, and ending in a few special things bought from designer outlets or antique shops.

In that time, the taking of a pregnancy test became a routine disappointment.

Her friends began to have children. They came for dinner, round, glowing, with the same conversation repeated. Due dates, names, nurseries. He was angry with her that she was so upset. He didn't see why it mattered what they had. At least, he said he didn't see it.

The boys took him out to let off steam. They drank steadily. He was the centre of things. They were gentler with him than sometimes. At ten thirty, they had some shots. At twelve, he was drunk, with a wild, whirling intoxication he'd never felt before. At three, he kissed a girl with tanned shoulders and fat knees.

In the morning, he could smell her still.

The third round of IVF worked. The baby was red and wrinkled, like all babies, but it moved with delicate shivers. He cried when it was born, because he expected to, but when they were back home, and he was holding his son, it seemed to him that if this was what he had been waiting for, it wasn't enough.

When his son smiled, though, six weeks later, something very different happened. The love that struck him was so intense, and so impossible to measure, that he realised every other time he'd felt love was nothing.

And when his son was eighteen months old, and walking, he realised that, although he loved him, it still wasn't enough. And so he left.

*

Their friends were shocked. She lived with a rage that bubbled out incontinently in every conversation. It pushed her into corners and held her under the surface of her daily life. She watched people, normal people, from the depths of anger, as from the bottom of a clear pool, holding your breath until your temples are hot and your chest tight and you rise and inhale fury, clear and fresh as air.

*

He got a flat. He furnished it cheaply. He had to. There was no money for branded goods, and he was happy with IKEA.

The boys settled into relationships. They seemed less embarrassed about it than he had been.

He had his son on alternate weekends. Two weeks was long enough for him to forget how to hold him, and increasingly, as his son grew up, this meant they rarely touched. They spoke about topics, or activities. They often had fun together. Sometimes it seemed to him that he had the best deal of anyone he knew. He watched other men, other friends, struggle with young children, and he revelled in the space he had to be himself.

When he remembered marriage, it was as a series of decisions not made by him. It seemed that everything they had been together was something decided by her, and he simply went along with it. But when he reached thirty-nine, he looked back at the last five years, and now it seemed to him that in her absence, all the decisions he had made were wrong.

*

He went out with the boys for his fortieth. They had a few drinks, but the night ended early. They all had families to go to.

*

A few weeks later, he met someone new. There had been brief flings before, two, three nights, seasoned with disappointment and selfishness. But this was more. His new girlfriend – that was what he called her – was lean and boisterous, with a streak of savagery that lit up a strange feeling of adulthood in him.

They drank together. They drank white wine in pavement cafes and kissed sweet-breathed vinegary kisses, arm in arm, on sunny benches. When they fucked it was akin to wrestling. He saw himself, male, next to her. She smelt rich and female.

They moved in together, and the flat grew thick with rugs and fabrics. He had a gut, now, and he wore jackets over T-shirts. His son came to stay for a night or two every now and then. When he met the boys for a night out, they looked both old and young to him. They walked like men defeated. He had a swagger now, in his forties, he'd never managed when younger. He grew a beard.

*

One year they met at midsummer. He was forty-six. A picnic had been arranged, and for the first time in many years, they all gathered with their families, apart from him, of course.

He came with his girlfriend.

They met on a curl of the river. The grass was neat, down to the muddy edge. At one end of the green was a willow. Within the bounds of the willow tree, the rhododendron bushes, and a bank of laurel, the families let their children roam. Most were between four and eight. The parents sat on rugs, next to baskets, occasionally rising to intervene.

He lay back, his head on his girlfriend's thigh. The sun was warm on his face, and he allowed himself to feel that he was happy.

Sometimes his eyes were closed, and sometimes they opened. He watched the boys. He had known them for twenty-seven years. It was hard to say when changes happen – when hair recedes, or grey begins, or a chin thickens – but they were all different. He looked from face to face. He imagined himself at nineteen.

His girlfriend rested a hand on his forehead. In the first few seconds it felt blissful, but then the weight and heat of it began to press down on him. He moved her hand away. The place where it had been felt different. They broke up later that day.

*

The first of the boys to die was Harry. They met, as they felt they ought to, in the pub afterwards. They sat carefully, guarding their solemnity. They were in their fifties, now. They were men, whether they felt it or not.

He looked across the table. Their faces were marked. They were not old men, not yet, but they would never have been mistaken for young. They talked, quietly. After a pint or two, the stories loosened into tearful laughter.

He listened more than he spoke. He listened to stories of Harry. Harry had two children, he had a wife, he was loved. He had a job, a home, hobbies. He was kind.

He had never known Harry.

*

That night he called his son. He was at university. They spoke about food, and work. They spoke about football. He held the phone to his cheek. As he spoke, he pinched the bridge of his nose between finger and thumb, as if by squeezing, he could hold the grief in.

ASYLUM DECISION

TAWSEEF KHAN

Home Office
The Capital
New Hall Place
Liverpool
L2 9PP

Our Ref: O4537821
Your Ref: Shah/Ile/215

Date: 19 November 2010

Folake Ilesanmi	Nigeria	27 August 1982

Dear Ms Ilesanmi,

ASYLUM DECISION

You have applied for asylum in the United Kingdom and asked to be recognised as a refugee. I have considered your claim on behalf of the Secretary of State.

Summary of your claim and future fear

1. The following paragraphs are a summary of your statements and evidence in support of your application for asylum. These are based on: your Screening Interview (SCR) conducted on 19 January 2010, Statement of Additional Grounds (SAG) dated 27 January 2010, and Asylum Interview Record (AIR) dated on 28 January 2010.

2. This claim is based on your fear that if you returned to Nigeria, you would face mistreatment because you were born and raised in the Niger Delta, where there is a conflict occurring related to the oil industry.

3. You have claimed that:

    a. You were born in the town of OB, Rivers State, to a Yoruba-speaking family. **Alternatively**, your father was Yoruba and your mother belonged to the ethnic Ijaw tribe (AIR).

    b. You were the middle of five children. Your father was a fisherman. He also owned a small crop of land, which he used for farming.

    c. When you were seven years old, a pipe burst (Q31). It was connected to a nearby oil field. Oil spilled across your town. Your water supply was fouled and your crops were destroyed. The land could no longer be used for farming. **Alternatively**, you were nine or ten years old when this happened (Q123).

d. A foreign oil company owned the pipes and fields in your area. After several years of negotiation, your chief was able to secure compensation with the help of an international NGO. The company agreed to pay $100,000. The NGO encouraged your village to reject this offer and negotiate for more money, but the council of chiefs chose to accept it. Your family's share of this amounted to approximately $200.

e. With this money, your family relocated to the nearby town of EK. Here, your father would be closer to his family. With their support, he was able to fish and farm again. You say that this happened in 1995. **Alternatively**, this happened in 1996 (SAG). You lived there until 2005.

f. In 1999, the neighbouring town of PA sold some land to an oil company. This field bordered both of your towns. Nobody in your town knew about this. The field lay untouched until 2004, when officials came to prepare the land for drilling. This brought the sale to your chief's attention, who believed the land belonged to your town. A dispute arose over ownership. It lay unresolved for some time.

g. The same company hired your eldest brother, Shakale, and some other youths to provide security to the oil operations in your town and nearby villages. **Alternatively**, your brother was part of a militant youth group, which was responsible for stealing oil by breaking into the pipelines, a practice known as 'bunkering' (SAG).

h. In February 2005, PA sent a convoy to your town to settle the matter. This boat of councillors was attacked. Most of the councillors died. Your brother's group was blamed.

i. Several days later, the Nigerian army entered your town. Your chief thought they were coming to resolve the matter once and for all. Instead, they raided the town and destroyed it. They fired at the villagers. Your brother, Shakale, disappeared. Your father went out of your house to find him. He was caught in the crossfire and shot dead.

j. After the raid, your mother fled the town with you and your remaining siblings. You moved to the capital of Rivers State, Port Harcourt, where your mother had relatives.

k. You stayed there with your mother's aunt. Eventually, your second brother, Ayodele, also became involved with a local gang. **Alternatively**, he was involved with the Rivers Oil Force, a group wanting greater control of Delta oil resources on behalf of the Ijaw people (SAG).

l. As a result, your mother decided that you had no choice but to relocate again. In 2007, your mother borrowed some money and moved again from Port Harcourt to Benin City, Edo State.

m. Each of you worked to survive. Your mother and brothers hawked food. You and your sisters worked as housemaids.

n. One day in late 2008, you were at the market with your mother buying produce to cook and sell. A woman approached your mother and, taking a look at you, offered to help you find a job. She regularly fixed jobs for bright, young Nigerian girls, she said. She found them jobs in countries like Italy and the United Kingdom. She promised that you would be able to send money back home and this way, better support your family. This woman was called 'Elizabeth'.

o. Your mother agreed to the proposition. Elizabeth handled everything. On 13 January 2009, you and Elizabeth's contact, 'Michael', travelled to Heathrow Airport. He provided you with a passport and ticket. After passing through immigration, he took the passport from you.

p. Michael drove you to a house outside of London. Once there, he informed you that you would have to do sex work to repay the money spent on bringing you here. If you did not, he would kill you. He knew your family and he would kill them too.

q. You were scared. You did not know what to do. From the next day, men started entering the house and you were forced to have sex with them. If you refused, you were beaten and denied food. You had sex with eight, maybe twelve men a day. You could not leave.

r. After three months of living like this, you managed to escape. One afternoon, Michael was busy in another room talking on his mobile phone.

The front door was locked, but the key was still in the door. You seized the moment and ran out. **Alternatively**, this happened in April 2009 (SAG).

s. You kept running until you reached a large park, where you hid for several hours. You were too afraid to go to the police in case they returned you to Michael, or sent you back to Nigeria.

t. Eventually, a British man saw you crying and asked if you needed help. You lied and told him that you needed to leave this place and go to Manchester because you had friends there. He helped you take the coach and leave.

u. When you arrived in Manchester, you slept in the coach station. On the third day, a Nigerian woman took pity and offered to take you home. You told her your story and she advised you to claim asylum. You refused, insisting that you were too afraid.

Future Fear

v. If returned to Nigeria, you fear persecution from the security forces in the Niger Delta. You believe that your Ijaw identity and residence there, and your siblings' involvement in the conflict, will make you a person of interest to them.

w. You also fear persecution at the hands of your traffickers.

Substantive Consideration of your Asylum Claim

4. We have thoroughly considered your claim for asylum and decided to reject it. The material facts are found to be unsubstantiated. In reaching this decision, we have compared the evidence you have provided with the objective information we hold about your claim and country. This is in accordance with the approach set down in the Court of Appeal case of *Karanakaran* [2000] EWCA Civ. 11.

Material Facts Consideration

5. Consideration has been given to your claim that you fear ill-treatment amounting to persecution at the hands of the security forces, who work in the interests of the oil companies operating across the Niger Delta.

The **Nigeria Operational Guidance Note (OGN) (April 2009)** states:

3.6.2 The oil-rich Niger Delta remains the scene of recurring violence between members of different ethnic groups competing for political and economic power, and between militia groups and security forces sent to restore order in the area. Violence between ethnic militia groups often occurs [...] over control of crude oil. [...] Local communities remain vulnerable to attack by militia groups and criminal gangs (Human Rights Watch, World Report: Nigeria, 2009).

3.6.3. Members of the security forces have reportedly been responsible for extrajudicial executions, torture, and the destruction of homes in the Niger Delta. In 2008, several dozen civilians were killed in clashes between security forces and gangs. Members of the security forces alleged to have been responsible for abuses are rarely brought to justice.

3.6.4 Oil companies in the Niger Delta have not always been held to account for the impact their security arrangements [...] have on the situation in the region. [...] Several companies are signatories of the Voluntary Principles for Security and Human Rights (including Chevron and Shell). These principles are intended to guide companies in maintaining the safety and security of their operations within a framework that ensures respect for human rights. They [...] have no monitoring mechanism, making it difficult to evaluate companies' adherence (Amnesty International, Nigeria Ten Years On: Injustice and Violence Haunt the Oil Delta, 2005).

6.   There are various inconsistencies regarding your claim to be affected by the armed conflict in the Delta region. You claim to be part-Ijaw. This is considered significant because the Ijaw are heavily involved in the Niger Delta conflict.

25.02 The current conflict in the Niger Delta has its roots in the differences between foreign oil corporations and the ethnic minority groups in the region, such as the Ogoni and Ijaw tribes, who believe that they have been exploited and squeezed out of the area's substantial oil wealth.

25.04 The HRW briefing paper 'Rivers and Blood: Guns, Oil and Power in Nigeria's Rivers State' (February 2005) reported that:

'On September 27, 2004, the leader of a powerful armed group threatened to launch an "all-out war" in the Niger Delta, [...] unless the federal government ceded greater control of the region's oil resources to the Ijaw people, the majority tribe in the Niger Delta. The threat, made by Alhaji Dokubo Asari, leader of the Niger Delta People's Volunteer Force (NDPVF), followed the deployment of federal government troops to quell months of intense fighting between the NDPVF and a rival armed group, the Niger Delta Vigilante (NDV). [...] A Human Rights Watch fact-finding mission to Rivers State in November 2004 found that months of fighting between the armed groups has led to serious human rights abuses against ordinary Nigerians. The violence has created a profound climate of fear and insecurity in Rivers State, leaving local people reluctant to return to their homes or to seek justice for the crimes committed.'

When you were asked if you spoke the Ijaw language, you said that you did not. When questions were put to you about the Ijaw tribe and about their involvement in the armed conflict, you were not able to answer. Given that you also failed to state your Ijaw background at the SCR and in your SAG, it is not accepted that you are of genuine Ijaw ethnicity. It is likely you have fabricated this detail to bolster your asylum claim.

7. Another inconsistency relates to the incident of the burst oil pipe. At Q31, you stated that you were seven years old when this happened. But later, at Q53, you

said that you were nine or ten years old. When this discrepancy was put to you (Q58), you said that you couldn't remember your exact age, but it happened around this time. It is reasonable to expect you to remember when exactly this occurred. Similarly, it is reasonable to expect you to remember which year specifically your family left the town of your birth and relocated to another. Here, you provided contradictory answers too.

8. Moreover, at interview you stated that your second brother, Ayodele, became involved in a local gang in Port Harcourt, but when pressed on the identity of this gang (Q226), you said you couldn't remember. But in your SAG, you said he was involved with the Rivers Oil Force, an armed militia group. Again, if your brother belonged to a militia group so integral to the Delta conflict, you should have been able to recall its name.

9. You submitted NGO reports on the armed conflict and environmental impact of oil extraction on the Delta region. These reports describe the situation in highly generalised terms. They do not refer at all to the events you have described as taking place in the towns where you lived. The documents are thus weighted accordingly.

10. In conclusion, due to the high level of inconsistencies in your account, the particulars of your asylum claim are rejected. It is not accepted that you are of

Ijaw heritage, or that a burst oil pipe caused you to relocate from your village. It not accepted that your brothers were involved in the conflict, causing your family to flee these towns and later, Port Harcourt.

11. Even if the material facts were to be accepted in your claim, you would be ineligible to receive Refugee Status or Humanitarian Protection.

Sufficiency of Protection and Internal Relocation

12. We recognise that security forces are responsible for ill-treatment in the Niger Delta, often with impunity. Victims are, therefore, generally unable to rely on protection from state authorities.

13. But your fear relates to the Niger Delta region only. There is no evidence to suggest that the security forces would remain interested in you or your family if you resided in another part of the country. Therefore, you can relocate internally within Nigeria to avoid being harmed. Your family has moved around Nigeria multiple times, so this would not be unreasonable or unduly harsh. You are clearly a bright and resourceful young woman. You speak English and Yoruba, two official languages in Nigeria. This will aid your reintegration into Nigerian society.

In summary, your claim has been carefully considered but it is clear that you do not qualify for asylum or Humanitarian Protection.

Your claim to be a victim of sex trafficking will be considered under the National Referral Mechanism (NRM). A separate decision will be communicated in due course.

If you have not yet taken advice on your position, you are strongly advised to do so now.

Yours sincerely

T. Kapadia
AS.Team.1

WE'RE MADE OF ELECTRICITY

JANE CLAIRE BRADLEY

It starts in the heatwave summer. There are power cuts and no rain and we play out as long as we can, until Imogen and Amber go missing.

Before we know about them, we are satisfyingly feral, roaming the estate until dark. There have been storms, on and off, and the air tastes of tin. On the park, there's a burnt tree everyone says was struck by lightning. When the fat raindrops start coming, we stand underneath its blackened branches. Half believing it won't hit the same place twice, half as a dare to the sky. We are defiant, soaked through and shivering in our thin summer holiday T-shirts, watching the clouds shift and churn. The rain, when it hits us, is like being pelted with coins. Stephanie and I lean against the tree's scorched trunk, come away with our shirts charcoal-smudged. We smack the stains from each other's backs before we go in for tea.

The first couple of days that they're missing, rumours teem, circulate, shift shape. The most common is that they've run away. But where do you run to when you're only nine years old? Steph and I are two years above, going to big school in September and not babies anymore. We feel like wise old grandmothers when we point this out to the other bickering kids on the street. By then, the search parties are in full swing and our parents are nervous. We are banned from going beyond our back gardens and the bit of dead grass by the pub visible from all our front doors. That way, they can see where we are, see that we're safe. Our informal committee meetings happen there each afternoon.

'It was on the news,' little Joey from number thirty-three mutters stubbornly. 'They found Imogen's jacket on a train going to London.'

'Doesn't her dad live in London?' someone else asks. 'They could have gone to his.'

'It wasn't her jacket, it was misidentified,' Steph says. Whenever the topic comes up, she pretends to be bored. Still, she knows everything. 'Plus, he's got an alibi.'

That week, TV vans and reporters with cameras and microphones set up camp on the pavements outside both their houses. We're all given warnings not to talk to them, or to any strangers. For once, we do as we're told. We have our parents' suspicion of outsiders already, showing itself in our glares when we see the journalists getting cigarettes and chocolate in the corner shop.

'I'll get those for you,' one says one day, when he sees me waiting with our blue Jubbly lollies. Steph is outside, minding our bikes, even though all we can do with them now is go up and down the street. If she were with me she'd probably have a biting answer, but she's not and I don't. So I scowl and shake my head, fierce.

'Go on,' he says, motioning again. 'I'll pay.'

'No, you won't,' says Yusef, from behind the till. 'I know the law. You gotta have parental permission to talk to minors.'

'Not if it's not on camera,' the man mumbles, but Yusef pulls himself up from his perma-slouch to his full imposing height, cracking his knuckles. The journalist doesn't say anything else. He puts too much money down, snatches up his stuff and stalks out without waiting for his change.

We don't nick any sweets from Yusef for the rest of the summer, not even our favourite sour jelly strawberries or pink sugar mice. We have our own sense of justice. We believe in karma.

At first the media circus is exciting, but we soon become desensitised. After about a week, we stop looking for ourselves in the backgrounds of shots of the estate. To start with, we read all the reports, but we soon realise how many mistakes the papers make. They get the street name wrong, or their ages, or the colour of Amber's eyes, even when it's next to a photo of her in her school uniform that clearly shows they're blue. Bit by bit, our faith in the media and the authorities crumbles away. With the others, we concoct and swap our own theories. The tabloids do the same. Imogen and Amber don't get found.

Mum doesn't watch the reports when I'm around. 'Too upsetting,' she says, chucking me under the chin, then holding my face in place a beat too long, like I don't know she's checking if I've been crying.

After I've been sent to bed, I hear the *News at Ten* bongs. The presenters say the search area's been widened, that suspects have been arrested, questioned, then released again. That Imogen's and Amber's parents have increased the reward. That the police don't know where they are. Sometimes, the sound cuts out mid-sentence, and I have to check the digital display on my bedside clock to see whether Mum's turned the TV off or if it's another power cut. Sometimes I hear her moving about, scuffling in the drawers for the emergency candles. Sometimes I hear what could be sniffling, or the squelch of the fridge being opened and wine being poured. Sometimes there's just nothing.

The hot summer days start blurring together. Steph at mine while I'm doing the ironing: slurping one of my home-made Ribena ice-lollies, trying to get enough of her legs out of the window to keep working on her tan. With Mum at work, I had to promise to stay in. Steph says her stepdad doesn't care, but she only lives seven doors down, so sometimes she puts her music on, slips out the back door, and it can be hours before anyone even realises she's gone. From her place on the windowsill, she keeps watch over what's going on.

'That slag from over the road's had her hair done. Red. Looks good.'

Then, after a bit: 'Another two police cars.' But not with their sirens on. We know what that means. They're just patrolling, or doing enquiries, or arrests. But nothing urgent. Not anything that could change anything, really. Probably not even anything to do with Imogen or Amber.

More thoughtful slurps. 'If they find them now, it'll be ambulance, right? Not police?'

The iron hisses hot steam.

'I don't even know why I'm asking,' Steph says, and her voice is that pretend-hard one she uses when she's talking back to the teachers after being told off, or when Joey's brother pushed her down the school steps and she landed bad but swore it didn't hurt. 'They're definitely dead.'

The search continues for weeks, then the sightings start coming in. Liverpool. Edinburgh. Cornwall. Some resort in Tunisia. People phone the hotline and say they've seen Amber and Imogen, together or separately, in all sorts of odd places. Some say their hair is different now. Some say they're in disguise. Some say they were there with someone else, a stranger, but then that person looked away for a second, and the girls mouthed the words 'help me' to some onlooker nearby.

These all get reported. The police investigate. Nothing comes of it.

'Cranks,' Steph says, digging her spoon into her mum's payday chocolate ice cream that we've smuggled upstairs to her room. 'They're making it up, for attention.'

'You said they were dead.'

'They are.'

But Stephanie eats the entire tub in a furious sulk, muttering about nutcases telling lies to the tabloids. When she's sick later, I hold her hair back. Later still, I hide the tub in my bag to get rid of on the walk back to mine.

Stephanie will blame her brothers for its disappearance and her stepdad will shout, but with no evidence on either side, nothing will happen. Her house is too chaotic for proper investigations into these sorts of petty misdeeds.

We start big school. Stephanie is funny and popular, like she is everywhere. I am clever, but not clever enough yet to hide how smart I am. Even though I know it doesn't do much good. Even though I know it only creates more pressure, more expectation, more disappointment when teachers think you're not meeting your full potential.

Steph never gets told she's not reaching her full potential.

I mention this one afternoon, after I've been kept back in English and told off for talking.

Steph blows a big, wet Juicy Fruit gum bubble, then cackles when it pops. 'This is my full potential, bitch,' she says, pulling a sexy pose like the dancers in our favourite music videos.

I laugh like I'm supposed to, and because it weirdly does make me feel better to always know what Stephanie won't take seriously. Mum picks us up and we go back to mine to do our homework. The afternoons are starting to get darker. There are no cameras by now.

For birthday parties or big football matches, the pub relaxes its rules on under-eighteens. We're not supposed to be in there unattended, but when its dark rooms are teeming with noise and tension and the warmth of bodies, the bar staff can't keep count of who's with who. Before

Amber and Imogen went missing, we'd be outside with the others, taking turns jumping from the falling-down garages behind the beer garden. It was an ongoing competition to see who could clear the wild tangle of thorns and nettles that came up halfway as high as the garage wall, to land unstung with ankles and kneecaps intact.

'Watch out,' Stephanie would crow like a wrestling announcer, when I scrambled up to take my turn. 'Cass can take you all on. She's fearless, y'know.' The others would make bets about how many bones I'd break, but I made it, every time. Steph sometimes talks about missing that mid-air reckless feeling of flight, but for me it was the impact that made the most sense: the spine-jarring jolt as my feet smacked back down, the sting of gravel on my palms. I liked knowing I had it in me to be brave, to hurtle myself into nothingness. To scuff my trainers on the rotting roof edge and then put two fingers up at the scoffing lads below and jump: to press my bruises or wiggle my loose teeth after and feel I'd done something important. Stephanie only did it once: she sprained her ankle and had to be given ice in a messy, wet wad of paper towels from behind the bar. After that, she'd only commentate.

When the girls were first reported missing, the garages were searched, then demolished. By now, we've somehow decided we should be more grown-up than that. We stay at the adults' tables instead of joining in with the other kids' rampages. Sometimes we take the glasses back, to be helpful, but also so we can down the last dregs of beer or rum and Coke, wincing and comparing which tastes we like. We've heard the phrase 'what's your poison' on films and TV. We have a lot of discussions about what our poisons will be.

That Halloween, no one is allowed out to go trick-or-treating. I use Mum's make-up to transform me and Steph into vampire queens, even though we're not going anywhere. Our faces itch with the weight of powder, eyeliner, mascara, adulthood. Still, we keep it on. In the morning, our pillows have pale prints of our skin and twin blotted moons from our eyelids.

Tinsel and mistletoe go up, then come down. The nights get lighter again. I spend hours on my bed with pencil crayons, paintboxes, oil pastels, drawing the cherry blossom branches outside my bedroom window. The petal blizzards remind me of confetti: delicate as paper, pastel-pretty. They catch in our hair, on our clothes. They clog in the gutters and make a grimy whimsical mulch. Stephanie says she loves my pictures but that real flowers should be banned. She wheezes on her inhaler but still steals spritzes of my mum's honeysuckle perfume whenever we're bored, home alone, ransacking her dressing table. Pretending to be older than we are.

On the anniversary of the girls' disappearance, there's a big appeal. Posters everywhere: all the rain-faded ones stripped down from the lamp posts and replaced with new laminated ones that look wrong in how rich their colours are. There's a re-enactment for *Crimewatch*, and although we're at school while it's being filmed, my guts churn all day.

'What's with you?' Stephanie asks, sitting on the sinks at breaktime, when I let my rucksack fall to the tiled floor and then slump down to follow it.

'I don't know. I feel weird.'

'Is it them?'

'Who?'

'Amber and Imogen. Maybe they're annoyed, about the re-enactment. Wherever they are.' She twists on the counter to look in the mirror that isn't even proper glass, just a sheet of metal buffed to a near-shine. After a spate of the bathroom mirrors getting smashed with no culprits identified, the school stopped replacing them. Steph peers into the metal murk, licks her finger and smooths her eyebrows into shape. 'They're sending you a message,' she says.

My stomach clenches. I fold my arms over it hard to keep the ache in. 'Like what?'

'You gotta disrupt the filming. They don't want to be found.'

Steph proclaims this with the lash-batting sincerity of the naff pretend-psychic woman on the lottery results show.

I shoot her a scowl. 'I can't even tell if you're joking or not.'

Her reflection in the almost-mirror blows me a sarcastic kiss.

We didn't know them, not really. Not enough to have a proper claim to the black fog feeling that seeps in whenever they get mentioned. But we went to the same school, shared the same playground, saw them on their skates in the street sometimes, span their skipping rope or yelled ourselves hoarse on sports day. Sack race for Amber, Imogen the undisputed champion of egg-and-spoon. By sight, we knew them: Imogen's freckles, Amber's big curls. That's enough to make this weird. The proximity feels sinister and contaminating, as though we've been infected by something. We're not scared, or no more than we are about other things we see on the news: the dead bodies found in binbags on the moors, the random knife attacks, the big bomb in the shopping centre. But it feels too close, a woozy, out-of-focus, edge-of-thought feeling, like the pressure before a thunderstorm. As though we should be doing something for them and aren't.

I pull my knees up and rest my head on them, let the cool black of my skirt press my eyelids blank.

'Fuck's sake, Steph. They're supposed to be in juniors, making pictures out of pasta or something. Learning their times tables. Writing cute poems about the rain-forest.' Steph's had enough practice to understand my muffled voice.

'Fuck their times tables,' she says. 'They could be anywhere. And they're probably somewhere better than here. They could be in New York, or Hawaii. Maybe Tenerife. Eating McDonald's every day.' Her voice goes dreamy, summoning chocolate milkshakes and chips. I raise my face to meet her gaze.

'Woah, Cass, you gonna puke or something? You've gone dead pale.'

I lurch upright and into a cubicle. 'Something's up with me. I'll be alright in a minute, I think. Just let me have a wee, will you?'

The lock's broken. Nearly all of them are. Without asking, Steph's hand appears on the top edge of the door, holding it closed in case anyone comes in. I lean my head against the graffiti-scarred wall. When I try to focus on the scribbles and compass-scratches, the writing seems to swarm.

My knickers, when I pull them down, are wet with red-brown gore.

I wedge a wad of tissues in place and Stephanie walks behind me in the corridors so no one sees the stain on my skirt.

The re-enactment brings in a record number of tips to the hotline. On the estate, people talk about how the look-alikes didn't look right. The latest theory in the tabloids is that the girls were burnt in the meat factory incinerator. The police say there's no evidence for that. We still feel suspicious and sick whenever we smell smoke.

By the following summer, we are thirteen and convinced that's old enough to do anything we want. On Fridays, we babysit for Steph's cousins. We're old enough now to prefer it to the pub, where grown-ups ask us cutesy-patronising questions about homework and boys, ignore us entirely or leer when they ask our age. At Auntie Nic's, we turn the music on loud, let the kids trampoline on their beds until they're tired. Once they're asleep, we're allowed one beer each. We slurp gold bubbles from green glass and belch the alphabet. Then we find Nic's stash of erotic novels.

'Is this really what it's like?' I ask, after reading Steph a scene involving sex on horseback at sunset.

'Definitely,' she says, riffling through another. 'Watch this.' She kneels up on the settee and drops the book. It lands pages up on the cushions with a soft flump of dust. I watch her, nonplussed.

'It's a trick,' she says, snatching it up. 'To find where the dirty bits are.'

And it works: that page is the start of a chapter-long sex scene, where the woman gets tied up and the man wears a mask and makes her say please, then leaves her bound to the bed when he goes. The last line describes the growl of his motorbike as it disappears into the distance.

'This is stupid,' I say. 'Like, how long is she supposed to stay there? What if she needs the toilet?'

'You're right,' Steph says, but her cheeks look hot and her eyes are starry as she frisbees the book across the room. 'It's ridiculous.'

At age fourteen, the bad things that have happened on the estate since Amber and Imogen have all been boring and ordinary enough that we're allowed to walk to and from school on our own. Sometimes, Steph has detention and I walk back most of the way on my own, then wait for her in the library. But it's not just that I don't want to go by myself past the corner where the girls were last seen. The library is cool and quiet and relieves some of the pressure that school seems to build up in my head. There are massive tables and an entire shelf of books on fashion and photography, with models like sexy skeletons in circus make-up, flower headdresses, cage skirts. I paw through them for the oddest poses and use them to practise drawing. After a few exploring sessions, I find a book on witchcraft. When I take it to the counter to borrow, the librarian gives a half-smile that she smooths away before I've even properly seen that it's there. She looks like Janine from *Ghostbusters* and has a million badges on the denim jacket hung on the back of her chair. The smile is like a secret, or a password. I put the book in my bag. I don't show Steph when she turns up.

That night, I stay up reading. I dig out the power-cut candles and line them up on the windowsill, watching the flames sputter. By morning, I feel strange but in a good way, and I want Steph to share it too.

'Look at this,' I tell her, when she meets me on the corner to walk to school. There's a smear of toothpaste on her cheek and the scent of vanilla body spray. She hands me a silver foil packet so we can share the last strawberry Pop Tart, then glances over to see me slide the book from my satchel.

'What is it?'

'I got it from the library. There's all sorts in here. How to be more psychic. How to find lost things. How to be invisible. How to be more powerful.'

'And you reckon it's real?' I know her well enough to hear the layers in her voice: wafer-edge of hope muffled by uncertainty, then almost-scorn ready to tip out on top.

'Maybe,' I shrug, matching her tone. Knowing she'll recognise the fizziness under the surface anyway. 'Only one way to find out.'

For the rest of that term we share custody of the book, taking turns checking it out from the library. We go to the counter together, so it doesn't get re-shelved in between. One of us returns it, the other one takes it back out.

'You know,' says the librarian, when this has gone on for months, 'if you ever lose a book, we can just look up what the original price would have been, and you can pay to replace it. You don't need to worry. You wouldn't be in trouble.'

Today, she's wearing black nail polish and a matching T-shirt with a pink triangle on it. Steph stares like the entire thing's a trap, but the kind smirk in the librarian's voice me tells me she's trying to help.

'So, say something happened to this book,' I say, and her eyes crinkle in encouragement. 'You know, like it got left on the bus or returned to the school library by mistake and we didn't know how to find it again?'

'Happens all the time,' she soothes. 'I'll find the cost for you. Just in case.'

Once the book is ours, we take it to the lightning-bolt tree. More even than our bedrooms, the air there is wild and dangerous and ours. We sit cross-legged in the shadow of its branches, on brittle grass scorched by another hot summer. A red money spider crawls over the book's pages. Sweat slicks the back of our knees. We do the spell for finding lost things: rattle the lighter until the flame catches, then ask the candle where Imogen and Amber are. Every time we finish the question, the candle flickers and goes out.

'I told you,' Steph says, leaning back against the tree's blackened trunks. 'I told you years ago. They're gone.' There's a wet ripple in her voice. I put my arm around her and she leans her head on my shoulder. We're bigger than we used to be, but still fit together perfectly. Steph rips up handfuls of grass and I stare at the jellyish puddle of melted wax cooling round the candle wick.

When we look up, I think I see something: a flash of red fabric in the overgrown weed tangle, like Imogen's T-shirt in those last pictures of them on all the posters. From the sharp inhale next to me, Stephanie's seen it too.

'Come on,' I say, pulling her up. 'We have to look.'

Steph stays quiet and keeps tight hold of my hand as we get closer, but when we get there it's nothing. Just an old carrier bag, snagged on brambles and breathing in and out with the wind.

By the time we're fifteen, we're sucked back to the pub. We still do spells sometimes. To make boys like us, or leave us alone, or to keep us safe from serial killers or getting kidnapped or being blown up with bombs. By now we wear make-up to school every day, and to the pub or wherever we go afterwards. When we pass them, we hear the little kids doing dares to summon Imogen and Amber by saying their names three times or running back and forth past their houses. Their names give us a twinge like long-ago imaginary friends.

When it's the England game, Steph nicks twenty quid from her stepdad's wallet. We press through the half-time scrum at the bar.

'Two pints of lager and two rum and Cokes. Doubles.'

Not what we want, but believable.

'These for your folks, yeah?'

'Course.'

We take all four drinks and sit on a picnic table outside to drink them even though it's drizzling.

'What will he say when he realises the money's missing?'

'He'll think he spent it.' Steph draws in the condensation on the side of her glass. 'Or lost it, the pisshead.'

'You know,' I say, remembering the spells we used to do to make ourselves invisible. 'I bet he's not the only one.'

The game goes into extra time, then penalties. We wriggle through the crowd. We see Auntie Nic with her new boyfriend, and I wonder who's watching Steph's cousins. Maybe they don't need babysitters anymore. Everyone's focus is on the screen, jackets and bags abandoned on nearby chairs. We let the crowd jostle us, let things get knocked to the floor, return them with apologetic smiles. No one even notices.

By the time we get through the crush of people and into the disabled toilet on the other side of the room, I've got three wallets up my sleeve. Steph's got two and two purses. We empty our spoils into the sink.

'Don't show me whose they are,' I tell Stephanie, as she starts rifling through them for cash. 'I don't want to feel guilty.'

'You're too nice,' she grins, but tilts the one she's rummaging through away from me, so I don't see the driver's licence.

'We must have a death wish to do this here.'

'That's what makes it fun.' As if to prove her point, she holds up a small clear plastic packet she's just unearthed from someone's wallet. Pills. In the next purse, an origami paper square. We smooth out the folds carefully to find a snowdrift of pale powder.

We dump the wallets in the sanitary bin as England score the winning goal. The pub shakes with victory chants. We divide the money and drugs, hide them in our bras before slipping out of the pub towards home. There are slurred choruses of 'Three Lions' in the street all night. Steph falls asleep, curled up at the end of my single bed. I try to draw her but after the rum and the beer, the lines are too slippery and soft. Still, the finished sketch has something to it. A rebellious sort of sweetness.

The following Saturday, we've taken two each of the mystery pills: a pink, shimmery candyfloss feeling in the ends of our fingers making us laugh on the bus towards town. On a whim, we convince the lad in the piercing place that we're over eighteen, then take it in turns to squeeze each other's hands as he threads the metal in.

There's a storm on the way back. We stand under our tree, Steph prodding at the silver hoop in her belly button through the blood-speckled dressing, my chin webbed with drool from the bar in my tongue.

She cackles when thunder rumbles overhead. 'Stick your tongue out, dare you.'

'What for?'

'So the lightning will go to you and not me.'

I remember a TV show about it and tell her so. 'That's a myth, stupid.'

'Prove it.'

I stare her down, grinning, then stick my tongue out. I feel like a witch about to be burnt at the stake.

Another vicious clap of thunder over our heads makes us jump, then dissolve laughing again. We slide down the tree, streaking black grime down our backs. Lightning forks the sky, so bright that once its sudden camera flash is over, everything in its wake seems gloomy and strange.

We look at each other and crack up again. My tongue aches when the bar trips against my teeth.

'We've got lightning in us,' I lisp to Steph, excited and urgent. The drugs have made me hyper, mapping in all the invisible connections between everything. 'Babe, we're made of electricity. It's in our veins. We've got powers.'

'Superpowers,' Steph shrieks, gleeful, trying to haul me upright and overbalancing so we end up collapsed in a pile again. We stumble home arm in arm, Stephanie pretending to shoot lightning bolts from her fingertips at everyone we pass.

We are bleary and subdued when we meet to walk to school on Monday. We somehow miss the headlines on the board outside the newsagents. They've been boring lately: the election and the football and the latest wave of blackouts. But this day, it's different. By the time we get to class, everyone's talking about it.

'It's them. Amber and Imogen.' Steph finds my hand and grips tight.

'They found the bodies.' I can't make sense of what they're saying, but the conversation keeps going. Everyone wants to put in what they know.

'They arrested someone, late last night.'

'They've put up one of those white crime scene tents.'

'They think there might be more bodies there.'

'I saw them bringing the digger in, early this morning.'

'My dog was howling all night.'

'My grandma said something was going to happen. She's psychic, you know. Hasn't stopped crying all week.'

'I was in the pub last night, when the news came in. You should've seen all the dads. Full sobbing. Like, enough to give you chills. I'll never forget the noise.'

'Bet you anything there's gonna be a special assembly today. We should ask for the day off. We can't do any work today. We should tell the teachers that we're traumatised.'

Steph storms to the toilets and I follow. I hold her hair back while she pukes. We sit on the cold floor for ages, not talking. I want to smash a million mirrors, but it's just metal on the wall, so I can't. No one comes to find us. There is no lightning and no thunder. The world goes on like before.

GOD HATES WITHERNSEA

ADAM FARRER

'**H**ello from the clifftop in Scarborough.'

Richard Whitely had just begun a live news broadcast from outside the Holbeck Hall hotel when the scene behind him dramatically changed. There was a brief, low rumble as a huge section of the building broke away and fell from sight over the cliff edge, a cloud of brick dust billowing in its wake. He turned to point at the scene, momentarily flustered.

'Holbeck Hall, a building here that has stood for a hundred and ten years, as you can see losing its battle – its grim battle – to cling on to the crumbling cliff.'

The report cut to an aerial shot of the hotel, the remains of it hugging the cliff edge above a great scoop of missing land. Following a night of torrential rain, a 200 metre-wide landslip had taken place, causing 27,000 square metres of soil to take on the consistency of damp sponge cake and slither down towards the beach. This was in June of 1993. Our family had been living in the small town of Withernsea on the same stretch of coast for less than a year, and for us, Holbeck Hall was big news. I watched this report with no small amount of concern.

'Fucking hell!' I said, then blushed. I was seventeen and in the trial stages of swearing in front of my mother. While I'd successfully road-tested 'bloody' and 'shit', 'fuck' was new ground. But she smirked and let it slide, realising that the report had troubled me. 'That won't happen to us,' she said, having been reassured at the time of purchase that it would be at least another hundred years before the sea became a problem for our home. 'We're nowhere near the cliffs.'

What happened to Holbeck Hall was alarming, but at the same time it was viewed as an outlier. A rare combination of factors, it was said. So, not knowing what the future held for us, my mother was more intrigued by the sight of Whitely presenting the news. Having spent the majority of our lives in Suffolk, we only knew him as the presenter of the daytime quiz show *Countdown*. It was a novelty to watch Yorkshire TV and see him in this role, as if he'd won the chance to present the news in a charity auction. And because my mother was not worried, I tried not to be either. Instead, I would go on to use this situation as a handy way of geographically pinpointing Withernsea for people who had never heard of it.

'It's near Bridlington,' I'd say. 'Waxholme? Hornsea?' Mentally tracking the coastline for somewhere they might be familiar with. Summoning names of resort towns that are more likely to be mistaken for Dickens characters than places where you might stop and build a sandcastle. Eventually, getting nowhere, I'd plump for disaster: 'Do you remember that hotel that fell off the cliff?'

'Oh, right!' they'd reply, lighting up with recognition. 'You're from Scarborough?'

The demise of Holbeck Hall was a reference that no one loaded with sympathy or fear, because generally no one thinks about the problems of the north-east coast. This is because no one thinks about the north-east coast at all. Chances are, if the person I was talking to had previously looked at this part of the country on a map, it would have been to see where Hull was, then decide not to go there. Withernsea is another eighteen miles further out from that decision, away from the city and along winding rural roads clotted with unremarkable houses and industrial fruit farms. It's not on the way to anywhere. It is not a region that anyone *just passes through*; it's a destination. If someone accidentally ends up in Withernsea, it's likely to be because they've washed up on the beach, having first tossed themselves off the Humber Bridge. So, a lack of interest in the area is completely understandable. Had my family not moved there, I wouldn't have thought about it either. But once we did, its fate was pretty much all I could think about. The fall of Holbeck Hall only amplified these thoughts.

*

I'd moved to Withernsea the previous summer, and wasn't due to start college until the autumn, so I had no friends and a lot of time on my hands. To fill my days, I'd swim in the sea, then walk the cliffs and beaches, trying to calibrate myself for this next stage in my life. And while I did, it was tough to ignore the regular changes in my surroundings. I might sit on a clifftop tuffet and ponder the bleakness of my existence, then, revisiting the same spot a week later, discover that it had shuffled several feet down the face. It seemed clear to me that the cliff edge was heading, apparently determinedly, towards our home. I mentioned this to my family and to my mothers' new colleagues at the pottery works in town, but no one seemed to be talking about it.

'Don't be soft,' my mother told me, knowing that I could be dramatic and keen to nip this panic in the bud. 'You think too much, that's your problem.'

This reaction just made me feel like a character in a disaster movie, someone who was able to see an incoming threat that no one else could see and was dismissed as unsound. The problem, it turned out, was that I just hadn't been speaking to the right people.

Spend any time standing on the seafront at Withernsea, particularly during bad weather, and you'll see dozens of people staring out to sea. Generally, they're elderly, many of them bearing an expression of grim resignation, as if they'd all committed themselves to waiting for a bus they knew would never arrive. Others lean against the railings, watching the waves crash and spit geysers into the air, occasionally whooping like excited children at a fireworks display. And some are very still and considered, staring hard at the horizon line, as if willing it to snap and unravel the whole world. But common in each, when I'd position myself alongside any of them, has always been a sense of welcome. Hard features would soften, there would be a loud exhalation, and this, I recognised, was a precursor to a chat.

One of the first I spoke to was an old man who sidled up to me on the promenade, his hair sparse and precarious-looking, as if all it would take was one strong gust for the whole lot to be blown off his head like the seeds on a dandelion clock. I guessed he'd been staring into storms his whole life, his face so cragged and deeply pleated you could have used it as a change purse. But when he spoke, I learned that one way you got that kind of a face was by concentrating on impending doom.

'There used to be towns and villages all along here,' he told me, scything his arm across the sea view. 'Dozens of 'em. All gone. It'll be us next.'

I'd heard this sort of thing before. Tales of the places that were swallowed up by the sea. You could pick up a map of them in tourist information leaflet racks, labelled *The Lost Villages of Holderness*. Dimlington, Turmarr, Old Kilnsea, Sunthorpe. Records go back to Roman times of the coast's inability to withstand the waves, which chomped through acres of land and anything unlucky enough to be standing on it. Yet it was local habit to talk of these places as if they'd not been destroyed, but merely submerged as a whole, hidden by the rising sea levels. I imagined a future Withernsea in the same way, sitting intact under brown waters. An East Yorkshire Atlantis with a bustling bingo hall, bubbles rising from the bar-nacled caller's mouth as he yells out, 'Two fat ladies.'

'They say you can see the tip of Owthorne church tower at low tide,' he said. 'And sometimes, during storms, you can hear the bells ringing.' He fell silent, staring out into the spray. I followed his eyeline and squinted, both of us imagining a plaintive, ghostly clang. He pulled his coat tighter around him. 'Course, it's a load of bollocks,' he said, laughing, patting me on the shoulder. 'But you keep looking, lad.'

I knew it was nonsense, but I liked the idea all the same. Stories like this are a charming testament to the human capacity not only for producing bullshit, but for swallowing great steaming handfuls of it and asking for more. To me, though, it was the details of grim reality that really captured my imagination. I'd been told that when the graveyards fell, skeletons appeared on the cliff face, poking out like chunks of hazelnut in a chocolate bar. The morbid part of me longed to see something like that when I looked down the coastline, but all I ever saw was exposed pipework. Collapsed outbuildings. Crumpled, static caravans slumped on the cliff edge, like aspirational suicide victims, too depressed and exhausted to even throw themselves over. These are the kinds of sights you can still see all along the Holderness coast.

It stretches for sixty-one kilometres, from the story-book chalk cliffs of Flamborough Head down to the Spurn Point nature reserve, where you can find an abundance of brown-tail moth caterpillars and, sometimes, a bloated dolphin corpse. Spurn Point is a three-mile-long arc of land, reaching out into the mouth of the Humber estuary, partially built from the eroded cliffs that have washed down from the rest of this coastline. Walk along its beaches and you are more than likely treading on the ground-down and transported remains of a once happy and laughter-filled family home that succumbed to the sea generations earlier. The composer Vaughan Williams wrote 'Andante sostenuto in E flat' after visiting there – a swooning and pastoral piece, which suggests he did not encounter a dead dolphin or stand contemplating the bleak provenance of the sands while a determined storm attempted to blow his head from his shoulders. But for me, admiring the beauty of Spurn Point while knowing how it came to be began to seem perverse, like severing your carotid artery then using your final minutes of life to applaud the elegant way that your blood pools around your body.

'Don't be weird,' my mother would say when I voiced my concerns in this way. 'It's fine, someone will do something.'

'But it *is* like that!' I'd tell her. 'It's like that woman with the steamroller!'

My mother claims to have known a woman who was run over and killed by a steamroller while riding her moped. She'd been travelling through temporary traffic lights just ahead of it, when the lights malfunctioned and showed green in both directions. She was forced to brake by another vehicle heading towards her, and while she panicked and contemplated her next move, the steamroller gradually caught up with her.

'There she was,' my mother would say. 'Flat as a pancake, squashed into the tarmac with her bike.'

The improbability of this story is great, and I dare say it was told to me as a moral lesson. My mother has lots of stories like this. The boy whose eyes fell out while headbanging to heavy metal music. The musician who was impaled on his drum stool in a prank gone wrong. Whatever point the steamroller story was intended to make, it was lost on me when I chose to take it literally. It's the visual that most often comes to me when I consider the predicament facing the people of Withernsea. The threat of erosion is devastating, but there is time to avoid it. It's not so fast that nothing can be done about it, but instead, people have just decided to wait and hope it doesn't kill them.

In 1997, I decided not to wait. Exhausted by the anxiety that I was one day going to wake up and find myself in the sea, I moved inland to Manchester. In my absence the sea did to the land what it has always done: consumed it. When I moved away, the edge of the cliff was still a few minutes' walk from my parents' house. On each trip home I'd be shocked by the change, in the way you are when you visit a child or an elderly relative after a prolonged absence.

'Fucking hell,' I said on my first visit back, looking towards the cliffs. 'Didn't there used to be a road over there?'

'Never mind that,' my mother said. 'Watch your language.'

With every subsequent visit the edge was noticeably closer, and the assurances about being a hundred years away from threat were starting to feel much less bankable. At the time of writing I reckon that, with a fair wind and the right dose of indignant anger, I could kick a football from our front lawn into the sea. In a few years it's likely that the ball would be able to float away of its own volition, because our garden will be on the beach. It's hard to watch the rate at which this coastline is being dashed into the sea and not imagine a near future where the United Kingdom has been reduced to an aspirin-sized speck on the world map, labelled *Birmingham*.

'You should sell up,' I'd tell my mother on my regular phone calls back home, urging her and my father to move inland.

'You're like a broken record,' she'd say. 'It'll be fine, they won't just let these houses fall into the sea.'

'They let Holbeck Hall fall into the sea!'

'They didn't *let* it, it just happened. Sometimes bad things just happen.'

But I wouldn't be told. Back in Manchester, I began researching the rates of erosion, sifting through government reports, geographical studies and dusty old self-published books on East Yorkshire history. I learned that several miles of coast had been lost over the centuries, and that I was not unique in my concern. Look through the historical records, pick an era, and you'll always find someone like me, freaking out. They could be a concerned Roman administrator or a medieval fisherman mourning a lost tavern. Or the Georgian vicar who stood on the remnants of his clifftop graveyard, watching a pair of robins building their nest in a newly exposed human skull, and calmly noted in his parish journal that the situation, in words more appropriate to his time and station, was extremely fucked up. Sitting at my kitchen table with my stack of printed-out reports and a laptop bearing a boringly sanitary browser history, I realised I was one of those people and deeply committed to becoming my generation's Withernsea crank.

What I was learning confirmed what everyone already knew about this town: that *they* have always let houses fall into the sea and there's no reason why our era should be any different. Still, there is an almost determined lack of concern among the people in Withernsea. A crocodile could be eating them alive from the feet and they'd still be insisting that everything was *fine,* even as their heads disappeared down its throat. They're not fools, they know the truth: they'd just rather not think about it. It's unfair of me to expect people to look around at everything they know and love, then admit that none of it is permanent and everything is doomed. It's much easier for them to consider lost undersea villages while they watch in real time as the buildings crumble into the waters. But for me, with the luxury of distance, it's frustrating. Especially as the very tangible indication of what is about to happen to Withernsea is already taking place in the village of Skipsea, a couple of miles down the road.

Make your way past the picturesque houses and over to the sands, and Skipsea becomes a post-apocalyptic land of ill-fated buildings and roads to nowhere. What remains of the former main road now fringes the cliff edge like a string of tattered bunting. The sea is drilling through the clay, revealing layers of peat and post-glacial forests in the cliff face on its way to consuming the few remaining houses in its path. And its appearance sings of all the things that are to come in Withernsea, exposing the fallacy of any comforting idea that someone will step in and do something. To the south of Withernsea, beyond the sea wall and rock armour, an embayment has already begun, one that will not stop until it hits cretaceous chalk. To get to that, Withernsea first has to fall.

Working my way through my research materials, I occasionally found myself thinking of the old shelter in Hull station for the 76 bus to Withernsea. For many years it bore a piece of graffiti, scrawled in black marker: 'GOD HATES WITHERNSEA'. Catching this bus home from college, I'd occasionally wonder how it would feel to be one of those religious people who viewed natural disasters as visceral evidence of God's fury at decadent human behaviour. To be the sort of person who'd watch their grandparents' house teetering on the edge of a cliff and think, 'Woah, what has Nan been up to?'

After all, it's local legend that God has form in this part of the country. Like with Ravenser Odd, a place I'd come across while reading up on the history of lost towns. It began as a sand bed that rose from the mouth of the Humber during the twelfth century, and soon after was established as a renegade port and a vile pirate haven, aggressively leeching business from Grimsby and Hull for around a hundred years. It was believed to have so angered God that he destroyed it with a storm known as *Grote Mandrenke*, the low Saxon for 'Great Drowning of Men', remodelling the region entirely and killing 25,000 people in the process.

When my mother joined a mature burlesque troupe and began a post-retirement career touring the clubs, I let this concern about a capricious, conservative God get the better of me, and phoned her up.

'You should sell up,' I told her again, this time insistent.

'Don't worry,' she said airily. 'We'll be dead before the house falls into the sea.'

'Is that supposed to make me feel better?'

'No, we'll be *dead*. Why would that make you feel better?'

'I feel like we've got a little off topic.'

'Ooh, I've not had a Topic for years. Do you think they still sell them?'

'You're doing this on purpose, aren't you?'

'*Yes*.'

So, I changed tack and brought up Ravenser Odd, at which point she brightened up.

'Oh, I was in a play about that once,' she said, referencing a production from her time in a Withernsea amateur dramatics group. 'I played a groyne.'

'Of course you did.'

Her responses would become less flippant in the late 2000s, when it became clear that several houses in south Withernsea were in imminent danger, including her own home. A committee was formed, the local MP petitioned, and my parents added their voices to the campaign.

'Something needs to be done!' they yelled at protest meetings, along with their neighbours, all engaged with a pressing issue and no longer believing in *fine*. It may have taken two thousand years, but it seemed that finally, erosion had become an overnight success. Emboldened by her place at the heart of a movement, my mother collared her MP about the issue at one of his street surgeries, then phoned to tell me all about it, still salty with outrage.

'He said that if you buy a property at the seaside, you should expect that it'll fall into the sea at some point. Then he said that there's no money for sea defences and I just need to "get used to it". Anyway, your sister complained about it on Facebook and tagged him, so we'll see what happens.'

What happened was that she received a letter from her MP, apologising for his tone, but the line remained the same: there was no money for Withernsea. *Get used to it*. Instead, protesters were fended off with terms like 'collateral damage' and 'inevitable environmental change'.

Words that are of no comfort when you're faced with the prospect of paying the mortgage on a home that is lying on the beach, more closely resembling a dropped pie than a four-bed semi with well-appointed gardens.

After their protests refused to die down and the MP's thoughts moved to those of re-election, a new response emerged. 'The council is looking into funding for sea defences,' and word got out that an EU grant had been secured. The pressure group dissipated, and all was calm again. But I had little faith in the notion of this funding; it was a mantra I'd heard many times throughout the years, as plans were made then unmade. Money has rarely been available for declining towns like Withernsea, so instead the people are offered hope. This has meant, in short, that the people there are in a long-term abusive relationship with the concept of sea defences.

Trawling social media for contemporary accounts of people affected by the lack of sea defences, I discovered Angela, who lives at the Golden Sands chalet park, just over the road from my parents. Each day she tweets images of her chalet and its accompanying view. There are shots of a double rainbow, dramatic sunsets, but also, most alarmingly, of her chalet resting on the lip of the cliffs, ready to fall at any moment. It was Holbeck Hall minus the press attention. So, I sent her a message, asking if she'd mind me paying her a visit. She agreed, and when I pulled into the car park a few days later and almost drove off the edge of the cliff while backing into a space, I knew I had come to the right person.

I tapped on the door of Angela's chalet and introduced myself. 'Hello,' she replied, shaking my hand, and with the same breath announced, 'Next door's just been condemned.'

I looked to my left and saw a cooker and a number of boxes waiting to be placed on a van. It looked fine, just like all the other remaining chalets. The problem lay in what was behind it. Or rather, what *had been* behind it but had just fallen into the sea, making the chalet too precarious to survive and destined for demolition.

Angela invited me into her home, a neatly ordered space the approximate size of a one-car garage, and into the small area that functioned as her living room. We sat on opposite sides of the building but were still close enough that we could have played patty cake, each of us perched on a section of a modular sofa. She began telling me about her life, and I learned that before she'd moved to Golden Sands she'd worked for English Heritage, portraying a sixth-century medicine woman and using mocked-up dog turds to form amulets that would ward off diarrhoea. Now she lives off her savings and spends her days blending hearty soups, wandering the quiet southern end of Withernsea and embracing the risks of her existence.

'Two things you need to know about me are that I hate heights and I can't swim,' she said. 'I had reoccurring nightmares about falling off a cliff. So, this is a way of confronting that. It seems odd, but I've never been happier. I like being on the edge. People ask me why I don't move over there,' she said, gesturing to the safer chalets on the other side of the site's access road. 'But it wouldn't be the same if I didn't have all this behind me.' She meant the view, the lack of anything else behind her, rather than the peril. 'Lying in bed, I like to think that no one in the world has their head closer to the sea than I do.'

To most people this would seem like madness, and Angela knows it, but she has an acute awareness of the small details of her environment, the ones that indicate big changes. Each day she walks the coastline, looking out for hairline cracks or subtle tilts in the cliff edge, knowing the signs of a forthcoming collapse. This is her second chalet, the first having been lost to the sea during the previous winter. The park has lost many homes, and when she took me on a tour of the site, she pointed out a number of heaped, overgrown rectangular patches of weeds next to the edge, where now-demolished homes once stood.

'I call them "chalet graves",' she said, smiling sheepishly. 'That's a bit dark, I know.'

'No,' I replied. 'It's perfect.'

'I never really got to visit mine. When my first place went, I thought it'd at least live on as a patch of plants, but, well ...' she said, pointing at an area several metres out to sea, to an absence. 'It's there now.'

We walked down to the place where the chunk of land had fallen away behind next door's chalet, taking some of the perimeter fence with it. When Angela first moved to Golden Sands, she'd calculated how long she could live there by eking out her savings, based on the published statistics for average coastal erosion. She had been told to expect to lose two metres a year, so did the maths and it all checked out. But there is a chaos at play here and government statistics couldn't necessarily be treated as gospel. The section that disappeared next door had easily been two metres deep and five metres wide.

I took a photograph of this area just as two men appeared at the cliff edge and began heaving the fence back onto land. They looked our way. Not wanting to cause a scene, Angela ducked from sight behind her chalet. One of the men called out to me.

'Are you a journalist?'

'No,' I said, heading over to him. 'I'm a fascinated local.' He relaxed and we got chatting. I learned that he was the owner of Golden Sands, so I asked him about the future of his site, which now consists of a dozen or so chalets.

'I'm hoping to save it,' he said. 'And they're talking about putting sea defences around the edge here.' He pointed around the base of the cliffs. A muddy soup of sea and clay was sloshing around against it. 'But that could be next autumn, so who knows what'll be left.'

I watched as the men shifted the fence into position along the newly formed cliff edge, then said goodbye to Angela. Later, heading home to type up my notes, she sent me a message telling me that the section the men had just repaired had fallen into the sea too, making the rate of erosion now faster than I can type.

The proposed sea defences won't be an extension of the robust concrete sea wall that currently protects most of Withernsea, but will consist of riprap, a rock wall made from chunks of granite, each the approximate size and shape of an industrial washing machine. This is not a new tactic. Over the years, the occasional ship would arrive from Norway bearing a number of these blocks, which were then arranged as a rough wall in front of the cliffs. And each time the sea has looked at these blocks, laughed and thrown them about like hacky sacks. It's a temporary measure akin to shielding yourself from a shotgun blast by holding up a paper plate. They will never be enough; they only ensure that catastrophic erosion will always be both news and history for this place.

I spoke to James, who runs Withernsea lighthouse, home to an RNLI museum and a memorial to Kay Kendall, a Withernsea-born actor who starred in the film *Genevieve* and became Rex Harrison's third wife before dying of leukaemia in 1959. James has lived in it for the last decade and was, I'd been told, the man to talk to when it came to Withernsea's fate. We sat at a table in the lighthouse cafe, a map of Yorkshire laid out before us.

'How far inland would you need to move to be safe?' I asked him.

'Here!' he said, bringing his hand down on the map like a karate chop, slicing off not only the Holderness coast and Hull but most of East Yorkshire. 'All this is built on boulder clay, left over from the Ice Age. The rock doesn't start until you get here,' he said, his hand wafting in the general direction of York, sixty miles inland.

Later, I phoned my mother to tell her that all of her notions of environmental certainty were built on a lie.

'That's a shame,' she said wearily. 'Will I have time to go to the shops?'

'Why aren't you taking this seriously?'

'Because we're getting new sea defences.'

'You're messing with me, aren't you?'

'Yes.'

'... fucking hell.'

Some geologists now say that they expect sudden, violent landslides of the type that destroyed Holbeck

Hall to occur along this coast every few years, confirming what people have known for generations: that these cliffs are a conveyor belt, rolling villages and towns into the sea and ensuring that the inhabitants will always be familiar with the rumble of buildings losing their battle to remain on land. As much as the locals cling on to the notion that it will never happen to them, Withernsea is as inevitably doomed as the lost places that went before it. But like those places, Withernsea could birth new legends. New bullshit. And in years to come, people might say that, if you listen closely past the roar of the cold waves, you can sometimes hear the ghost of a fretful man pleading with his parents to 'Move inland!' while he struggles to outrun the ground, always slipping away beneath his feet.

ACKNOWLEDGEMENTS

T his book was a collaborative effort and it relied from the very start on the shared vision of a number of organisations. New Writing North, C&W Literary Agency, Bloomsbury Publishing and Dead Ink all came together to deliver the book that you have in your hands today. Not an easy feat when we were all working under lockdown!

Will Mackie of New Writing North was a huge help in delivering this project and putting this book together. Without him I'm sure chaos would have reigned, and it was his thorough knowledge of northern writers and their work that made this book as full of variety as it is. He is truly a champion of the North.

Sara Helen Binney of Bloomsbury Publishing was a great source of advice throughout, who was able to keep things moving and translate between independent small publishing and big Bloomsbury publishing. Her assistance in editing this book was invaluable and I think it was her support that kept everyone calm – at least it was for me! Thank you also to Paul Baggaley at Bloomsbury who enthusiastically partnered with us on this book and got the wheels moving. From the start he understood what *Test Signal* was about and believed in its purpose.

Sara Helen and Will Mackie were joined by myself, as well as Lucy Luck and Emma Finn from C&W Literary Agency, to make up the judging panel for the open submissions. We all brought interesting insights to our discussions, and I know that we all had favourites who didn't make it. In the end, I think we are all proud of the final selection and are expecting great things from them in the future.

Laura and Jordan at Dead Ink, as well as Dan Coxon out there freelancing, were all key members of the team who made this book. They are also the more competent and talented members of the team who I could never survive without. Thank you also to Amelia, who always keeps me going and also tells me when to stop.

Speaking of key components to the success of this book, I must mention all of the Kickstarter backers who are listed overleaf. They quite literally got this thing going and I hope all of you are pleased with the work that we have done.

We received a great deal of submissions to the open call for *Test Signal*, so a degree of thanks is owed to everyone who sent in their work. If we didn't already know that writing was alive and well in the North, then we certainly did after reading all of their work. There was more talent than could ever be included in one book.

In the end, the biggest thanks must go to the North of England itself for always being an inspiration, and investing in all of us a sense of ambition.

CONTRIBUTORS

Andrew Michael Hurley's first novel, *The Loney*, was originally published in 2014 by Tartarus Press and then John Murray a year later, after which it won the 2015 Costa First Novel Award and the 2016 British Book Industry awards for Debut Novel and Book of the Year. *Devil's Day* was published in 2017 and went on to jointly win the 2018 Royal Society of Literature Encore Award for best second novel. *Starve Acre*, published in 2019, was adapted for BBC Radio's *Book at Bedtime*. The author lives in Lancashire and teaches Creative Writing at Manchester Metropolitan University's Writing School.

Amy Stewart is a freelance copywriter by day, writer of feminist speculative fiction by night. She has an MA in Creative Writing from York St John University and is currently studying for a Ph.D. at the University of Sheffield, looking at carnivalesque women and the modern circus. Amy's work can be found in *Undivided Magazine* and *Ellipsis Zine*, and she also received a Highly Commended Award in the 2019 Bridport Prize for her short story 'Wolf Women'. She's most often found ambling around the Yorkshire countryside with her partner, Phil, and rescue dog, Wolfie. Twitter: @AStewartWriter. Instagram: Amystewartwriter

Melissa Wan was awarded the inaugural Crowdfunded BAME Writers' Scholarship to study Creative Writing at the University of East Anglia. Her story 'The Husband and the Wife Go to the Seaside' was published by Bluemoose Books (2018) and reprinted in Salt's *Best British Short Stories*. She was 2019's Northern Word Factory Apprentice, mentored by Carys Davies, and currently lives in Manchester, where she is completing a collection of stories. melissawan.com

Kit Fan is a novelist, poet and critic. *Diamond Hill*, his debut novel about Hong Kong, is published by Dialogue Books/Little, Brown and World Editions in 2021. His second poetry collection, *As Slow As Possible*, was a Poetry Book Society Recommendation and one of the *Irish Times* Poetry Books of the Year. He was shortlisted twice in the *Guardian* 4th Estate BAME Short Story Prize. He was a winner of a Northern Writers' Award, *The Times* Stephen Spender Poetry Translation Prize and *POETRY* magazine's Editors Prize of Reviewing. Twitter: @Kit_Fan_ Instagram: kit_fan_

Matt Wesolowski is an author from Newcastle-upon-Tyne in the UK. His debut novel, *Six Stories,* was published by Orenda Books in the spring of 2016, with follow-up *Hydra* published in the winter of 2017, *Changeling* in 2018, *Beast* in 2019 and *Deity* in 2020. *Six Stories* has been optioned by a major Hollywood studio, and the third book in the series, *Changeling*, was longlisted for the Theakston Old Peculier Crime Novel of the Year, 2019 Amazon Publishing Readers' Award for Best Thriller and Best Independent Voice. *Beast* won the Amazon Publishing Award for Best Independent Voice in 2020. Instagram: MattJWesolowski. Twitter: @ConcreteKraken

Naomi Booth is a fiction writer and academic. She is the author of *The Lost Art of Sinking*, *Sealed* and *Exit Management*, and she was recently named one of *The Guardian*'s 'Fresh Voices: Fifty Writers to Read Now'. She is the recipient of a Saboteur Award for Best Novella and her short fiction has been longlisted for the *Sunday Times* EFG Short Story Award and the Galley Beggars Short Story Prize. She was commissioned to retell the northern folk tale of the boggart for the Audible Original/Virago anthology *Hag*; the resulting story, 'Sour Hall', has been adapted into an audio drama series. Naomi grew up in West Yorkshire and now lives in York.

Jenna Isherwood lives in Leeds where, among other things, she is co-organiser of the writers' social night Fictions of Every Kind and a documentary programmer for Leeds International Film Festival. She was selected to be part of the Northern Short Story Festival Academy in 2019 and has published fiction online at *Litro*, *Disclaimer* and *Long Story, Short*. A while ago she studied literature at University of Leeds and Bowling Green State University. Twitter: @JennaIsherwooo

Laura Bui teaches and researches criminology at the University of Manchester. Her writing received a 2017 Northern Writers' TLC New Fiction Prize from New Writing North.

Désirée Reynolds is a writer, editor and creative writing workshop facilitator living in Sheffield. She started her writing career as a freelance journalist for the *Jamaica Gleaner* and the *Village Voice* in South London. She has written film scripts, articles, short stories and flash fiction. Her stories are in various anthologies, both online and in print. *Seduce*, her first novel, was published by Peepal Tree Press in 2013 to much acclaim. Her fiction is concerned with Black women, internal landscapes, race and being, history, class and the stories in the ordinary. She continues to work as a writer, journalist and broadcaster. You can find her on Twitter: @desreereynolds and Instagram: desiree_reynoldsu2

Robert Williams grew up in Clitheroe, Lancashire. His first novel, *Luke and Jon*, won a Betty Trask Award. His second novel, *How the Trouble Started*, was shortlisted for the Portico Prize for fiction. *Into the Trees* is his latest. His books have been translated into ten languages. Robert has spoken at the Edinburgh International Book Festival and the Berlin International Book Festival, among others. He is also a songwriter and his songs have been played on Radio 6 and Radio 2. Twitter: @redwardwilliams

Sara Sherwood grew up in Dewsbury, West Yorkshire. Her short story 'Likes' was Highly Commended in the 2018 Bridport Prize. She lives in Leeds and is working on her first novel. Twitter: @sarasherwood. Instagram: sarasherwood

Carmen Marcus is an author, poet, creative practitioner and campaigner for untold voices. Her debut novel, *How Saints Die,* was published with Vintage in 2018, and won New Writing North's Northern Promise Award and was longlisted for the Desmond Elliott Prize. As a poet she was selected as a BBC Radio 3 Verb New Voice, and her poetry has been commissioned by BBC Radio, the Royal Festival Hall, Durham Book Festival and New Writing North. With support from Arts Council England she has pioneered a form of co-creative storytelling and created a route map for working-class writers with funding from the Booksellers' Association. She regularly teaches online workshops on creative writing which you can read more about at carmenmarcus.co.uk. She is currently planning a new project to support emerging writers and working on her second novel. You can find out more about her and her work by following @kalamene

Crista Ermiya's first collection of short stories, *The Weather in Kansas* (Red Squirrel Press, 2015), was chosen as a New Writing North 'Read Regional' book and included in *Best British Short Stories 2016* (Salt). She was a winner of the Decibel Penguin Short Story Prize (*New Voices from a Diverse Culture, Vol. 1*, Penguin 2006) and was one of the short story writers featured in *The Book of Newcastle* (2020), part of Comma Press's 'Reading the City' series. Originally from London, of Filipino and Turkish-Cypriot parentage, Crista lives in Newcastle-upon-Tyne with her husband and son. Instagram: dayofthedodo

J. A. Mensah is a writer of prose and theatre. Her plays have focused on human rights narratives and the testimonies of survivors. Her short stories have been published in various collections, and her debut novel, *Castles from Cobwebs,* won the inaugural NorthBound Book Award.

Lara Williams is a writer based in Manchester. Her novel, *Supper Club,* was published in Spring 2019 by Hamish Hamilton (UK) and Putnam & Sons (US). It won *The Guardian*'s Not the Booker Prize and has been translated into six languages. Her debut short story collection, *Treats,* was published by Freight Books in 2016 and in the US by Flatiron in 2017 under the title *A Selfie as Big as the Ritz.* The collection was shortlisted for the Republic of Consciousness Prize and longlisted for the Edge Hill Prize. A new novel is forthcoming in 2022.

Tricia Cresswell's professional background is in public health medicine and the writing of scientific papers and formal reports. As a dedicated reader of fiction, and aspiring writer, she completed the MA in Creative Writing at Newcastle in 2017. Her first novel won the *Mslexia* Novel Competition in 2020 and will be published in hardback in March 2022. Her work reflects her concerns about social justice, women's reproductive rights and the ethical complexities we all face. Creative response to the climate emergency has now taken priority in her writing, though, like everything, this has been disrupted by the COVID-19 pandemic.

Rebecca Hill lives and works in Sheffield, where she received her MA in Writing from Sheffield Hallam University in 2016. Her work has previously appeared in *Matter*, and in 2020 she received a commendation in the Hive South Yorkshire Young Writers competition. She is currently working on a Ph.D. application.

Sharon Telfer grew up on Teesside and now lives in East Yorkshire, where she works as a freelance editor. In 2018, she was awarded the New Writing North/Word Factory Short Story Apprenticeship. '7.43' began life during that apprenticeship, under the wise and generous mentoring of Jenn Ashworth; Sharon would like to thank Jenn and all who made this happen. In 2020, Sharon placed second in the Bath Short Story Award and also won the Bath Flash Fiction Award for the second time. Her flash fiction collection, *The Map Waits*, is published in 2021 by Reflex Press. Twitter: @sharontelfer. Instagram: sharontelferwriter

Sammy Wright is vice principal of a large secondary school in Sunderland. He sits on the Social Mobility Commission, and is the lead for Schools and HE. His stories have been published in a variety of places, by Galley Beggar, Tangent and Tartaruga among others, as well as winning the Tom Gallon Trust Award and being longlisted for the *Sunday Times* Short Story Award. In 2020 he won the Northern Book Prize with his first novel, *Fit*, due to be published in October 2021 by And Other Stories. Twitter: @SamuelWright78

Tawseef Khan is a qualified solicitor specialising in immigration and asylum law and a human rights activist with over ten years of experience working on refugee and Muslim issues. In 2016 he obtained a doctoral degree from the University of Liverpool, where his thesis explored the fairness of the British asylum system. He was a recipient of a Northern Writers Award in 2017 and an Arts Council grant to develop a novel about life as an immigration solicitor. In March 2021, he published his first non-fiction book, *The Muslim Problem: Why We're Wrong About Islam and Why It Matters.* Twitter/Instagram: @itsmetawseef

Jane Claire Bradley (janeclairebradley.com) is a queer working-class writer, therapist and educator living in Manchester. She is the winner of a Northern Debut Award for her first novel, and has been longlisted for the *Mslexia* Novel Competition and the Lucy Cavendish Prize for Fiction. Jane is also the founder and director of For Books' Sake (forbookssake.net), the non-profit dedicated to championing women and non-binary writers. janeclairebradley (Instagram) / @jane_bradley (Twitter)

Adam Farrer is a writer, spoken word performer and the editor of *The Real Story*, an Arts Council England-funded journal and spoken word event series, specialising in creative non-fiction. He has been a photo lab technician, an illustrator, a ceramicist and a music journalist, but now works at the University of Salford, where he is the Writer in Residence for Peel Park. He is currently working on his first collection of essays, titled *God Hates Withernsea.* Twitter: @adamjfarrer

BACKERS

With thanks to the following people (and those who chose to remain anonymous) who backed *Test Signal* on Kickstarter and made this book possible:

Aisling Holling
Alexa von Hirschberg
Alexander Cochran
Alexandra Bowie
Alexandre
Amber Greenall-Heffernan
Amy Lord
Amy Slack
Amy Zamarripa Solis
Andrew Kenrick
Anna Pendleton
Arlene Finnigan
Barney Walsh
Becky Kearns
Ben Pester
Ben Webster
Benjamin Judge
Beth Lincoln
Bex Hughes
BobbyRoo Smith
Catharine Mee

Cem Ozer
Chris Gribble
Christian Lisseman
Claire Dean
Colin Watts
Dan Coxon
Daniel Carpenter
David Coates
David Hartley
David Hebblethwaite
David Riley
Dipika Mummery
Doug Winter
Eamonn Griffin
Ed Baines
Eddie Robson
Edi Whitehead
Eleanor Equizi
Eli Allison
Eliza Clark
Elri Vaughan

EM Woolerton
Emma Sweeney &
  Jonathan Ruppin
Evaline Farrer
Francesca Emmett
Gabriel Vogt
Gareth Durasow
Gemma Seltzer
Geoff Cox
George Royle
Georgina Kamsika
Grace Helena Watt
Graham Hardwick
Hannah Preston
Harriet Hirshman
Heidi Gardner
Hilary Elder
Iain Broome
Inez Munsch
Jack Redfern
James M Lindsay
James Powell
James Tawton
Jane Roberts
Jane Spencer
Jenna Warren
Jennifer Corcoran
Jessica Greenall
Joe Luscombe
Johanna Robinson
Jonathan Carr

Jude Cook
Justine Pendlebury
Kate Harvey
Kathryn Garner
Katie Hale
Kitty Hyde
Kristin Wieler
Kym Nicholls
Laura Elliott
Laura Fisher
Lewis Johnson
Lindsay Jackson
Lindsay Trevarthen
Liz Turner
Lizzie Huxley-Jones
Loren Cafferty
Louise Corcoran
Louise Wilkin
Lucie McKnight Hardy
Lyndsey Ayre
Marian Womack
Mark Little
Martin Feekins
Matt Dowling
Michelle Collier
Natalie Ross
Nathan Wescott
Neil Campbell
Niall Harrison
Nicky Kippax
Nicola Humphreys

Nikki Brice
Noel Johnson
Paul Corry
Paul Handley
Rachel Wild
Robbie Guillory
Robert Hamilton
Róisín Finn
Rosemarie Cawkwell
Rosie May
Samuel Edney
Sandra Nimako-Boatey
Sarah Dodd
Sarah Jeffery
Sarah McPherson
Sarah Pybus
Scott Pack
Seona Bell
Sharky shark
Sharon Telfer
Simon Craven
Simon Holloway
Stephanie Gallon
Stephanie Wasek
Steve Clough
Steve Dearden
Stuart Evers
Stuart Gresham
Tamar Shlaim
Tobias A Carroll
Tom Houlton

Tony Burke
Tracey Sinclair
Unsung Stories
Valerie O'Riordan
Victoria Penrose-Jones
Wendy Mann